PF

A DEED OF DREADFUL NOTE

"Meredith revitalizes Anna Katharine Green's legacy while creating an intriguing new mystery. She captures the spirit of *The Leavenworth Case,* yet adds her own strokes to Green's original characters, placing the author herself as the protagonist. Anna emerges as a strong young woman, college-educated and confident in her intellectual ability, a sleuth who knows the law and is comfortable in New York society. As a reader, I look forward to reading more of Anna's detective adventures in the future." — Patricia Maida, author of *Mother of Detective Fiction: The Life and Works of Anna Katharine Green*

* * *

"I don't think that there is a weapon in writing that Patricia Meredith doesn't know the use of. She continues to inspire me. Her work always draws me in and I feel stuck between wonder and amusement. Another murder mystery that keeps you on the edge with such dramatic events that follow the climax. Her work is so incredible, it can be read in one sitting. Only Patricia has the power to give everything a meaningful end. Bizarre and unusual events are detailed with such literary techniques that will keep you interested. A murder mystery cannot get better than this." — Kini Sunny, @purposeofabook, Bookstagram Reviewer

* * *

"*A Deed of Dreadful Note* is a delightful stroll into the birth of a mystery, with fresh characters and exciting drama. A fascinating glimpse into the life of a budding author and the world that surrounds her." — Rebecca Writz

* * *

"Amazing! Incredible! She's done it again! Patricia Meredith's best work yet!" — Sue Walker, Historian

* * *

"Patricia Meredith brings the story of Anna Katharine Green to life while creating a compelling new mystery!" — Niko and Layla Sollazzo, @nikosbookreviews, BookTuber

* * *

"Thoroughly engaging... beautiful and impactful..." — Lydia Pierce

* * *

"The way Patricia portrays Anna Katharine made me fall in love with this real life woman, whose memory will never be forgotten, as she inspired all the great mystery and detective writers in her day. The humor, real challenges for women in that era, inspiration from this incredible woman and her brilliance, and relationships in the story had me hooked. I found myself cheering for the heroine and crying through real, relatable heartache. Beautifully written. I can't wait to read the next ones in her series!" — Anne Fischer, Goodreads Reviewer

PRAISE FOR THE SPOKANE CLOCK TOWER MYSTERIES

"Gosh! This book is incredible and that might just be an understatement. Not only surpassed my expectations, it also fired up my brain and I still can't get the feeling out of my head. A murder mystery with all the Agatha Christie elements... The storyline is ingenious and the characters are flawlessly presented.... Her books are a high that no drug can match." — Kini Sunny, @purposeofabook, Bookstagram Reviewer

* * *

"Page-turning addicting...absolutely brilliantly written! You're going to be reading late into the night because you want to find out what's happening. Let me tell you: it's so good!" — The Ginger Selkie, @thegingerselkie, Bookstagram Reviewer

* * *

"Another taut and tightly plotted thriller...one not to be missed!" — *New York Times* bestselling author William H. Keith

* * *

"A page-turner... The characters were compelling and likable, and the murder itself was something that made me fascinated to discover how everything would come together in the end." — Corin Faye, author of *The Beautiful Era*

* * *

"Historical mystery with all the Agatha Christie vibes I could want.... Contains the energy and aura of the turn of the century: the new ideas, the mixing of different cultures, the inventions, and especially all the lovely literary references... The dialogue makes me want the characters to be my neighbor and the details of the time period are spot on." — Bibliobrunette, Bookstagram Reviewer

* * *

"I can't get the book out of my mind." — Kathy Buckmaster, Historical Fiction Reader

* * *

"I was in suspense the whole time. A fun mystery plot, cleverly and compellingly written, with excellent integration of historical persons and events." — Alex Fergus, Spokane Historian

* * *

"From her ingenious title to the well-formed characters with quirks, Patricia Meredith has crafted a mystery that is unique and entertaining.... Meredith's historical knowledge of Spokane shines, as does her mastery of blacksmithing and clocks.... Overall, a strong beginning to a new mystery series!" — Tonya Mitchell, author of *A Feigned Madness*

* * *

"Find a comfy spot to read this and don't be surprised if you can't put it down! The story and characters will have you locked in to find out what happens next and you will not be disappointed. The ending is so unpredictable and exciting you will be on the edge of your seat to solve this mystery! You will be addicted. There's charm, wit, mystery, irony.... You will love these characters!" — Anne Fischer, Goodreads Reviewer

* * *

"I can't WAIT for the rest of the books in the series... Absolutely loved this book! Could not stop!" — Corina, Amazon Reviewer

ALSO BY
PATRICIA MEREDITH

Anna Katharine Green Mysteries

A Deed of Dreadful Note

The Spokane Clock Tower Mysteries

Butcher, Baker, Candlestick Taker

Cupboards All Bared

Crazy Maids in a Row

Short Stories and Poetry

Happenings: Poems

Murder for a Jar of Red Rum

A DEED OF DREADFUL NOTE

A Deed of Dreadful Note

BOOK ONE IN THE ANNA KATHARINE GREEN MYSTERIES

Patricia Meredith

Games Afoot, LLC

This book is a work of historical fiction. Incidents, characters, names, organizations, places, events, and dialogue are products of the author's imagination or are used fictitiously to breathe life into history's narrative. Any resemblance to actual events, locales, or persons living or dead is entirely coincidental...except where it isn't. For more on this, see my historical notes.

First Printing, 2023

This book is dedicated to my husband,
Andrew Meredith.
You are my lodestar.
I love you more than you love me no changes.

"A deed of dreadful note."
—Shakespeare, *Macbeth*

"I have found that the incidents in books which people pick out as improbable are the very ones which are founded on fact. Truth *is* stranger than fiction."
—Anna Katharine Green,
"Why Human Beings Are Interested in Crime"

Dear Reader

It is my pleasure to introduce you to an author who has inveigled her way into my heart and mind, as I'm sure she will yours. In fact, she may have done so already without your knowledge.

Have you enjoyed Sherlock Holmes and his deductive reasoning, as well as his friendship with Dr. Watson, wondering how Sherlock accomplishes so much when afflicted with rheumatism in his later mysteries?

Have you lost yourself in Agatha Christie's first novel, *The Mysterious Affair at Styles,* loving the moment when Hercule Poirot realizes the importance of his straightening over the mantelpiece for a second time?

Have you been drawn in by Dorothy L. Sayers's second Lord Peter Wimsey novel, *Clouds of Witness,* which opens with a coroner's inquest and the description of the murder victim and possible murderer from the first page?

Have you flipped to a crime scene map? Read a locked room mystery? A manor house mystery? A mystery set in New York City? A detective series following the escapades of an American detective? A mystery entwined with a romance that seems doomed from the beginning?

All of this and so much more began with one woman back in 1878, when she introduced the world to *The Leavenworth Case,* an overnight bestseller proclaimed for decades as one of the best detective stories ever written. Fifteen years before Sir Arthur Conan Doyle's Sherlock Holmes, this female author of American detective fiction began writing the book that would sell over a million copies by her death, not to mention the thirty-six other books that later caused the papers to declare she had "changed mystery fiction," giving her the title of "the Mother of Detective Fiction."

This author was Anna Katharine Green.

Her first novel, *The Leavenworth Case,* and her Detective Gryce would set the stage for the creation of future detectives like Sherlock Holmes, Hercule Poirot, and Lord Peter Wimsey. She'd go on to write of an elderly spinster amateur detective, inspiring Miss Marple, and a young girl detective, inspiring Nancy Drew. Anna's writing is really at the heart of almost every device and convention we now recognize as standard in detective mystery fiction.

Although much of her process and inspiration can be found in her letters to friends, as well as published articles and interviews, there are still many nooks left to be filled regarding how she came to write the book that would redefine the mystery genre forever. Perhaps the following will fill in some of those crevices.

To that end, this story is a piece of historical fiction, created by blending *The Leavenworth Case* with Anna's personal history, recorded thoughts, and relationships since, as she said herself, "Truth is stranger than fiction." Where possible, I have used Anna's own words to capture the grace and wit with which she approached the world and her writing, in particular.

It is my honor to reintroduce you to this woman overlooked by history for far too long, the woman who invented mystery as we know it today, Anna Katharine Green.

—Patricia Meredith, 2023

1

New York City, 1872

"I never write a single story unless I am in the mood for it. I cannot. I have to feel and live the parts."

—Anna Katharine Green, quoted in "Life's Facts as Startling as Fiction," by Ruth Snyder

Jane Austen was wrong. Dead wrong.

If it really is a truth universally acknowledged, that a single man in possession of a good fortune, must be in want of a wife, then Howard Jackson clearly broke the mold. Either one of two things must have been true: his fortune was built upon false pretenses, or he didn't know good wife material when it sat demurely fanning herself across from him in the front parlor.

I know I'm getting on in years, but this is the nineteenth century. My father may say twenty-five is closer to thirty than twenty, but my stepmother would be the first to warn against counting eggs before they've hatched. Mr. Jackson's egg had clearly hatched twenty years ago, and all that remained was the rank stench of a pig-headed, undesirable old bachelor.

Of course, I couldn't say any of this aloud, but I thought it loudly enough even mostly deaf Mr. Jackson should have heard me.

I'd done everything my father asked. I hadn't corrected Mr. Jackson when he said that "The Bells" was Edgar Allan Poe's last poem—it was "Annabel Lee"—nor when he proclaimed the wine to be the best "cabaret" he'd ever tasted. I'd even bitten my tongue when he'd argued that servants should only be allowed a half day on Sunday, rather than the full day he'd overheard my father offering to our cook so she could celebrate her grandson's baptism. The man made it clear he thought of his servants not as a critical, integral part of his home, but as cattle to be milked when the master called for cream.

But even the best of us have our limits. When he dared to pick up my copy of *The Mysterious Key* by L.M. Alcott—after I'd proclaimed how much I was enjoying it—and he said that he never could understand women's morbid fascination with crime, I could no longer hold back.

"I believe we are all interested in crime, Mr. Jackson, no matter our gender. If your next-door neighbor killed his wife, would you not be more interested in that than in anything else he might do? Just suppose that your neighbor's young daughter was caught in the act of shoplifting. Do you mean to say that you wouldn't be incredibly more interested than you would if the young lady won the highest honors at school, or announced her engagement, or even died? If a young man in the next block should poison his sweetheart, wouldn't you be more excited than if he won a decoration on the battlefield? I don't think there is the slightest doubt of it."

"It's all well and good for a man to read of a crime in the papers and share it with his wife," Mr. Jackson said. "It's quite another for a woman to take it upon herself to read...*mystery* novels as though they were anything close to reality. More full of romance and poppycock than anything," he grumbled under his mustache.

"I disagree. A good mystery novel is inspired by true events. Truth is stranger than fiction, after all. If a crime is committed, not by someone we know personally, but by people *like* ourselves, or like the kind of people we want to be, we are intensely stirred. If a society woman shoots her husband, or a college student murders a young girl, or a businessman is killed by one of his competitors, the story of it is of the highest interest to all—whether in the papers or in a fictionalized account."

"Miss Green, you speak of that which you do not understand. Do you mean to tell me that such things are included in the books you read?"

I thought through my recent reads. Indeed, I had read worse things than those I'd just listed for Mr. Jackson. Poe's "Tell-Tale Heart" and "Cask of Amontillado," with dismembered corpses and walled-up living men left to die of suffocation—I had held back these particular examples.

"You know of my interest in *The Moonstone,* Mr. Jackson," I said. After all, it had been this novel which had brought us to this moment.

Only a month ago, Mr. Jackson had first joined our family for dinner, having met with my father about some legal matter or other that had required he stop by our home rather than my father's office downtown. Over creamy mashed potatoes and roasted lamb, my father had revealed that Mr. Jackson had spent some time in India.

"Oh!" I'd said, quite interested. "I'm reading a book about India right now—Wilkie Collins's *The Moonstone.* You didn't accidentally steal a Hindu diamond while you were there, did you?"

At first Mr. Jackson had blustered at this. But then, upon realizing the book to which I was referring was fiction, he'd stated he'd had far more interesting adventures than anything a concocted story might offer.

And indeed, he had. An hour later, we were all still glued to our seats, so entranced were we by his tales of what seemed to us like something out of a storybook.

To be clear, I'd laughed and smiled and reacted to his stories as much as anyone else at the table, but apparently, Mr. Jackson had taken my interest as something more. Thankfully, my dear father had warned me of Mr. Jackson's intentions. In his late forties, I knew a man was bound to be set in his ways, but I'd been flattered he'd even considered me when I was nearly half his age. My father had said he understood if I was disinclined, but only requested that I might let Mr. Jackson down gently.

This was proving far more difficult than I'd anticipated.

"A man's stomach is made of sterner stuff, Miss Green," he said now. "Why, the things I saw during my time in India... But you will have to wait to read my memoir."

"I was under the impression, based on your last statement, that I should not read your memoir, Mr. Jackson, given the delicate lining of my stomach," I said, gripping my fan in hopes that it would give me the strength and poise necessary to voice my thoughts in a ladylike manner rather than like a jumping hoyden —my father's words, not mine. "I believe men *and* women are not so much interested in crime itself as they are in the *reasoning* behind the act. Why would someone do such a thing, whether it be stealing, kidnapping, or murder? To be interested simply in crime, merely as crime, should not be considered either morbid or scientific. Most of us are neither. We are just human; and with us it is the motive which rouses our curiosity."

Mr. Jackson shook his head. "What is there to be curious about? The motive is always the same: someone wants something that's not theirs. Take it from a wealthy man. Should I ever die, you can be certain greed is the motive."

"Indeed. In nine times out of ten the motive could be put down as selfishness. Money is obvious, as you said, but there are also the crimes people commit to be freed from some obligation or duty which they were too selfish to meet. Men kill their wives, women kill their husbands, because they want the liberty to go with someone else," I continued. "Jealous men, jealous women, kill because they couldn't have the love they wanted or because someone possessed some secret which would disgrace the murderer if it were known. In Emile Gaboriau's *The Lerouge Affair*, for example—"

Mr. Jackson stood. "As I suspected, you *are* one of those women fascinated by crime." He scoffed in a most ungentlemanly manner. "I would recommend that your father encourage you in alternative pursuits. As a lawyer, he must understand the detrimental effect crime can have on the minds of women."

I stood as well, my grip on my fan restraining me from slapping the man's face. Even then, I was certain there would be no hope of slapping sense into him.

"Then it appears we are at an impasse." I offered my hand. "Thank you for your interest in courting me, Mr. Jackson, but I am afraid I must decline your offer at this time. Perhaps we might continue our acquaintance in another manner in the future."

He bowed over my hand as I curtsied, and I could see where his head was balding in the middle. I restrained a smile as he stomped his way to the foyer, grabbing his hat himself on the way out, rather than awaiting assistance from our butler, Teagan, as his station demanded. The front door slammed shut. Clearly, the man was incensed.

"I suppose that might have gone better…" Mother Grace said with an odd smile, approaching from where she'd been seated as chaperone to the entire conversation in a back corner of the parlor.

I sighed and tossed my fan on the table. "I am afraid there will be no wedding bells this summer," I replied, echoing her smile.

She and I had both known before the start of the visit that Mr. Jackson's entreaty was not going to end with courtship, even if he hadn't been so rude and disrespectful toward my interests. But his last barb against Father? He was lucky I hadn't hit him with the fan itself, right in the middle of his balding head.

I plopped myself into my chair, allowing my skirts to billow about me as I did so, my chatelaine jingling and jangling like bell chimes that followed me everywhere I went. I could tell my stepmother did not disapprove of my response, and in fact, thought my reaction quite fitting.

"I never much cared for Mr. Jackson anyway," she said, taking her seat in the exact opposite manner of myself, crossing her ankles and sitting forward on the edge of her chair as properly as she had most likely done since the first day of finishing school. Her graying chignon was fashionable and elegant, her gray-blue eyes sharp and perceptive.

Grace Hollister had swept into my life like an answer to prayer. When my mother passed away while I was yet a young thing, my father had attempted to raise the four children left to his care as well as he could.

As I said: "attempted to raise." Dear Father did what he could, but to this day I could only imagine how we might have all turned out if he had not found Grace.

"Clearly Mr. Jackson hasn't the slightest idea of who I am, other than the young daughter of his lawyer. Why would he want to court me?"

Mother Grace picked up her needlework. "I believe most men come to a point in life when they're desirous of a young lady to...come alongside them in their later years."

"What you mean is he's middle-aged and looking for a wife before he's truly old."

"I'd remind you your father and I are yet sixty. It is a shame forty appears so old to your young eyes."

I blushed. "I would never consider you nor father 'old,'" I objected.

Mother Grace smiled at her embroidery. "Mr. Jackson may not be as young as you might wish, but he's a most distinguished gentleman."

Maybe it was simply his character that made his craggy face so objectionable to me. He could not help being an old—that is, middle-aged—rich man looking for someone with whom to share his wealth.

"Mr. Jackson's tea fortune may be enough to warrant him a home on Fifth Avenue, but I could care less about where a man lives. I'm more interested in where a man *dwells.*"

Mother Grace raised an elegant brow at me.

"What I mean is, does his mind dwell on the mundane everyday things of this world—like tea—or on the higher philosophies of justice, perspective, reality, or truth."

"Your aspirations are lofty for one so young."

"I'm twenty-five years old, Mother Grace. I think I'm old enough to know my own mind."

"It all comes of sending you to college," muttered a low voice from the hall.

"Father!" I cried, standing as he joined us in the parlor. My father's thick white beard tickled my lips as I stood on tiptoe to give him a quick peck on the cheek. "I'm afraid it's true. My education has made me unfit for marriage."

I pulled back with a smile that matched his own.

"What nonsense is this?" he said, his eyes twinkling. "You are too lovely for your education to be of any hindrance." My father brushed my cheek affectionately at these words. He was the only man in my life to as yet call me beautiful, but such was a father's prerogative.

"I fear the possession of great loveliness is incompatible with the possession of good judgment."

My father frowned. "The bloom upon a handsome sister's cheek will fade with the roses of departed summer. But a woman who trains the mind builds up an endless storehouse of wealth from which she can produce treasures for her own enjoyment, as well as those about her."

"It is clear where Anna gets her talent, James," said Mother Grace.

As the youngest of four, some might have said Father's affection for me was what had kept me from marrying thus far, but this would be false. My older sister, Sarah, was still living with us, and I had a suspicion she would never marry. Even after our father had taken a new wife, Sarah had continued to dote upon him as though she intended to do so until his passing.

The truth was, I had no interest in marriage. Perhaps someday, yes, but not anytime soon. I had ambitions of my own that would suffice for a lengthy time before any marriage need be considered.

Not that I had anything against marriage. I had been blessed to witness many a successful and happy marriage. Both of my brothers, James and Sidney, for instance, were happily married and settled down with families of their own.

But I had dreams. Aspirations. I was going to be a Poetess.

Father's quick eyes took in the empty room. "I take it things did not go well with Mr. Jackson, then, my love?"

Mother Grace gave a slight shake of the head as I did the same, leading my father to the couch where we might sit together.

"I'm afraid he was quite rude to me, Father, but indeed that is no excuse. I fear I was quite rude in return."

"I see," he said, taking my hands in his. "I only want what is best for you. You know that."

"I do, which is why I feel I must apologize to Mr. Jackson."

Mother Grace put down her needlework. "I don't think—"

"I would hate for you to lose one of your most important clients on my account, Father," I said.

"You needn't worry about such things."

I bit my lip. Father hadn't heard me, and even now as I recalled the conversation, I worried what I'd meant to deliver as a treatise on the mystery genre might have sounded more like a criticism of Mr. Jackson's lack of interest in such matters. I'd felt defensive; had my tone been more biting and cruel than I'd intended? I should not have said the things I'd said. I should have skipped to the part where I declined his courtship and left the room, venting my frustrations into my silent bedroom rather than into the ears of Mr. Jackson.

"You cannot help your intellect," Mother Grace said.

"But I can control my temper. An intellect without temperance is of no use to anybody, and is much less likely to be heard," I said.

"Did you ever hear back from Mr. Emerson?"

I shook my head, but my cheeks glowed red. In fact, I *had* heard back from Ralph Waldo Emerson. I had been honored to meet him while at Ripley College in Vermont, and he'd been kind enough to read some of my poetry. When I'd written to him in request of his thoughts, however, he had not replied at first. After I'd written him a second time, inquiring as to whether he might honor me by becoming my sponsor—since a poetess required a male sponsor for publication—his response had been none too comforting. I still had the letter somewhere, though I was not eager to re-read his words. Just the thought of them made me cringe deep inside.

Although complimentary, he'd suggested I not give up on other ventures to concentrate on publishing my poems. In essence, he'd told me to focus on getting married, rather than write.

"I am certain when he does reply it will be with a glowing review," Mother Grace said kindly from her chair.

My stepmother was my biggest supporter in my writing, second only to Father, who thought my writing skills were something to rival even the greats.

I knew I had thrived under tutelage, had excelled according to my professors, who had been unafraid to remark that had I been a man, I would have joined my father at the bar within a year. But I am not a man, I am a woman, and women cannot be trusted with such heavy yokes as law and justice.

I was only just finding it within myself to return to writing poems since receiving Mr. Emerson's critique. I wondered if he realized how long his words had set me back in my writing progress. Of course, it was useless to blame him. It was not his fault. He had most likely thought he was offering me some indispensable advice: don't waste your time.

But writing wasn't a waste of time for me. Through my poetry, I'd found a calm I'd never felt before. It was a place of belonging, a place of *querencia,* a Spanish word a professor had given me once to define that place of peaceful fulfillment. I'd later learned it was also used to define when a bull in a bullfight stakes his claim upon a corner, his back against the wall, and makes his most dangerous last stand.

Then again, perhaps that was still a good definition.

Father nodded and patted my hand. "I will go with you to give Mr. Jackson this apology. He was quite reticent to speak with me of his intentions toward you, for he feared that his…experience might make him less amenable to your young and ambitious spirits."

I blushed at this. "Thank you, Father."

2

Mr. Jackson

"For, as you know, dead men tell no tales."

—*The Leavenworth Case*

My father and I climbed into our carriage after luncheon the next day. In hopes of presenting myself as an upright woman of the best society, even if I didn't want Mr. Jackson to offer courtship again, I had put on my best red-and-white striped skirt, with a tight-fitted red jacket over a white waist. It was my favorite day dress, making me feel elegant and fashionable, as close to fitting in with Fifth Avenue society as possible. I may not be one who normally cared to follow the latest fashions, but when a certain cut flattered me, who was I to turn up my nose at what the latest season dictated?

"Do you think Mr. Jackson will be quite upset?" I asked, rubbing my gloved hands together as we drove. I had run through our entire conversation all night, listening to it over and over again in my head like the chorus to a hymn.

"From what Grace told me, you have nothing to fear," my father said with a smile.

I returned his smile, pleased Mother Grace had been listening in. It made it much easier to believe I hadn't put my foot in my mouth if Mother Grace had heard him say the same things I had thought I heard.

That was the problem with reconsidering a past conversation. Every time I stopped and pondered, I wondered if I'd simply misremembered. Had he really said those words? Perhaps Mr. Jackson had merely been interested in a dialogue, rather than a diatribe? What if he hadn't meant to be offensive? Had I misunderstood his meaning? Was I truly the one at fault? A person's memory could be—

A gunshot echoed across the sidewalk, bouncing between the brick buildings on either side of Fifth Avenue.

I ducked my head inside the carriage, as did my father, in an involuntary reaction.

Once the initial shock had passed, however, I quickly realized that there was no bullet, and no gun to be seen, either. The carriage had stopped without our saying so, and my father sprang outside to look about him.

I peered out through the carriage window and was not surprised to find my reaction on every man, woman, and child in the flow about us. Wide eyes met mine and open mouths muttered, "What was that? It sounded like a gunshot!"

"Where did it come from?" I asked Father.

"I don't know," he said.

I took a good look at his face and began to fear the worst.

"People are saying it came from the house on the corner," he said, pointing in the same direction as others in the crowd.

Gloved hands were all waving excitedly as bystanders conferred with their companions, as well as with strangers who were now considered companions in the shared strife of the moment.

"Mr. Jackson's house," I murmured, my face blanching at the realization.

Father reached out to take my hand and help me alight.

"It may not be," he said.

But I could feel the tremor in his hand.

"I saw my life flash before my eyes," a woman said theatrically beside me, her hand on her chest.

"Who lives there, I wonder?" a man muttered, and I was surprised when someone else answered.

"That's the home of Mr. Howard Jackson," a young woman said matter-of-factly. "My father says he's the biggest tea magnate in Manhattan."

I glanced at my own father, who was tight-lipped, his eyes focused on the front door of Mr. Jackson's abode. I followed his gaze and watched as a young maid poked her head out of the imposing black door and said something to the nearest man. A cry rippled through the crowd that a surgeon must be called. A boy was chosen from the front of the crowd to run for the surgeon, and he shot off like the bullet we'd heard.

"Should we see if we might be of any assistance?" I whispered to my father.

He nodded and began pushing through the crowd toward the front door. It was astonishing to realize that though we'd alighted almost as soon as we'd heard the shot, already there was such a crowd of people in the streets, one would have thought a parade was due to pass through at any moment.

"Excuse me," Father said. "Pardon me."

"That was quick." I pointed toward a black cab as it pulled up before the limestone steps, the thickening mass of bystanders slowing down the horses' progress.

The surgeon rushed inside, black bag in hand. He did not stop to knock, so I assumed he was either known to the household, or that the boy had made clear the urgency of the matter.

I held my breath with the rest of the crowd. As we finally neared the steps, another cab pulled up and stopped to the northwest of the house, the crowd now keeping anything from reaching Mr. Jackson's front door.

Out stepped a middle-aged man whom I knew quite well by sight; he was the coroner who often met with my father regarding cases he was representing. His name was Leroy Hammond, and he was an unforgettable character. Tall and broad-shouldered, his balding black-haired head made his face seem larger-than-life, which matched the brains I knew were hidden behind that impressive forehead.

He pushed his glasses up his nose as he disembarked from the cab and pressed through to the front door, knocking with the door-knocker before he was beckoned inside by a butler who matched him in size and figure.

"That cannot be a good sign," muttered my father upon seeing the coroner.

We tried to press through the mass to enter behind Mr. Hammond, but the butler closed the door as we began to ascend the steps.

My father hid his perturbation, and merely reached up to the door-knocker and knocked.

It was a few moments before it was answered by the same butler I'd glimpsed before. I knew he was the butler because everyone's butlers looked the same these days. Tall, distinguished, pompous, and if the red glint to his hair told me anything, Irish or Scottish—though with the current trend leaning toward Irish staff, I placed my bets on Irish.

"Good afternoon, Boyle," said Father, handing the butler his card.

"Yes, Mr. Green, yes, please, come in," the butler said with a slight Irish brogue.

"This is my daughter, Miss Green."

The butler bowed to me in a distracted manner, leading us swiftly into the front parlor.

"Has something happened, Boyle?" my father asked. "I thought I saw Mr. Hammond..."

Boyle glanced up the stairs and back to us. "Yes, Mr. Green. I'm afraid Mr. Jackson will be unable to attend you."

"What happened? Is there anything we can do to help?"

The butler did not answer, but instead said, "If you would please wait here." Boyle deposited us onto the Chesterfield beside the fireplace and left to climb the main staircase.

"It must have happened upstairs," I murmured.

"Now, now, we cannot even be certain what *it* is, yet," said my father, removing his hat and running it through his hands. "I wish Boyle would have simply answered my question. I don't like the look of things..."

I took the opportunity to take a turn about the parlor as we waited, admiring the furnishings and remarking on a beautiful Turner oil painting that looked to be an original, given its prominent placement above the fireplace. I hoped it would distract my father from his morbid thoughts, for I worried he and I had the same thought running amok through our brains.

This was my first time in Mr. Jackson's home, and for all my commentary regarding where he lived, I could not help but be astonished by his choices in decoration. Paintings and sculptures displayed an appreciation for the arts, with pieces that reminded me he was a man who'd traveled and lived in foreign countries.

Perhaps I had judged him too harshly. Perhaps I had jumped to conclusions. Perhaps he was really simply a man looking for some companionship.

I found myself drawn to the bookshelves lining the walls, as I'd found the best way to learn about a person's character was to see what they read.

Or didn't read, as the case may be. Although it was clear a maid of some level had taken the time to brush a feather duster over the edges of the books, she had neglected to brush the tops. As I reached forward to pull out a beautiful green-backed edition of William Wordsworth's collected poetry, I uttered a small note of dismay at the amount of dust that left the book to collect on my white-gloved finger.

"Mr. Green, Miss Green," said a soft voice behind me.

3

Lenore

"...a confusion too genuine to be dissembled and too transparent to be misunderstood."

—*The Leavenworth Case*

I turned as a young lady entered in the finest red silk taffeta ensemble I'd ever seen. Her dress was a gathered confection dripping with lace trim, ruffles, bows, even macramé fringe, all bustled in the latest fashion, complete with a jacket-style bodice with a high, square neckline that perfectly accentuated the woman's delicate neck.

The young woman had the quintessential compilation of features, from the petite nose that no doubt wrinkled adorably when she laughed, to the sparkling blue eyes that probably captured a man's heart the instant they locked onto him. Her hair was the color of the first daffodil of spring, softly curled as it hung from a twisted roll atop her head.

And yet, beneath the perfection lay an innocence, a naïveté, that evoked pity in me.

"I am afraid we have not been properly introduced," said my father, rising to greet her. "If it is not too much to assume, you must be the niece Mr. Jackson has mentioned to me. Miss Kelthorpe, was it?"

Mr. Jackson had made no mention of her to *me*. Neither had my father. Perhaps he'd assumed my relationship with Mr. Jackson would not make it as far as meeting the family.

"Oh, yes, how rude of me… I'm all aflutter at the moment… I…I am Miss Kelthorpe, but you may call me Lenore."

"Lenore?" I repeated, latching onto the familiar name.

"Yes, like Poe's dead woman," she said, her voice taking a surprising dip. "Not an alluring history, I must admit, but it was my mother's favorite poem, and so my father named me such upon her death."

"So a loving memorial, nonetheless," said my father.

"You are both most welcome," said Lenore, motioning that we should be seated as she settled across from us. "How gracious of you to come on such short notice, Mr. Green. However did you hear so quickly?"

I gathered my own now fearfully simple red-and-white bustled skirts about me as I sat. In this young lady's presence I no doubt looked more like a candy cane than a woman worthy of conversation, but I tried to collect myself and sit up straight and proper, all the while wondering why Mr. Jackson had failed to mention that he had his young and beautiful niece staying with him. It put quite a different light on his interest in me. He had no need of a young woman to dote upon him in his old age; it looked like he already had one.

"We intended to visit Mr. Jackson this afternoon, and only just happened to be approaching when we heard what sounded like a gunshot," explained my father. "Please let us know how we might be of some assistance to your household."

"How considerate. But I am afraid..." Suddenly it became apparent that it was tears which had made the blue eyes sparkle so, as Lenore removed a handkerchief hidden amongst the lace edges of her left sleeve. "Oh, it is too terrible to comprehend. My uncle—it appears he has shot himself!"

I merely nodded my head. It was as I had suspected. There really was no other reason why a gunshot should be heard echoing down Fifth Avenue.

But then an even more terrible thought occurred to me: had *I* been the cause?

No, I shook my head at myself in my mind. No. It couldn't be. My dismissal of him couldn't possibly have caused him to give up on life altogether.

My heart pounded and I was thankful for the gloves on my hands which hid my suddenly sweating palms.

I was grateful when my father beat me to the question that threatened to pass my lips.

"Are you...certain?"

"Well, yes!" Lenore stammered. "Why... What do you mean?"

I shook my head. "I wonder the same. Mr. Jackson does not seem the type of man to kill himself."

"Have you notified the police?" my father asked.

Lenore seemed shocked at the suggestion. "Why would we?"

"It is possible it was not suicide, which means the police should be informed, as well as the coroner. I saw Mr. Hammond upon our arrival, but I have not seen a constable."

Which was surprising, given by now the corner cop most assuredly must have heard reports of the gunshot from the milling crowd.

"But...it must have been... We all heard the gunshot and ran to his study," said Lenore with a frown. "When we opened the door he was—my uncle was—he had a hole—"

Surprisingly—or perhaps not since I'd only ever seen it happen in novels—no one fainted, not even Lenore at this suggestion, though she did grow pale and seemed to think it best to distract herself with her handkerchief rather than dwell on the image no doubt doomed to grow into a nightmare in her head.

"When you say 'we all,' who do you mean exactly?" I asked Lenore, eager to turn her from the memory.

"Why, the entire household: myself, Mr. Farwell, Boyle, Bridget, Kate, and Murphy, my lady's maid."

"You must excuse my impertinence, I am not familiar with your family other than your uncle; are all those people staff or...?"

"Yes. I'm sorry. We're quite devoted to one another here. Other than my uncle, I'm alone, so I think of the staff as my family."

Immediately Lenore rose in my estimation.

"Did Mr. Jackson feel the same?" my father asked.

Lenore shook her head sadly. "No. I'm afraid he did not." The newness of her situation was evident in the tremble of her voice whenever she mentioned her uncle. "I often have to remind myself that he was of a different generation, of a time before the War, when battle-lines had to be drawn, including within one's own house."

It had only been seven years since the end of the War between the North and the South, but the scars remained indelibly across America. The first poem I'd ever published had been entitled "Ode to Grant," which I wrote when Ulysses S. Grant had become the eighteenth President. I glanced at my father, who knew as well as anyone what the War had cost.

"Mr. Farwell is—was—the only one my uncle really appreciated," Lenore continued, smiling slightly at the thought. "He was working with my uncle as his private secretary, writing a book regarding his experiences in India—"

The sound of a man clearing his throat interrupted her statement, and we turned to find the coroner had joined us. Mr. Hammond nodded to Father in recognition, but turned his focus to Lenore.

"Miss Kelthorpe, if I might have a word."

"Of course." She stood swiftly and excused herself, stepping out into the hall with the man who seemed a giant beside her.

My father and I sat quietly together, our ears perked toward their conversation.

From out in the hall I could hear the low baritone voice of Mr. Hammond saying, "I'm afraid an inquest must be called under these circumstances."

"An inquest?"

"Yes. The surgeon does not believe your uncle killed himself, and I am inclined to agree. We must call a detective immediately whilst I collect a jury from those outside."

"A detective?"

"Yes, Miss Kelthorpe. It is standard practice to hold a coroner's inquest as soon as possible when the cause of death is called into question. We must collect evidence while we can. I will assemble a selection of peers from the crowd. They will view the body, then listen to witness testimony from everyone in the house, including yourself. If you would like, I can call someone to come sit with you during this period. It is a lot to take in."

I stood before my father could stop me.

"Pardon me," I said, joining them in the hall. "Perhaps I might be of assistance? I would love to sit with you, Miss Kelthorpe, if you'd allow."

I nodded my head and was pleased to see Lenore, lost in shock, nodding her head in mirror image.

"Very good. I shall ask the staff to prepare a room for the event, then send for the detective and assemble the jury. There is no need for you to worry, Miss Kelthorpe. Everything will be arranged for you. You are excused until such time as we have need of you," said Mr. Hammond with a bow.

4

Practicing Patience

"Any attempt at consolation on the part of a stranger must seem at a time like this the most bitter of mockeries; but do try and consider that circumstantial evidence is not always absolute proof."

—***The Leavenworth Case***

I have never been good at waiting. Why is it that the only way for God to teach us patience is by throwing us into situations where we must practice exactly that? There must be a simpler way...

I was itching to return downstairs, where I could hear the men filing in off the street after being randomly hand-picked by the coroner to sit in as a jury. There would be at least seven men, who would probably offer their time willingly, given the state of affairs and the interest shown by the crowd we'd encountered outside. Unlike Lenore, I did not need Mr. Hammond's explanation; I knew from personal experience with my father that this was common practice. There was nothing like a quick coroner's inquest to get the ball rolling for the police when it came to judging whether they should treat a case as a suicide, murder, or unknown.

I also knew my father would not be picked, since he was personally involved with the deceased on several levels. I wondered if he'd be called as a witness.

Would *I* be called as a witness?

My heart raced at the thought, though not entirely with dread. To be honest, a large part of me wished and hoped I would be called. Although I had attended my fair share of inquests and court cases alongside my father, it would be my first time taking the stand.

As I turned from the window peering out over Fifth Avenue, my thoughts echoed my movement and I assessed the room.

My father had remained below, while Lenore and I had retired to her private salon connected to her bedroom. It was a beautifully appointed room, with tasteful furniture and a homey feeling decidedly disparate from the downstairs parlor. It was clear that the parlor was for the formal invitation of guests, while upstairs was where the family *lived*, even if there was a sorry lack of books for distracting myself.

I had a mind to spend the time questioning Lenore, so as to be capable of offering further information to my father, who would no doubt wish to know what we'd discussed while we waited.

Unfortunately, Lenore seemed to be of the quiet sort, and my presence was quickly overcome by Murphy, Lenore's lady's maid.

Murphy was middle-aged, with dark brown hair that might have had red tints through it once, but years of indoor work had stripped the color down to a browned bronze. Her eyes were dark, and entirely focused upon her mistress. She was as attentive as any mother I had ever known, and I wondered if Murphy mightn't have started her employ as Lenore's governess.

"How long have you had the benefit of Murphy's guidance?" I asked, once we were settled with tea and I finally saw my opening.

Lenore looked fondly at Murphy, seated beside and a little behind her. "She came as my governess first, when I was, oh, eight? And she remained as my lady's maid once I became too old for governesses."

I almost hummed, so pleased was I at my deduction, though given Lenore was no more than eighteen, I wondered how recently she'd "become too old."

"I've been grateful for every moment, *mavourneen,*" said Murphy, her Irish lilt only truly apparent on the final word.

She reached forward to take Lenore's hand in hers as they exchanged a glance. It was a tender moment, and I suddenly felt the presumptuousness of my pressing myself into the situation. For me, this whole matter was a mere quandary, a chance to test my legal knowledge and deductive powers, but for Lenore and Murphy and the rest of the household, it was something much, much more.

"'*Mavourneen?*'" I asked, sipping my tea.

"An Irish term of affection," explained Lenore. "Something like 'my darling,' wouldn't you say, Murphy?"

The Irish woman nodded and let go of Lenore's hand, allowing her to sip from her own teacup.

"Have you always lived here, in this house with your uncle?" I asked. "Or did you join him in India first?"

Lenore shook her head. "I never lived with him in India. That was before my time. Fortunately, my parents did not pass away until he had returned to his life here in New York."

"It must have been such fun, growing up hearing about all his adventures." No matter how our relationship had come to its end, I had to admit to enjoying his repertoire over dinner that first night I'd met him.

"Yes, indeed," was all Lenore said, sipping at her tea.

I glanced about the room for memorabilia. "Did he ever return to India while you were with him? Did he bring you back anything unique?"

"Oh, yes. My uncle loved to travel, and he was generous with his gifts." She nodded toward where a golden elephant stood on its hind legs on a shelf, its head and back sparkling with a variegated design of red, blue, and white jewels.

"How lovely!" I cried in true admiration. "Did you ever go with him?"

Lenore swallowed before responding. "No," she said simply. "I never had the opportunity."

A sudden sadness reminded her that this was no normal tea, no normal day. With a sudden movement, she set down her cup and saucer and picked up her embroidery from a basket beside her chair, seeming to indicate she didn't wish to speak further.

It suddenly occurred to me that perhaps I needed to give the girl a chance to mourn, so I turned to Murphy for company instead, talking about the weather and other inane conversation simply in an attempt to pass the time. At one point, Lenore excused herself to her bedroom, reaching for her chatelaine as she went; it wasn't until I saw her rise that I realized quiet tears had marred her cheeks.

"This must be a lot for her," I murmured as Lenore's bedroom door shut behind her.

"It is. I've spent my time around a young girl or two—though Lenore is the only one who's been my *mavourneen*—and yet, they all go through a similar moment at one point or another."

"You mean the loss of a parent or guardian?"

Murphy nodded. "Not only that, but the disparate nature of grieving for a man with whom she argued constantly—as is the way of most young ones—and yet loved and felt great affection for. Naturally, she may not have realized to what depths she held the man in such regard until his demise." Murphy set down her cup and saucer and whispered, "The girl has spent the better part of the past year yearning to be free of Mr. Jackson's guardianship. Not for any fault of his, other than the protective nature that has persuaded him that what is best for a young girl in New York City is to remain closed off from society until she is much older."

I understood. It was standard practice for a girl to come out into society sometime between her sixteenth and eighteenth year, but some parents chose to hold back on that moment until even later, hoping that by doing so they might protect their young charge from the pain of young love.

"Lenore cannot be more than eighteen?"

"Aye, she is no more. She hoped this autumn might be the season she'd finally be allowed to attend her first ball. You can imagine the struggle she's having at the moment. Her young heart was no doubt at odds with her uncle, and yet, to lose him on the eve of—"

Lenore returned with a face the somewhat blotchy red of someone who'd been crying. I wasn't certain if I should remark on the fact, and was pleased when Murphy rose and went to her charge with a handkerchief and a reassuring murmur.

"I'm fine, Murphy," Lenore said, though she did take the handkerchief. "Fine as can be, I suppose." She picked up her work, but almost immediately returned it to her lap. "May I ask you something, Miss Green?"

"Please do," I said with a smile.

Lenore fingered the red silk of her skirts for a moment before continuing. "I understand my uncle was pursuing you in courtship?"

I blushed that she should be aware of this and yet I'd been unaware of her existence until this morning. "Yes," I said softly, "but we had agreed that we would not be courting only yesterday. My father and I were coming to speak to him regarding the matter this afternoon—to be certain there was no ill feeling between us."

Lenore glanced at Murphy and then back to me. "Did he seem…was he much distressed by the decision, do you think?"

I considered, not much caring for the direction of the questioning. "I…do not know. He left most abruptly."

Lenore nodded and fingered her embroidery. "He returned home yesterday quite discomposed over some matter or other, but I hadn't the heart to ask him directly."

I bit my lip, my worst fears rising once more, the tea churning in my stomach. "You don't think… Oh, dear… I hope I didn't…"

Lenore waved a dismissive hand. "I'm not suggesting you were the cause of his suicide, especially since the coroner seems to think it was not self-harm after all, but done by some person or persons unknown. Do you know the name of my uncle's sister?"

I was taken aback by the sudden turn in questioning. "Mr. Jackson had a sister?"

Lenore's eyes fell at my answer. "I take it you do not know then."

I set my teacup and saucer upon the table. "I am afraid I do not, but my father must."

"Yes, I am certain he does." Lenore nodded, returning to her embroidery again, signifying she had no more to say.

Who was Mr. Jackson's sister? Was she the only relative outside of Lenore who must be notified of Mr. Jackson's passing?

My thoughts were interrupted—as so often happens in novels—by a knock at the door, and a maid asked if Murphy was ready to give her account before the coroner. Lenore gave her a quick squeeze of the hand and a comforting smile, and then her lady's maid left, leaving a silent void in the room.

I wished I could think of some excuse to join the crowd downstairs. Why had I been so eager to offer my presence to Lenore? They had no doubt filled the parlor by now, where

Mr. Hammond would set up the inquest. My father had found it intriguing to query me after attending an inquest as to my thoughts in regards to it all. Did I notice the way the man's hand moved when he spoke? The tightening of the wrinkles around his eyes? What did I think that meant? Was the man lying?

What felt like an hour later, we were still waiting. My multiple attempts to engage Lenore with friendly talk had backfired to the point she had finally excused herself to her bedroom, saying she would take the opportunity to lie down in quiet while she could, in preparation for the ordeal she knew was soon to come.

What could the coroner possibly be obtaining from the servants' statements that would require such time and consideration? Perhaps the surgeon was giving a more lengthy description than usual because he was able to be on the scene so quickly?

The detective assigned to the case had arrived half an hour after Mr. Hammond sent for him—not nearly so quick on the draw as the surgeon or coroner, it would seem. He had only given Lenore a few minutes to provide a statement before depositing her once again with me and Murphy. He was a large, bulldog-faced man whose gut and reddened cheeks spoke to the kind of work he preferred, no doubt one of those types who liked clean-cut cases, and when a case was not to his liking, forced it into a little box until it looked like one to his superiors, so he could get back to the bar where he "kept tabs" on the local riffraff.

Perhaps I might do a bit of digging myself, so as to assist the detective in his inquiries? But what could I tell, locked up in this small room, with the only witness worth questioning succumbing to a headache behind closed doors?

I glanced around at the furniture—elegant, but hiding nothing—the tables—adorned with lamps and nothing more—and shelves covered in bric-a-brac, some of them the gilded wonders of India, and others the clearly homemade items of woven sachets and framed embroidery, rather than books. I took a turn about the room, taking a closer look at some of the paintings, then at some of the items on display. A particularly ornate wooden box with a gorgeous etching of pipes, elephants, and flowers engaged my attention. I reached for it and pulled it down from its higher shelf.

I opened the lid and immediately snapped it closed again when music began to play. I glanced toward the closed bedroom door and listened intently. No sounds of movement came from within, so I returned to my find.

Carefully, with unhurried and deliberate movements, I opened the box just enough to slip my finger under the lid, feeling for the small catch that triggered the music.

I found it and kept my finger upon it as I cautiously lifted the lid once more. This time the music did not play.

I breathed a sigh of relief, glanced toward the closed door one more time, and then pulled out the stack of letters hidden within the box.

Closing the lid, I left the box on the shelf, turning to the letters.

"My dearest darling, when shall we meet again? 'When to the sessions of sweet silent thought I summon up remembrance of things past, I sigh the lack of many a thing I sought,' I sigh for you, my dove, my love, my one and only."

A Shakespeare lover, it would seem. I flipped to another letter. More Shakespeare.

"'Shall I compare thee to a summer's day? Thou art more lovely and more temperate...' Write soon and very soon if not sooner, my love."

I glanced toward the door. One more...

"My fellows tell me I am too young. That I am lost in the dream of love, wrapped in lines from a play, merely playing the role of the young lover. They attempt to dissuade me from your love, but they fail altogether."

Apparently Mr. Jackson's attempts to keep his Rapunzel in her tower had failed. She had somehow managed to fall in love without his knowledge.

Perhaps just one more letter...

"I know you fear your uncle, his distress over our relationship, saying we are too young. But one is never too young to experience true love. I tell you truly, no other has ever made me feel like this. I am yours, forever and always. You must tell him. You must—"

Footsteps sounded in the hall.

In a frenzy, I shoved the letters back into the box, lifting the lid so quickly to return them that the music only sounded a single note before it was closed again, and the box was slid back onto the shelf where I'd found it.

There was a rough knock on the door and the Bulldog himself entered.

"They want you downstairs," he barked.

I turned from the shelf as though I'd been simply pondering its curios. "Me? I think you mean Miss Kelthorpe," I said.

"I know very well whom they want, Miss Green," he growled. "You, downstairs, now."

5

Inquest

"[Anna Katharine Green is] 'the foremost representative in America today of police-court literature;' yet to us this reference seems unsatisfactory, inadequate. It conveys no hint of the constructive skill, the imaginative power and the perceptive faculties necessary for the praiseworthy writing of police-court literature; and, furthermore, it offers no suggestion of Anna Katharine Green's exquisite sense of humor."

— E.F. Harkins and C.H.L. Johnston,
"Anna Katharine Green," ***Little Pilgrimages Among the Women Who Have Written Famous Books***

I practically tripped down the main staircase and into the parlor, my heart beating faster than my feet were traveling.

My breath only evened out when my eyes fell upon my father, James Wilson Green, lawyer extraordinaire, his calming presence precisely what I needed at this point in time.

He looked up as I entered and crossed to me, his hands out. "Daughter," he said formally, taking my hands and giving them a squeeze as he whispered, "Do not worry, my dear. They only want to know your connection to the deceased, and the reason for our presence here today."

"Yes, Father," I whispered in return.

"And watch your tongue." He winked. "All you say will be recorded from the moment you take the stand."

"I know, Father." I smiled.

He squeezed my arm tenderly, then led me to the chair set beside the table which was working as the coroner's bench for this afternoon. I adjusted my skirts about myself as I demurely took my seat with my hands clasped before me, my face set in a manner as to tell the jury that I was honest, trustworthy, and decent, and could be taken as a reliable witness.

It was quite a lot to ask of my face, but I knew I was up to the task. I felt confident I could set my face in whatever manner the situation called for.

The men seated in the jury chairs smiled at me pleasantly. Their faces varied from a double-chinned man whose flat face looked like a closed pocket watch, to a ferret-faced individual who squinted at me with beady little eyes that made me want to squint back. I turned my focus instead to the kind features of Mr. Hammond so as not to mar my appearance of reliability.

"Miss Green, thank you for joining us," the coroner said in a deep voice of assured respectability. "I assume you are familiar with such proceedings and are prepared to give honest answers to all you are asked."

"Of course, sir," I said with a nod.

I avoided looking at my father where he sat just to the left of the jury, for I knew if our eyes met, my poised and practiced face would crack.

"Very well then." Mr. Hammond raised his voice so all in the room could hear him clearly as he continued. "Miss Green, tell us how you came to be here this afternoon."

"My father and I were on our way to visit Mr. Jackson when our carriage was stopped by the sound of a gunshot."

"What time was this?"

I considered. "I'm afraid I cannot say, sir, as I did not think at the time to check my pocket watch." I held up the watch that hung from my chatelaine, a beautiful Seth Thomas I had been gifted just last Christmas.

"And you both heard the gunshot?"

"Everyone heard it, sir. The entire street stopped and ducked, believing it had come from somewhere on the street itself."

"But it did not?"

"No. Once the shock had subsided, it was clear it had come from an upper window. Everyone was pointing in that direction. The direction of Mr. Jackson's home."

"And you were familiar with Mr. Jackson's residence prior to today, he being a client of your father's?"

I shook my head. "This was my first time visiting Mr. Jackson in his home."

"Then why were you accompanying your father on this particular visit?"

I hesitated only briefly. There was no use attempting to hide something that would come to light one way or another.

"Mr. Jackson and I had suffered a...disagreement yesterday. My father and I were visiting to ensure our acquaintance would remain intact."

A susurration traveled through the watching crowd. Having engaged in a recent argument with the victim was never a good place to find oneself in the midst of a murder inquiry. But it was always better to be honest about such things up front, or so my father had often indicated.

"And what was the nature of your 'disagreement?'"

"I had declined Mr. Jackson's proposal of courtship."

The men of the jury didn't seem to find it odd that someone my age might be attached to Mr. Jackson. A middle-aged man could have any young lady he set his fancy to, should his pocketbook be large enough.

"Was Mr. Jackson much displeased by this?"

My mind flashed to the same question being asked by Lenore.

"I honestly do not know, Mr. Hammond," I said, raising my chin. "My father and I merely felt it was the Christian thing to do, to inquire as to his emotional state on the following day. My father must maintain an amicable relationship with all of his clients, after all. I would hate to learn that their business relationship had been somehow marred by our...lack of compatibility on another plane."

A soft chuckle could be heard amongst the jury, but I kept my eyes glued to Mr. Hammond.

"Perhaps that question would be better asked of those who knew him better, such as his niece."

The coroner nodded. "Yes, I was coming to Miss Kelthorpe. I take it you knew her well?"

"I am afraid I only met her for the first time today."

"Oh?"

"As I said, this was my first time visiting Mr. Jackson's home. I was unaware Miss Kelthorpe lived with her uncle until she introduced herself to me and my father upon our arrival."

"Which was after the shot. Was she much distressed?"

"Quite distressed," I affirmed. "She told us her uncle had committed suicide, but I thought she must be mistaken."

"And why was that?"

"From what I know of Mr. Jackson, sir, it would be most unlikely for him to commit such an act." I was tempted to make a wry smile at this remark, given that the pompous man most assuredly would not have considered taking his own life. But then my heart sank, recalling the manner in which Lenore had implied that he truly may have been so afflicted by our lack of courtship that his only recourse was to—

"But Miss Kelthorpe did not think it unlikely?" Mr. Hammond asked.

I considered. "I believe she took what she'd witnessed and came to the most likely conclusion, given the gunshot and the hole in his head."

The jury rumbled at this phrasing, the Ferret's eyes slitting further, and I bit my lip. *Demure and decent, demure and decent.*

"And you have been with Miss Kelthorpe ever since?"

"Yes, sir."

"How would you describe Miss Kelthorpe's character? Broadly speaking and given your relatively short acquaintance."

I considered for only a moment as Lenore's blotchy red face appeared in my recollections. "She is young, sir, and alone. I believe she is frightened and obviously grieving for her uncle. To have an inquest follow so quickly on the heels of her personal discovery—but I will let her tell you of that."

Mr. Hammond gave a sharp nod. "Thank you, Miss Green. Are there any questions from the jury?"

I glanced over the collection of men but did not linger long on any one of them, hoping they would not have anything further.

They did not and I was excused, but asked to remain in the parlor. I took a seat beside my father gratefully.

"Well done," he said softly, pausing in his notes to pat my hand encouragingly.

"What did I miss?" I asked.

"Later," he replied, tapping the pad before him, which was covered in his shorthand.

I wished I'd thought of bringing a notebook with me today. I might have recorded my descriptions of the Ferret and Watch-face jurymen and the Bulldog detective, perhaps used them in a poem about the disagreeable face of justice.

My thoughts were interrupted, however, as everyone turned to watch someone enter from the back of the room.

6

Witness

"The hand will often reveal more than the countenance..."

—***The Leavenworth Case***

The afternoon sun was streaming through the bay windows at just the right angle to provide a halo about Lenore's ringleted golden head. Her bow lips and heart-shaped face seemed to entrance the viewers—all of whom were men, besides myself and a couple of the servants. The way she held her chin aloft with her hands clasped before her, walking slowly, delicately, seemed to invoke the presence of her namesake.

She settled into the chair beside Mr. Hammond and surveyed the room. The poise she displayed was practically flawless, but I'd seen the crack in her armor upstairs. Perhaps it had been worth my time spent above, after all, to know that contrary to her appearance now, Lenore was struggling with the loss of her uncle.

"Miss Kelthorpe, thank you for joining us," Mr. Hammond said, quickly switching to his voice of authority. "I will be asking you some questions, which I would like you to answer honestly. Can you do that for me?"

"Of course, sir," said Lenore, her youth belied by her carriage, her head held high as though this was the moment she'd been preparing herself for all day. Perhaps her lie down had done her some good.

"Thank you. Please begin by telling us about your relationship with your uncle."

"Of course, sir," Lenore said again, turning to face the jury. She seemed about to deliver a monologue from Shakespeare; I half-expected Ophelia's "I cannot choose but weep, to think they should lay him in the cold ground."

I was suddenly reminded of the letters I'd found upstairs, forgotten in the apprehension of my own testimony. I mustn't forget them again.

"My uncle was a kind and generous benefactor. He took me under his wing after my parents' sudden and untimely death when I was young. Without his care and guidance, I do not know what might have become of me in this frightening world of wolves."

What Lenore delivered was not far from Ophelia's cries.

"How long have you been in the care of your uncle?"

"Fifteen years. He adopted me when I was only three, upon his return from India."

"And the loss of your uncle, what will this mean for you? Have you any other family?"

Lenore shook her head sadly, her eyes larger and sparkling again with the tears of loss. "No. I believe my uncle had an estranged sister, but that is of little use to me…" She took a deep breath, then softly whispered as if to herself. "I am alone in the world forever now."

Mr. Hammond proffered her a handkerchief and she took it gratefully, dabbing lightly at her eyes.

"You have no betrothed or intended?"

"No, sir," she said, but the hand which held the handkerchief tightened.

My brows rose in surprise. I knew for a fact she was lying. Not just by her hand, but by the letters I'd uncovered. I wondered who the lucky man might be.

A man shifted in his seat across from her, his eyes completely focused on Lenore in the witness chair.

Could this be the man? I wondered. I considered where he sat between Boyle and Murphy. I recalled Lenore's slight smile when she'd said her uncle had only shown appreciation for one member of staff: his private secretary. Perhaps she, too, felt a high regard for the man. It would explain how she'd managed to find love whilst remaining within her uncle's walls. Young love would always find a way, it was said.

He was nothing remarkable to look at. He had the plain, well-mannered, whiskered face of one who might have been lost in a sea of faces, had he not been in such close proximity to Lenore.

I recalled my own infatuation with a young man whilst summering with my cousin Mary Hatch in upstate New York after college. He had been a poet whom I would not have considered otherwise, except that we were in constant contact with one another that summer, and his words...his words captured my heart. We had promised to remain in touch after the summer, but we had not. Such was young love, and again I was reminded of the letters in Lenore's room.

"Do you believe your uncle will have made provision for you?"

"Of course, sir," said Lenore, her hands stilling. "He made it clear that he intended to leave his estate to me at the time of his...death." She lowered her eyes.

"Your uncle's lawyer has corroborated that remark," the coroner said, nodding toward Father and reaffirming what I'd already guessed to be true: I'd missed seeing my father on the witness stand. "Would you say you were close to your uncle, Miss Kelthorpe?"

Lenore hesitated and glanced toward the staff, who were all smiling at her in encouragement, as though by their positive thoughts and prayers they might help their young charge.

"We were as close as kin," she said, which didn't really answer the question.

"The servants also made mention of it," Mr. Hammond continued, speaking as much to the jury as to her. "They have described your relationship with the deceased as a reserved one, but they assumed quite dear."

"We are—were—private people," Lenore said, her eyes cast down.

"And are you aware that one of your staff is currently missing?"

Lenore's eyes widened and she looked fully at the coroner.

"No, sir. Who?"

"The downstairs maid," Mr. Hammond referred to his notes, "Emily O'Connell."

Lenore's poise was faltering, her eyes darting to the servants and back again, as though seeking assistance.

"When was the last time you saw her?"

Lenore's hands twisted and untwisted the handkerchief. "Yesterday evening. She came to me for some drops for a headache."

"Is it common for the staff to come to you for medicines?"

"Yes. I am the holder of the keys to the medicine cabinet." She touched her chatelaine at her side, from which hung the usual accoutrements. From my seat I could make out a tiny gold watch, a perfume ball, a small bottle, and a collection of keys. "All medicines are kept in my room, locked, so they will not be abused."

"Have you had instances where they were abused, to make this a necessity?"

"No, but it has happened in other houses, so my uncle required it to be so."

"How long have you been in charge of this cabinet?"

"About three years. I am quite familiar with its contents by now."

"So it was yesterday evening when you last saw Emily?" Mr. Hammond asked.

"Yes."

"Did you give her the medicine she requested?"

"No."

"No?" The coroner raised an eyebrow at her.

Lenore sighed. "I suppose I must tell you all in honesty?"

Mr. Hammond glanced at the jury. "Yes, Miss Kelthorpe, to the best of your ability."

Lenore nodded perfunctorily as though she knew what she had to do. Her grip on the handkerchief tightened. "Although she came to me for drops for a headache, it was not the real reason she came to my room."

"And what was the real reason?" the coroner encouraged her.

"She wanted money."

Mr. Hammond's dark brows rose nearly to his receding hairline. "Money?"

"Yes. She said she knew the truth about my uncle and his will, and wanted money to be kept silent."

The jury shifted in their seats and murmured. The Ferret's eyes slitted once more.

"Miss Kelthorpe, are you saying Emily blackmailed you?"

"Yes and no. She attempted blackmail, but was unsuccessful. I told her she had no idea what she was talking about, and sent her away."

"Back to her room?"

"No, away from the house. She is not missing, Mr. Hammond. She was dismissed."

A general stir traveled the length of the room. The juryman with the double chins shook his head as he clutched his pocket watch. Lenore's lady's maid, Murphy, was shaking her head and muttering something to the cook seated beside her, who was shaking her head right back. Apparently they had not known of this occurrence, and were as surprised as everyone else.

Mr. Hammond called everyone to order before returning his attention to Lenore.

"This is information that would have been better conveyed to Detective Billings this afternoon."

"I am sorry, sir," Lenore apologized. "I did not feel it was relevant to my uncle's suicide."

At the word, the jury muttered and swayed again.

"It is the object of this inquest to determine whether it was indeed suicide, Miss Kelthorpe, so if you can, would you please relate to us the events of today that have led to us gathering here."

Lenore nodded slightly. "Sometime around one o'clock there was a gunshot, causing the entire household to run to my uncle's study to discover he had shot himself."

I caught the juryman with double chins checking his pocket watch, as though to confirm the time Lenore had given.

"Would you mind embellishing the details a bit?" asked Mr. Hammond. "For instance, was the door to the study locked?"

"Yes, sir, from the inside."

"Do you have a key?"

"Yes, sir, but I could not find it, so flustered was I by the gunshot, and so it was Mr. Farwell's key which was used to finally open the door." She sent a smile his way and the young man with the forgettable features sat up straighter in his chair. I'd deduced his name, at least, correctly.

"Mr. Farwell, your uncle's private secretary?"

"Yes, sir."

"Very good. We have heard his account of events. Would you please tell us what you saw when you opened the door?"

Lenore choked in her throat and her eyes grew round like a startled bird's. "Must I, sir?"

"Yes, Miss Kelthorpe, I am afraid so," said Mr. Hammond gently, his demeanor suddenly tender.

"Well, I...I saw...my uncle's head—"

This time, she fainted.

7

Evidence

"At this critical time [Anna Katharine Green's] father was friend and counsellor.... When doubts arose, when discouragement appeared, he was nearby to cheer her and to advise. He enlisted her sympathy in different cases that interested him; he sharpened her wits; he discoursed to her on his own interesting experiences; he contributed judicious criticisms; above all, he fostered her confidence in her own powers."

— E.F. Harkins and C.H.L. Johnston, "Anna Katharine Green," ***Little Pilgrimages Among the Women Who Have Written Famous Books***

Above the hubbub that followed the rousing of Lenore, led by the private secretary who was the first to her side, the coroner adjourned the inquest until the following day, stating that Miss Kelthorpe would be required to return to complete her statement and answer any questions the jury might put to her.

Father and I led Lenore into the semi-privacy of the back hallway where he spoke to her in low tones, offering his assistance should she require it, as he'd been the friend and confidant of her uncle for so many years. Slowly, the rest of the crowd receded from the parlor, all too eager to hold on to this most interesting of experiences as long as possible. With a final gracious "thank you" falling from her lips, Lenore excused herself to her room, and her lady's maid followed, attentive and concerned.

Finally, all that remained were four people: the Bulldog, my father, myself, and one man who'd been seated in the back of the room, who now remained as though he'd always been a permanent fixture, sculpted into the large armchair which he'd made his own.

He leaned forward onto the head of his cane as the bulldog detective approached him.

"You will have to leave now, sir—ah, Mr. Sokol," he growled. "Of course it is you."

"You say that as though it is not a pleasure to see me," said the man, studying the head of his cane, which was shaped like a bird of some kind.

"Well, sir, if you did not insist on horning in on every one of my investigations, perhaps I would find it more of a pleasure to notice you forcing yourself, yet again, into my case."

"'Horning' is so close to a dirty word, and 'forcing' is no better. Perhaps you might pick another. 'Pressing' or 'pushing' still have an unpleasant accompaniment of thought. Would 'assisting' or 'helping' be too simple for you?"

The Bulldog growled again. "Mr. Sokol, I must ask that you not involve yourself this time."

"Nonsense, Detective Billings," said Father. "To not allow Mr. Sokol to share his insights would be a detriment to our case, if we hope to solve this murder efficiently."

The Bulldog's eyes snapped to Father's and back again to the man in the chair, who was now contemplating the embroidery lining the armrest.

"He's your pet, Mr. Green. Not mine. You take care of him, but I don't want him sniffing anywhere near me on this one."

"I shall attempt not to leave a mark on your territory in any manner whatsoever," said Mr. Sokol, a small twitch at the edge of his mouth telling me that he was as much aware of the dog-like aspects of the detective as I was.

The Bulldog tipped his hat to me, said he'd return on the morrow, and finally left.

The room felt lighter immediately.

"Ah," sighed Mr. Sokol. "Now I can breathe."

"I don't believe you've had the pleasure of meeting my daughter, Sokol," Father said, presenting me to the strange man in the chair.

He seemed to prefer admiring the hem of my striped gown rather than meeting my eyes.

"I have not," said the man, rising stiffly and bending over his cane in a bow that signified an age much older than he'd at first appeared, perhaps closer to Father's age. Or perhaps he merely suffered from some debilitating disease—arthritis or the like.

"Forgive me, Miss Green, for the rheumatism in my hands and feet prevents me from offering you a more sincere greeting," he said, and I smiled. My powers of deduction were finally hitting their stride, it would seem.

I gave him a polite curtsy. "It is a pleasure to meet you, Mr. Sokol."

I wished desperately to ask how Father knew this enigma, but it would have to wait. For now, I must simply gather the details I could from the man's features and aspect.

He was tall, though when he had stood he was slightly hunched to a height less than Father's, and he'd quickly retaken his seat in the armchair with a soft *whompf*. He was not thin, but neither was he as large as the Bulldog, so I put him down as comfortably portly. His clothing bespoke a man of means, though not quite a gentleman, but his manner said he was used to being listened to. Although he had seemed at odds with the detective, he otherwise seemed an agreeable personage, and I decided then and there that if my father liked him, I would like him, too. Even if he had yet to meet my eyes.

"Have you had a chance to walk about the house and note anything of interest?" Father was asking.

"I have," Mr. Sokol said, and I wondered how he'd managed to get upstairs and down again without my hearing a tapping cane in the hall. I must have been more distracted by the simple conversation that had taken place in Lenore's room than I'd realized.

"And?" Father asked.

"And..." Mr. Sokol's eyes flitted to the mantelpiece, to the witness chair, to the coroner's table, to the seats of the jury.

"I would be willing to discuss my thoughts further should you desire to take the time, but they are not appropriate conversation for this particular location," said Mr. Sokol, focusing on the top of his cane again and running one long finger up and down the beak.

"Of course," said Father. "We could entertain you for dinner, if you'd care to join us."

"It would be my pleasure," Mr. Sokol said with a nod to his cane, who apparently was also invited. He then stood and made his way slowly toward the door, replacing his hat upon his head as he went.

I couldn't help feeling an urgency as we called for a cab and finally returned to our own house on Twelfth Street.

Father informed Mrs. Heritage, the cook, that there would be one more for dinner and apologized for the late notice, but she took it in stride, as it was often the case that Father was either suddenly not in attendance or arrived with a guest, depending upon his caseload.

"Mrs. Green and Miss Green have gone out for the evening to the theater, sir, so it will be no bother to add another," she said with a bob.

Knowing this was the case, I dressed for dinner quickly. I gathered my long, brown hair—which, unbound, swept to the floor when I stood erect—into a magnificent concoction of chignon curls. I chose a navy-blue evening dress of finest silk, trimmed with caramel ruffles and a square-cut neckline that accentuated my shoulders and long neck, and brought out the blue in my eyes. I loved the sound the dress made behind me as I came down the stairs, clutching my fan to keep my hands occupied in the excitement of discussing the day's events with my father and a man I took to be an expert in his field.

I was not surprised when Mr. Sokol arrived before my father, and I curtsied respectfully as he entered.

By the light of the evening lamps, I took a moment to study his features. His nose was large and peaked, like the bird on his cane, and he was clean-shaven, so I could make out the cleft in his chin and the curves of his full lips as he spoke. His evening attire had changed his aspect once again, and now I thought he might be closer to thirty.

"You are wondering how old I am," he said, his hands playfully twisting his cane back and forth as he sat before the fire, revealing the handle to be in the shape of a falcon head.

I jumped slightly. "I am afraid you are correct, sir. It is impertinent of me, but—"

"How old do you think I am?" he asked the inkstand on my father's desk in the corner.

I paused, conflicted, but in the end deciding that honesty must win the day. "When we first met, I thought you middle-aged, until you referenced your rheumatism, which explained the stiff movements and the cane. Now, in the light of the gas lamps rather than daylight, and dressed in a dinner jacket and bow tie, I would guess you were...thirty-two."

Mr. Sokol's mouth twitched as he focused his gaze on me fully, on my eyes and face, and not on my hands or gown. His eyes pierced with intelligence like a falcon's straight through to my heart. I'd read that once in a novel and thought it a cliché, but now, feeling it, I understood why it was a worthwhile descriptor.

"I am thirty-one," he said clearly. "I suppose I should be offended you think me older." But he did not look offended as he continued his conversation with the intriguing inkstand. "Your powers of deduction are quite adequate, Miss Green. I can see why your father is so proud of you."

I could feel my face warm as Father entered.

"I am glad you feel that way, Sokol," he said, welcoming his guest. "I have shared many an interesting case discussion with my daughter. I would like her to hear what you have to say in regards to the Jackson case."

"So long as you do not fear her *friendship* with Mr. Jackson to be a hindrance."

He said the word "friendship" as though it were a dirty word, and his eyes actually flicked once again to mine before returning to his cane, a small smile on his lips.

Was he attempting to make a joke at my expense? Did he find it humorous that the day after I had declined courtship, Mr. Jackson had been found dead? There were more things in heaven and earth that were laughable, to paraphrase the good Bard.

"It will be no hindrance," I said pointedly.

8

Dinnertime

"All animated and glowing with his enthusiasm, he eyed the chandelier above him as if it were the embodiment of his own sagacity."

—*The Leavenworth Case*

I was glad the rest of the family had gone out, so we'd be able to converse about the case over the meal, and not be forced to wait until after.

Over the sparkling of glassware and the clink of forks against china, I found myself withdrawing from the tepid discussion between my father and Mr. Sokol about current affairs, until it finally landed once again upon the Jackson case.

"So, Sokol, tell us what Detective Billings missed."

"Besides everything, I'm certain," I said derisively, the glass of wine freeing my tongue of my honest opinion.

"You should not look so dimly on the New York Metropolitan Police Force, Miss Green," said Mr. Sokol. "They are not all so bad."

I cursed my inability to hold my tongue after just one glass of fermented grapes. It was beneath me to allow it such a hold, and I knew I should avoid it altogether, but the supple blend of sweet and bitter and joy was too much for me to deny at every meal.

"Sokol himself used to be one of them, but retired when they thought his rheumatism slowed him down—though nothing ever has nor will slow him down, as far as I can tell." Father lifted his glass across the table in salute.

"You are too kind." Mr. Sokol dabbed his lips. He did not continue, however, as the third course was cleared and the fourth—baked fish dressed with coleslaw, cucumbers, and tomatoes—was placed before us.

"Please, Sokol, don't leave us dangling," said Father once it was again just the three of us in the dining room.

"The detective only missed two items of import," Mr. Sokol told his wine glass. "The first was a key that fits the lock of Mr. Jackson's study, found in Mr. Jackson's personal fireplace in his bedroom."

"It must be Miss Kelthorpe's—the one she lost." I pushed my pernicious glass of wine farther out of reach.

"Ah, that's the question. Is this key," he removed the item with a flourish from within his jacket pocket, "Miss Kelthorpe's missing key? Or does it belong to someone else?"

"Whom else could it belong to? Mr. Farwell used his own key to open the study door."

"So we've been told, but one key looks much like another. Who's to say Mr. Farwell didn't take Miss Kelthorpe's key because *his* was missing? So in reality, I have found Mr. Farwell's missing key, rather than Miss Kelthorpe's missing key. You see where the confusion lies. We have yet to verify how many people in the house had a copy of that particular key. Mr. Jackson himself was certain to have at least one on his person, and we have not heard that his was found on his body," Mr. Sokol told the key as he twisted it between his long fingers.

"I'll be sure to verify that information with Mr. Hammond tomorrow," said Father.

"Whether it is her key or Mr. Farwell's," I said, "I wonder why it was in her uncle's personal fireplace? Why would she or he have reason to enter her uncle's bedroom?"

"I think the more important question is: Why would she or he murder her uncle?" Mr. Sokol said, and I bit my lip. Though he was still speaking to the key, somehow Mr. Sokol had noticed this small movement, and he asked me if the question made me uncomfortable.

I shook my head. "I just have a difficult time believing she could shoot her uncle. She is too young, naïve. She's never left her house. She knows nothing about the world..." But I stopped there. I was conflicted. How much did I really know about Lenore? I'd spent all of a couple hours with her, and in that time what facts had I seen, outside of emotions?

The letters.

"I do wonder if Mr. Jackson stood in the way of Miss Kelthorpe's marriage to an unwanted," I muttered.

Father looked at me and Mr. Sokol considered the chandelier.

"What do you mean? She said she didn't have a man in her life," said Father.

"Yes, but she was lying."

"How do you come by that?" my father asked, finally giving up on the fourth course and setting down his fork.

"Her hands," Mr. Sokol told the chandelier.

I quirked my mouth. "Yes, so you noticed, too? I thought all men in the room were completely enthralled with Miss Kelthorpe."

Mr. Sokol looked at the chandelier fondly. "Not every man."

"You see now why I wanted to include my daughter in this conversation?" my father asked, now lifting his glass to me, causing me to blush. "I usually notice when a witness is lying, but this particular time I must have been distracted by my notes. What did I miss?"

"You've told me before that the hands are the most reliable of testimonies against the truthfulness of a person's words," I said, taking the lead. "That poor handkerchief was almost rags, it was so wrung and twisted when she said she was not betrothed, and again when she told about the missing maid blackmailing her."

"So you do not think she was entirely truthful today," summed up Father. "Do you think it might have been nerves, given the shock she'd just endured not three hours before?"

I glanced at Mr. Sokol, who was regarding the candlestick in the middle of the table as though it was the most marvelous contraption he'd ever seen. I wondered what he was really admiring.

"It most certainly might have been caused by grief," I admitted.

"Grief can be affected," said Mr. Sokol, apparently done admiring the candlestick. "Actors on the stage bring about tears in many ways."

My heart leapt at the thought, remembering the tender moment I'd witnessed between Lenore and Murphy. No, Mr. Sokol was not there. He had not seen what I'd seen. And, indeed, if he never allowed his eyes to rest on a person, I wondered at his ability to see anyone fully at all.

"What cause would she have to feign grief before me? It makes much more sense that her performance was below, before the jury, and not above for only myself. Besides, true grief, the kind that distorts the features... I believe there are some emotions not even the best actress can feign, and someone like Miss Kelthorpe would never let her face become so unappealing on purpose," I said, recalling once again the obvious redness upon Lenore's features that had come after true tears.

"Besides," I said, preparing for my big reveal, "there were the letters."

"What letters?" my father asked.

"I found a stack of letters hidden in Miss Kelthorpe's private salon."

My father frowned, but Mr. Sokol was back to admiring the candlestick.

"She went to lie down for a moment and I was left alone to twiddle my thumbs until I was called upon. I happened upon a box that held a collection of letters, and since there were no other reading materials available to me at the time, I perused them. Not in any great depth, mind you, but enough to make sense of the contents."

My father still didn't look pleased to hear his daughter had taken to snooping, but his curiosity soon got the best of him.

"And?" he asked.

"I do not know who they were from, but they were most certainly love letters between Miss Kelthorpe and a young man, a young man with a penchant for Shakespeare."

"So you were correct," said Mr. Sokol. "She was lying."

I nodded.

"You also said she was never allowed to leave the house. So how did she meet this lover?" Mr. Sokol asked.

"I don't know. All I know is, she had letters secreted away. She must have met him somewhere at some time. Or," I paused for effect, "he was living in the house with her."

Father cleared his throat. "What do you mean by that?"

"I mean it's possible one of the staff is the secret lover. I'm certain Mr. Jackson would not have approved of such an affair."

"You think Boyle is in love with Lenore?"

I laughed lightly at the idea. "No, not Boyle—Mr. Farwell."

"Ahhh," my father said slowly, clearly seeing what cards I was laying down.

Mr. Sokol said nothing, but continued to look fondly at the candlestick.

"It is unfortunate that she is currently the only one who benefits from Jackson's death, which immediately makes her look guilty before the jury. And if she was hiding an affair..." Father waved his fork and sighed. "Thankfully, I don't believe there's enough evidence that might lead to Miss Kelthorpe's arrest just yet. There's still the missing maid, and the attempted blackmail, about which I must question Miss Kelthorpe further. All we can know for certain at this point is that the inquest will declare Jackson's death was not suicide. The surgeon confirmed that."

"Did he? I missed his statement," I said.

"Yes. He gave a detailed description of the wound, its location, and what it meant in terms of Jackson's position at the time of his death," said Father.

"Sir, are you ready for the next course?" the butler interrupted, with an admonishing look at our half-full plates, though Mr. Sokol's was surprisingly clean.

"Yes, Teagan, you may clear."

Roasted venison, potatoes, and green beans presented themselves swiftly, and I made a point of taking multiple bites before I became distracted by conversation again. It would never do to make Mrs. Heritage angry by sending back food, especially after surprising her with a dinner guest.

"So what did the surgeon say?" I finally asked.

"I'm not certain it's appropriate dinner conversation," said Father. "Let's just say the wound was clearly made by a gun held close to the back of the head while he was seated and looking down, most likely writing a letter or working on his book, and no gun was found nearby."

"So that was why the jury didn't like Miss Kelthorpe's insistence that her uncle had shot himself. They knew he couldn't possibly have done so." I shook my head.

"I'm afraid it's the little things like that which will give me a difficult time defending Miss Kelthorpe, should it come to it," agreed Father with a sigh. "But I must, for the sake of Jackson."

I reached out and gave my father's hand a squeeze.

"Now we just need to determine if she knows how to fire a gun," said Mr. Sokol smoothly after taking a draft of wine.

My mind flicked to Lenore's reaction to the hole in her uncle's head. "I somehow doubt she's capable, given her faint today. I should think it another point in her favor, besides her youth."

"Never underestimate a determined woman, no matter her age," Mr. Sokol counseled his knife. "There is a gun in the house, after all."

"Ah, I was wondering what the second thing would be," said Father, a smile revealing his pleasure at Mr. Sokol's ability to outwit the local detective.

"There was a small Smith & Wesson pistol in the drawer of Mr. Jackson's desk."

"The desk where Mr. Jackson's body was found?" Father scoffed. "How on earth did Billings miss that?"

"It is not enough to look for evidence where you expect to find it. You must sometimes search for it where you don't," said Mr. Sokol. "It was tucked behind a stack of clean manuscript paper, so one wouldn't find it unless one pulled the drawer out far enough to look. Unfortunately for Detective Billings, you will find that the ball extracted from the dead man was a No. 32 ball, which would fit perfectly into that pistol."

"Was it loaded?" Father asked.

"Yes—but!" Mr. Sokol raised his finger, stopping Father's look of disappointment. "I could tell that a bullet had recently been fired from one of the chambers. Although the barrel had been cleaned so that it showed no evidence, the cylinder had a bit of smut lining one of the chambers, which indicates a bullet had recently passed through it. Someone cleaned the barrel but not the cylinder, and in so doing, left unintended evidence behind. Should the coroner call for a clerk from a pistol and ammunition store, he will surely tell you the same."

9

Final Questions

"I own that I was surprised at the softening which had taken place in her haughty beauty."

—***The Leavenworth Case***

"How did you come to meet Mr. Sokol, Father?" I asked the next morning as we rode to the second half of the inquest.

Father chuckled. "How does one ever come to meet Mr. Sokol? Same as you did: at an inquest. I don't know how many times I saw him and yet never spoke with him until finally one day I asked him why his interest. He told me, 'I fear I have been bred to do so. As a retriever must retrieve, so I must detect.' I thought him an abrupt individual, rather abrasive in some ways, and odd, distinctly odd. But oddly perceptive at that."

"Is the rheumatism why he never looks you in the eye?"

My father smiled. "No, that's just Sokol. Always been that way, always will be."

I nodded. "So he's helped you before? On cases?"

"Yes. He's been invaluable in gathering evidence against or for persons involved. I believe he has something like a crew of information gatherers, who work for him when his rheumatism keeps him confined to his house," said Father. "You were lucky he was capable of joining us for dinner last night. I have invited him many times before and he's always passed on my offer, claiming pain in his joints."

The carriage slowed as we neared Mr. Jackson's house. "If I'm not mistaken," my father continued, reaching for the door, "the reason he chose to come last night of all nights...was because of you." He gave me a fatherly smile and then alighted from the carriage, reaching back for my hand.

I sat a moment, blushing ridiculously at my father's intimation. Why would any man show interest in me when there were others—Lenores—in the world, beautiful women who would meet a man's eyes with far more pleasure and less intellectual obstinacy?

I wasn't certain why my heart raced at the idea.

I alighted and my father led me inside, back into the coroner's lion's den. I wondered how Lenore had fared the previous evening, alone in the house where her uncle had been murdered.

I noticed the room had somehow swelled to accommodate even more onlookers than the day before, but someone other than Mr. Sokol had taken up residence in his armchair. I wondered where he was.

"I'm so thankful you returned," Lenore said, approaching me with arms outstretched.

I was surprised when she not only took my hands but leaned in to press her cheek against mine, as though we had been friends for far longer than a single day.

"Sit by me," she said, linking her arm through mine and leading us to the front row, my father taking a seat on my other side.

"How are you?" I asked, taking in her pale features, the darkness under her eyes causing me to guess at a sleepless night.

"I am quite nervous," Lenore whispered to me. "I couldn't sleep a wink last night."

"You look beautiful," I said, attempting to comfort her by admiring her mourning gown. The black bombazine was gathered in tiers to give the dress form, with a square-cut neck lined with black lace, echoed in the sleeves and hemline. She wore no jewelry, not even black, leaving the paleness of her neck to stand in deep contrast to the dress's color. "You must tell me your dressmaker. She does an excellent job of finding styles that suit you."

Lenore shook her head. "I am so grateful for Murphy. If it had not been for her assistance this morning, I fear I might have appeared in my nightgown." She tried to smile, but I could see the effort it required.

"Thank you all for returning," said Mr. Hammond, calling the crowd to order.

To my surprise, the coroner did not begin where we'd left off, with Lenore's testimony, but instead called a new witness to take a seat. Lenore breathed a sigh of relief at my elbow and I could practically feel the load on her shoulders lessen.

When the new witness declared himself to be a man who worked for a pistol and ammunitions store on Broadway, I couldn't help but scan the room for Mr. Sokol.

The coroner presented the man with the bullet removed from Mr. Jackson's body and the gun found in Mr. Jackson's desk, and the clerk began a lengthy explanation which amounted to the same things Mr. Sokol had said over dinner the night before. As the jury responded in loud appreciation of what this meant to the case, I glanced over my shoulder again toward the back of the room, but I still didn't see Mr. Sokol's cane amongst those present.

"He's not here," Father leaned in to whisper. "I've received a message from him asking that we take notes and inform him after the inquest of what he missed."

"Why would he miss this?"

"I assume his health," said Father.

Perhaps Father had been right and Mr. Sokol had pushed himself too far by coming to our house for dinner last night.

"Miss Kelthorpe, do you think yourself capable of answering a few more questions for us?" Mr. Hammond asked, and I heard Lenore's breath catch beside me.

"Yes, sir," she said slowly, rising with her head held high as she returned to her seat before the jury. Her laced ebony mourning gown accentuated her pale features and blonde ringlets, giving her even more of the appearance of a grieving angel today.

"Miss Kelthorpe, given the circumstances, I must ask if you were aware of your uncle's possession of a gun," the coroner said.

"Yes, sir, I was aware."

"And did you know where it was stored?"

"Yes, in his bedroom."

The coroner glanced at the jury and back to Lenore.

"Would you mind saying that again?"

"Of course, sir. My uncle kept his gun in the drawer of his bedside table."

Mr. Hammond cleared his throat and leaned forward. "Are you quite certain?"

"Yes."

A susurration flowed through the crowd, and I wondered if Murphy had told Lenore what had been shared by the other witnesses the day before. If so, Lenore was doing an admirable job of pretending she didn't know where her uncle's gun had been found.

"Then, how do you think it came to be found for this inquest in the drawer of his *desk?*"

Lenore opened her mouth in shock and her pale cheeks grew paler. "I'm surprised to hear that, sir. For I was always led to believe it was in his bedside table."

"You never saw it there?"

"No...," Lenore said slowly.

"And you never saw it in his desk drawer, either?"

"No, sir, but then I was not one to riffle through my uncle's things."

Mr. Hammond took a deep breath and straightened his notes before him after writing a few things down. When he finally looked up again, he asked, "Who else in the house do you believe was aware of the gun's existence?"

"Why, everyone, sir. He showed it to us all the night he brought it home. He said he wished to make clear that he intended to keep his household safe from burglars, and warned us that no one should be moving about the house at night after curfew unless they wanted an accident to get them killed."

The juryman with the watch-face actually widened his eyes before speaking, and I had to control the impulse to laugh at the thin and squeaky voice which emanated from above the double chins. "You mean he threatened you with it?"

The private secretary, Mr. Farwell, stood up from where he was seated with the other servants on the opposite side of the room, as they'd been the day before. "No, she means he made it clear there was a gun in the house and he wanted to be certain his household was conscientiously aware of it, so as to avoid any mishaps."

The other servants nodded in agreement about him.

"Thank you, Mr. Farwell. Please be seated."

Mr. Farwell took his seat once more, but the way his hands fidgeted with his tie told me there was something aggravating him.

"Miss Kelthorpe," the coroner returned to Lenore, "who in this house do you believe capable of firing this gun?" He held the small pistol out and she visibly shrunk back from it as though he'd held forth a snake for her to pet.

She took a moment to regain her composure before stating, "In all honesty, sir, I do not know. You would have to ask each person in turn."

"That's fine. Miss Kelthorpe, are you capable of firing this gun?"

Lenore glanced at Mr. Farwell, whose face whitened as he grimaced.

"Yes, sir," Lenore said softly, but the whole room heard her answer and murmured in surprise.

"Well, that answers that question." Father wrote in his notes beside Lenore's name: *can shoot gun.*

"That's enough outbursts from the room, thank you," said the coroner to the crowd. He turned back to Lenore. "Did your uncle teach you how to fire his gun?"

"No."

"Then who did?"

She glanced in his direction before saying, "Mr. Farwell."

The room turned to look at the private secretary again, who was paler still than before.

"Mr. Farwell. And why did he teach you?"

"Because I asked him to."

"Please don't hedge the question, Miss Kelthorpe. Why did you ask him to teach you?"

"Because...," she hesitated, "I knew my uncle wouldn't teach me, and I wished to be capable of defending myself, should the need arise."

"Why would you need to defend yourself, Miss Kelthorpe? Your uncle had already said he bought the gun in order to defend you, did he not?"

"Yes, but...I, well, I just wished to know." Lenore's hands were gripping each other so tightly they were going white at the knuckles. "There's nothing more to it."

The double-chinned juryman stood and asked, "Are you capable of cleaning the gun?"

"No," she said, her hands relaxing.

The jury asked a couple more questions, all mundane, about the layout of the house and how the rooms adjoined one another, but I did not listen closely.

Finally Lenore was told she could step down, and it seemed Mr. Hammond was about to ask the jury to withdraw and come to a decision, when the bulldog-faced detective marched up to him and leaned down to whisper something into the coroner's ear. Mr. Hammond's eyebrows rose and everyone murmured, wondering what the latest news was.

The coroner declared the Bulldog would take the stand. I decided I really must at least show him the respect of thinking of him by name rather than by feature.

Detective Billings seemed eager to be questioned and began his response before the coroner finished asking, "Detective, please tell us what you've discov—"

"It has come to my attention that the missing maidservant, Emily O'Connell, is indeed missing and not merely dismissed," he barked at Lenore, who flinched at his words.

I reached out to offer a squeeze of reassurance to her, returning the detective back to the Bulldog in my mind for his rude and unprofessional behavior.

"Her quarters were searched last night and her roommate, the upstairs maid Bridget Kelly, was questioned. Emily never returned to her room the night of the murder after going for drops for a headache. All her belongings remain untouched. We've placed an advert in the papers with a description of her. It will only be a matter of time before we find her." The Bulldog stared directly at Lenore. "And before we know the truth."

"Thank you, Detective Billings," said Mr. Hammond, cutting in as though worried the detective was about to arrest Lenore on the spot. It didn't make sense to me, this aggression toward Lenore. As far as I could tell, Lenore was the victim. "At this time, I will ask the jury to adjourn to an adjacent room in order to come to a consensus regarding Mr. Jackson's demise."

It did not take them long to return a verdict of "Murder by person or persons unknown."

"Now we wait for the detective to make his move," Father muttered as the crowd filed out.

Every juryman paused to express his condolences to Lenore, who eventually removed her handkerchief from her sleeve once again when the stream of well-wishes became too much for her.

"We may not have to wait long," I muttered in reply, as the detective approached Lenore after the final juryman let go of her hand.

But the Bulldog merely removed his hat and asked that Lenore keep him apprised of her movements, inquiring as to when the funeral would be taking place.

"I...I do not know...," Lenore choked out from behind her handkerchief, her eyes full of tears once again at the thought. "Excuse me," she said, and walked swiftly out of the room and up the stairs.

"I've already told Miss Kelthorpe she can count on me for legal representation," said Father, nodding his head toward her retreating back. "May I ask if she'll have need of me in the near future?"

"Quite near, I should imagine," said the Bulldog gruffly. "Why you insist on defending the guilty, I'll never understand." The detective returned his hat to his head with some force. "Good day, Mr. Green. I'll be seeing you soon."

I wanted to trip him as he left, but resorted to merely sticking my tongue out at him in my mind. Sometimes I was quite thankful my thoughts remained safely locked in my head behind a thick screen of propriety.

"I think I'll find out if Miss Kelthorpe would mind some company for tea this afternoon. What do you think, Father?"

"I think Miss Kelthorpe would be most grateful for the suggestion. However, I'd appreciate it if you'd take these notes to Mr. Sokol before returning. I must get to the office to begin preparations to meet Detective Billings head on, should the need arise sooner than anticipated."

I quirked a brow at my father. "You want me to take your notes to Mr. Sokol? Why not mail them?"

"He will be interested to hear what was missed today and I do not want to risk their being read by eyes other than his own." He gave me a quick whiskery kiss on the cheek, and before I could argue he was off to prepare for his latest, and perhaps most difficult case.

10

Sokol

"I even detected Mr. Gryce softening towards the inkstand."

—*The Leavenworth Case*

Mr. Sokol's place of residence was as mysterious as the man. The brick house was simple and withdrawn, set back amongst hedgerows that delineated a purposeful separation from its closely set neighbors. The shutters were closed as I approached, though I caught someone peeking out of the far left one on the third floor as I neared the front door. I knocked and was let in by a maid, who took my coat and hat before conveying me to the front parlor.

"Ah, Miss Green," Mr. Sokol said from the couch, where he lay contemplating the bandaged hands resting upon his chest.

"So good of you to come. Your father could not spare the time, I take it? Already preparing for Miss Kelthorpe's case?"

"Yes, precisely, Mr. Sokol," I said stiffly, uncomfortable to find myself alone with a man to whom I'd only just been introduced, and who, if my father was anything to go by, might even be interested in me. I suddenly found I wasn't certain what to do with my hands, and was sorry the maid had taken my hat.

"All I ask is that you drop the 'Mr.' My friends call me Sokol."

I gave a nod but did not return the favor. "I just stopped by with my father's notes and—"

"I've never been one to read notes. Please, I'd much prefer to hear the inquest as seen through your eyes," he said to the rug while motioning me to a chair nearby.

I sighed as I took a seat, ready to give him only the highlights since he could read the details in the notes he'd declined.

"You're under no obligation to stay, Miss Green," said Mr. Sokol quietly.

I looked up, and I realized he was looking at me.

At me.

Once again I was struck by a piercing intelligence. I could not draw my eyes away from his, and I wondered if the reason he did not look people in the eye when he spoke was because of the effect it had when he did.

"I'd like to stay," I said softly.

And then it was over. His eyes went back to studying the rug, though he looked at it affectionately.

"Please, tell me everything."

So I did. I told him about the ballistics report that matched his own to the letter, and that not only could Lenore shoot a gun, but she'd been taught by the private secretary with whom I suspected she was romantically involved. I told him every question and answer, including my own reactions and the little things I'd noticed. I ended with the declaration from the Bulldog about the missing maidservant.

It was only when I'd finished that I realized Sokol hadn't interrupted once. Not one question. He'd simply considered the rug with a puzzled expression like he was unsure if he'd noticed an error in the pattern or not.

I was silent for several moments, studying him, watching his face as it worked through something only he could see. He was clearly not asleep, and yet it took him a good ten minutes before he realized I'd stopped speaking and glanced up at the clock on the mantel.

"Miss Green, I apologize. Your attention to detail made me feel as though I'd been there with you, watching Miss Kelthorpe's hands turn white at the knuckles."

"And?"

"And?" he repeated.

"And what do you make of it? Have you solved it already?"

Sokol's mouth twitched at the corner, which I imagined was his way of smiling. "No. But I will say that signs of a guilty conscience do not mean Miss Kelthorpe is a murderer."

I was glad to hear it, but I worried how quickly others were jumping to that conclusion based on Lenore's testimony.

"We know she's hiding something involving a man in her life," continued Sokol. "That could be enough to color everything else."

"Not everything in a woman's life comes back to a man," I said derisively, but then cursed myself for being so forthright. I didn't know this man well enough to be so honest, but I couldn't seem to help it. There was something about him that made me want to say what I really thought, rather than holding it back like I usually did in mixed company.

"Indeed," Sokol conceded to the clock.

"Whom do you suspect?" I asked.

"Everyone and nobody. It is not for me to suspect, but to detect."

I had to bite my tongue from retorting that such a line sounded too rehearsed to be true, and yet, I thought, it sounded just like something a detective would say.

"Why did you leave the police force?" I asked.

"As your father said last night, it was not my decision to make." Sokol waved his bandaged hands before his face.

"He said you retired."

Again Sokol's mouth twitched, this time as though irritated or impressed that I should recall his exact words.

"Yes." He nodded. "I retired after they told me my services were no longer of any use. What good is a detective who cannot beat his witnesses and suspects into confessions to fit the prevailing theory?"

"Not all policemen resort to their fists. My father is friends with many and I have overheard their conversations regarding cases." I blanched. Once again I'd said too much. It was most unladylike to listen in on conversations not intended for one's own ears. But was it my fault my father would confer in places where it was impossible *not* to hear?

Sokol studied his bandages. "Mr. Green is the most discerning and dedicated lawyer I have ever encountered. But I must ask: Does your father truly care how he gets the evidence he requires? Does he ever ask how it was obtained?"

I bit my lip. The only thing worse than an innocent person hanged for a murder they didn't commit was the realization that many more of the guilty were set free simply because they'd acquired better lawyers.

"Why are you doing this?" Sokol asked the clock.

I glanced at the clock and back at him, but I knew he was talking to me.

"Doing what?"

"Why have you involved yourself in your father's case? Why do you delight in sitting in on inquests? Why do you continue to show interest in a murder, beyond the average woman?"

My shoulders stiffened. It was Mr. Jackson all over again. Another man who thought women had better things to do than "play detective."

"You can never be a lawyer like your father," he said succinctly.

"I know that," I said, my shoulders loosening with the truth of it. "Perhaps I'll get a poem out of it. I write poetry, you know."

Sokol frowned at the clock.

"You do not like poetry?" I asked, somewhat amused.

He cleared his throat. "I do not see the point of poetry. What has poetry ever done for humanity?" He turned his gaze suddenly upon me again. "Your intelligence is above that of any poet's. You can and should do more with your talents."

And with that he rang for the servant.

"Wait, we're not finished," I said, anger filling me as I stood to my feet. "How dare you speak to me like that."

Sokol's mouth twitched again. "And why not? If you're merely a poetess, I have no use for you."

"Use? Use?!" I cried, my fists balling at my sides. I knew it was childish. But...but... "Who ever said I was to be of *use* to you? I came on behalf of my father, who looks upon you with some degree of admiration, though I have no idea why. As far as I can tell you are prideful, conceited, arrogant—"

"You really ought to work on your disdainful monologues. The least you could do is use words that don't all mean the same thing."

"Argh!" I cried, throwing up my hands.

"I believe we should get to know each other better if you're going to behave in such a manner in my home."

His condescension rankled me, but what was worse was that he said it all with an almost-smile toward the sconce on the wall.

I marched across the room and stood in front of the sconce, blocking his view and forcing his eyes to lock with mine. I hoped he could feel the heat spewing from my eyes as much as I could feel it in my cheeks and down my neck.

I took a deep breath in and out to calm myself just enough to deliver the words that had leapt to my heart. "There is a melody born of melody, / Which melts the world into a sea: / Toil could never compass it; / Art its height could never hit; / It came never out of wit; / But a music music-born / Well may Jove and Juno scorn."

Another deep breath brought me back to the room, to the man lying on the couch, and out of that still, small place where poetry often took me.

Sokol's eyes were still upon me.

"My friend, Ralph Waldo Emerson, wrote that," I said softly, and couldn't stop myself from adding, "Perhaps you've heard of him?"

"Miss Green," Sokol said before letting his eyes dip to something on my right, "if this is the passion you pour into others' poetry..." He looked up into my eyes once more. "Perhaps I might be willing to give your own a try. But only if!" He stopped me with a bandaged hand. "Only if you promise to help me uncover the truth of this case for your father. I have no use for a poetess, but I could use an intelligent young woman with her wits about her."

I still did not care for his insistence on the word "use" but I did want to help my father, and I didn't think he'd care to hear I'd talked so boldly to a gentleman he admired.

"I'll help you, for my father and Lenore," I said. "And I'll make you see how poetry can change the most hardened of hearts."

11

Tea Time

"My imagination may be stirred by some detail or situation, but until I am thoroughly acquainted with my people, their environment, the thoughts they think, the glances they give, in fact every little element that goes to make up their relationship to the drama in which they are cast, I sit and think, feel and dream, but do not write."

—Anna Katharine Green, quoted in "An American Gaboriau," by Mary R. P. Hatch

I returned to the Jackson home at a quarter to three, noting the clumps of people in the street occasionally stopping and pointing at the house as I made my way to the front door. The morning newspaper had posted the inquest's decision, and a murder was always something people would clamor to be a part of. One of the city's favorite pastimes was to gather loved ones to have a picnic and watch a hanging.

As I'd said to Mr. Jackson the eve of his death, I truly did believe that normal people were not so much interested in crime itself as they were in the motive behind the act, or in the person committing it, or in the mystery surrounding it, or in some extraordinary circumstance connected with it.

I knew that was what drove my father: discovering the motive. I loved the way Father collected facts and opinions and arranged them methodically to ensure he had the best presentation possible for his defense.

Whenever he did lose a case, he always insisted on attending the hanging himself, though, of course, he wouldn't let me come with him. Once I'd sneaked out anyway. Escaping Mother Grace, I'd followed Father to the yard and watched as he crossed himself and said a prayer for the man on the gallows. My father had proclaimed the man's innocence to the end, but the man had admitted his guilt with his dying breath, asking God to forgive him his sins.

I was fairly certain this was what had caused Father to become solitary for a month, and not just the loss of a case. In the end, he'd been wrong. He'd defended a guilty man. I wondered if he ever worried he'd do that again.

It would be up to me to collect as much information as I could to mark the guilty party accurately. It was up to Sokol to stay out of my way.

I clenched my teeth at the thought. I couldn't forgive the man for his manner toward me. Why had I gotten so angry at his words? Was it really because of his remarks against poetry? Or was it the way he'd downgraded me based on my writing—which he'd never even read before, mind you—suggesting I had little to no role in the solving of this mystery?

No matter what Sokol said, I had a worthy part to play as "lawyer's daughter."

I'd be like Kate Warne, who'd walked into the Pinkerton Detective Agency and demanded Allan Pinkerton give her a job. How I wished I could be so bold.

Instead...was I "simply" a writer? What could a writer do to bring justice to a world dripping with a multitude of sins?

I sighed, lifted, and dropped the knocker on the front door, and waited for the butler to answer. I glanced over my shoulder and saw people on the street watching me in awe, but I was glad they were too timid to snare me with questions.

"Excuse me, miss," came a voice behind me. I jumped when I realized it was the Ferret from the jury. "You wouldn't happen to be Miss Green, who testified yesterday?"

"Indeed I am, Mr.—?"

"Mr. Fredericks, at your service," he said, sweeping his hat off to reveal a head as bald as a naked mole rat. Perhaps thinking of him as a ferret had been inaccurate.

"What can I do for you, Mr. Fredericks? I am about to join my friend for tea." *Where is that butler?*

"I merely wanted to inquire as to your thoughts regarding the case. Do you think your friend stands a chance if she goes to trial?"

The bluntness of the question frightened me.

"As far as I know, sir, she has not been arrested."

"The readers of *The Brooklyn Daily Eagle* are most eager to know—"

Thankfully, at that moment, the butler finally answered and I pressed myself into the hall as the butler slammed the door firmly in the reporter's face.

"Thank you,—"

"Boyle, Miss Green."

"Thank you, Boyle."

"Not at all, Miss Green. They've been latching onto everyone who's come to the door. I only apologize for not coming sooner." His Irish brogue was as thick as molasses.

"Thank you, again, Boyle. I assume Miss Kelthorpe is waiting for me?"

"Yes, miss, right this way." He led me into a reception room off the right of the hall, rather than to the left where the front parlor's pocket door was closed. I marveled at the marble columns draped in green silk which marked the room as being a woman's domain, unlike the front parlor which had smelled of dust and books. Here one could only smell rose water and tulips. And tea.

Lenore rose, her mourning gown crinkling as she did so, and welcomed me with a kiss on either cheek this time.

"How can I ever thank you for your friendship these past two days? I am afraid I have not been myself," she began, leading me to a settee before taking a seat across from me and asking if I'd like sugar or cream.

"A little of both, please," I said. "I am happy I could be of help. Thank you for having me for tea this afternoon. I am sure by now, with the news posted in the paper, you've had droves of friends coming by to wish you well, so I am most appreciative of your taking the time—"

"I'm afraid I do not have any friends outside this house," she said quickly, blushing slightly at the admission.

"I'm surprised to hear it, what with your uncle being a man of some means."

"Yes, and *mean,*" Lenore said, emphasizing the word. "Not a copper penny to be spent on leisure activities, no going out, no rides through the country. The only parties we attended were ones thrown in his honor. Otherwise, he was a skinflint and a recluse, happy to be locked up in his study working on his magnum opus."

I sipped at my tea as I marveled at the perfidious nature of Lenore's discourse. Where was the young woman who'd proclaimed her uncle was a "kind and generous benefactor?"

I could not decide what to make of this young woman. It bothered me like a loose tooth, and I determined to wiggle it until it removed itself.

"Perhaps you might call me Anna, then, if we are to be such honest friends."

Lenore beamed. "Dear, Anna," she said, her eyes welling with tears once again, but this time with rosy cheeks of pleasure. "If we are to be friends, then I feel I must confide in you something which has gnawed at me since discovering my uncle's death."

My eyebrows rose in interest.

Lenore looked about before setting her cup and saucer down and joining me on the settee. She leaned in close enough for me to smell the heavy Parisian perfume dousing her neck and wrists—something I had never done, abhorring the false scents of jarred flowers.

"I have a great secret, which you must allow me to relate in something of a long, digressive story, for it is all of great importance in regards to my uncle. I feared I must reveal the truth to your father, eventually, as he has so kindly offered to represent me should the worst occur. But I do not think it will be necessary as..." She paused and looked about the room yet again, clearly fearful of a servant's entering at the most inopportune moment. "I will not be in the country long enough for them to take me in." She smiled with excitement as I tried not to gawp in surprise.

"You must do no such thing, Lenore," I said firmly. "To leave the country is to admit guilt." I set down my cup and saucer. "You are not guilty, are you?" I asked tentatively.

"No!" Lenore cried, but then laughed like the young girl she was, so naïve and thoughtless. "At least, not of that."

"Perhaps you had better explain," I said coaxingly.

Lenore's smile grew. "It all happened last summer. My uncle took me with him to a hotel in Boston where he'd been asked to speak on the nature of the tea enterprises since the infamous Boston Tea Party. It was my first time visiting Boston, first time outside of New York, and I was given more freedom than I had ever enjoyed before." She blushed. "I'm afraid I went quite wild."

I raised an eyebrow. "Oh?"

"Nothing indecent, mind you. Little things like drinking cherry cordial—something I'd never been allowed to taste—and dancing—only in the hotel ballrooms, of course, and only the most sedate waltzes. I suddenly felt like Cinderella, free for the first time in my life. But like Cinderella, I, too, had a curfew, for I had to return to my room by ten o'clock every night.

"Then one night…I met my prince." Lenore sighed. The most wistful, tender look came over her face; I was honestly quite jealous. I may have often thought I did not intend to marry, but this didn't mean I never dreamed of finding that one man who could change my mind.

"A prince?"

Lenore giggled. "No, not a real prince. If he was, perhaps my uncle would have been more inclined to allow us to marry."

My mind returned to the private secretary Farwell who had fidgeted in the front row when Lenore had lied about having a man in her life. Though I had a difficult time imagining such a man being considered "a prince," forbidden love had a way of romanticizing even the most featureless of men.

Had he only recently been hired to join Mr. Jackson's household after meeting him in Boston last summer, perhaps?

"Someone your uncle would not have approved? For lack of money?"

"More because of his profession. He's an actor."

So *not* Mr. Farwell after all.

"An actor?"

"Yes," Lenore said, her eyes taking on a dreamy look. "I saw him in 'The Exiles' at the Boston Theatre one night and it was love at first sight." She sighed again. "So tall and handsome. A commanding voice that drew me to his side in an instant."

"How did you meet him if your uncle went with you to this show?"

"He had such a bad headache that he left at intermission to return to our hotel. It took a lot of pleading, but he finally allowed me to remain behind with Murphy, who was traveling with me as my chaperone."

The plot thickens, I thought. Of course Murphy would know all about the secret love affair.

"So...after the show...?"

"After the show I cajoled Murphy to take me down to the dressing rooms so I could meet him face to face. As I said, as soon as we met, we were in love."

I bit my lip. I hated to ask my next question, but it was necessary. "Does he...know your uncle is wealthy?"

Lenore's eyes flared suddenly. "What do you mean by that?"

"I mean exactly what I said," I repeated firmly. There was no way to beat about the bush. "Is this actor aware of your family's fortune?"

"Are you suggesting he's a fortune hunter? That his only interest in me is for my uncle's money?"

Well, yes. "It is possible he is not, but it is also possible he is. You are young, Lenore, and sometimes it is difficult to tell—"

Lenore stood with a rustle of skirts. "He loves me and I love him and we're running away tonight to be married!"

I sat back against the cushions. "Lenore...your uncle disapproved of a man to whom you were secretly engaged, and now your uncle is dead."

Lenore sat down again slowly. "I know, Anna. Believe me, I know how it looks. But I did not kill him. I swear, I did not!"

"And your prince?"

Lenore's face paled. "He...he was not in the house..."

"Are you certain?"

"I..." She faltered, her words stilling as she began to breathe more quickly. "He..." Lenore's mouth crumpled into a sob and she covered her face in her hands.

I reached out and put a sympathetic arm around her shoulders.

She looked up, real tears streaking her cheeks, ruddy with true, heart-breaking sadness. "But I want to marry him, Anna. It's the only thing I've ever wanted in the whole world."

"Is this the first man you've met outside of your uncle's walls?" I asked tentatively.

"Yes." She raised her hand. "I know what you're going to say: that I haven't met enough men to know love but...oh, Anna. This feeling inside me must be love! What else can it be?"

I did not discount that what Lenore was feeling was something she *thought* was love, but how could she possibly know? How often had my heart fluttered at the sight of a handsome man, a kind word? That didn't mean I was about to run off and marry him!

I remembered Murphy's words the morning of the inquest. She'd noticed Lenore's tension under Mr. Jackson's guardianship, her longing to make her own choices, and now here was a man who had offered her that freedom by way of marriage. What if all Lenore wanted was to be free of Mr. Jackson? Was she simply willing to believe she was in love in order to get it? What Lenore needed was a motherly hand to guide her, before she did something rash that could not be fixed.

Compared to Lenore, I was a world-weary pilgrim of the darkness that hid beneath New York City's shining lights. With a lawyer for a father, I was all too aware of the mistakes one could fall into if one was not careful.

"Lenore, perhaps you might reconsider. You are grieving, and it is common to feel with such deep feelings the need to be free—"

"This isn't a reaction to Uncle's death. We had intended to run away tonight. It was all planned." She caught sight of her reflection in the silver tea urn between us. "Everyone takes one look at me and thinks I need protecting," she murmured. "But I don't. I know what I want: I want to marry the love of my life. But now...I fear..." Her face crumpled again.

"Come, come, it is not over yet. If you are innocent—"

"I am, I am, I swear to you, I am!"

"And if he is innocent..."

This Lenore did not respond to, except by widening her eyes to show she feared the worst.

"You have nothing to worry about; all will be well," I said, though I did not believe my own words. "Your uncle is gone and you are his heir. Once this horrid business is in the past, you and your love will be free to live happily ever after."

"Just like Cinderella," Lenore murmured through her tears.

But I had the terrible feeling Lenore's story was echoing a different tale: the tragedy of Juliet and her Romeo.

12

The Theater

"I cannot but feel a desire to write him a play in which he may have an opportunity to show himself in a part equally strong but more sympathetic. Whether or not this will eventuate in anything has not yet been communicated to me by the muse."

—Anna Katharine Green, quoted in *Good Reading About Many Books Mostly by Their Authors*, by T. Fisher Unwin

By the time I left Lenore, I was more than a little concerned. Although I'd been able to convince her she should not run away with her lover tonight, she insisted she would be meeting him to tell him so in person. When I'd suggested I could come with her, she'd practically leapt at the chance to introduce him to me.

"Oh, Anna, you're going to love him! You will see in a moment he is no murderer!"

So it was agreed that we would journey to the Washington Square music stand together for the secret assignation.

At home, however, my plans were quickly complicated when Mother Grace and my sister Sarah insisted I join them for the theater that evening.

"We're going to see the play-that-cannot-be-named!" Mother Grace said excitedly, waving her hand before her face.

"I think you can say its name, so long as you're not standing in a theater," I said, picking up on her meaning.

"Where's the fun in that?" Sarah asked. "It *is* about murder after all, so I'm certain you will love it."

"I've seen *Macbeth* before, you know," I said. "I know who the murderer is and everything." I winked at her.

Sarah gave me a hug. "Will you come? You haven't come with us to a show in so long."

"I went with you last week!"

"Please?" Sarah gave me her biggest eyes.

I never could disappoint my elder sister, for she was as much a mother to me as Mother Grace. When our mother had died when I was just three, my sixteen-year-old sister had been forced into the role of caretaker to the point that I still thought of her as "mother-sister."

"All right," I agreed. If I left immediately upon our return from the theater, I could still make the assignation in the park.

"Splendid!" cheered Sarah. "Before we go anywhere, though, Father wanted to speak with you in his study."

After knocking on the study door and hearing, "Enter," I found my father bent over his desk, fountain pen busily scratching across paper as he took notes. He looked up as I closed the door behind me.

"And how is our client?"

I smiled to hear my father say, "our client" and wondered if perhaps he might be persuaded to allow my pursuance of a law degree after all, something he often said was the most genteel of the professions, and therefore one that strongly appealed to him for his most intellectual daughter.

"Miss Kelthorpe had quite a story to share with me, Father. Thankfully, she gave me permission to share it with you as well, as it may have great bearing upon her case, should she require your defense."

Father gave me his full attention, his eyes focused on mine as I spoke, causing me to wonder yet again why Sokol could not do the same.

Why did that man keep springing to mind? I tried to focus instead on the story of Lenore's secret love.

"Thank you for sharing this with me," Father said when I finished. "I'm uncomfortable with the idea of you joining her in her assignation tonight, however, and I must ask that you allow me to accompany you."

I nodded. "I had an inkling you would desire such a thing, and I do not see how Miss Kelthorpe could argue with such a noble request."

Father nodded and leaned back in his chair, running a hand through his gray hair that I knew would someday match his beard in color. "As you have done me the honor of informing me of your conversation, I will share what I have gathered from the coroner."

"You met with Mr. Hammond?"

"Yes, at my office. These are the facts." He brought his hands together before him in a steeple, as he was wont to do when about to relate important information. "First, I obtained a list of what was on Mr. Jackson when he was murdered."

"His keys?"

"Yes, his personal set of keys were in his pocket."

"So it was not his key that Sokol found in the fireplace?"

"Sokol? Not 'Mr. Sokol?'" Father asked with a raised brow.

I blushed. "He asked me to call him Sokol, but I can continue to refer to him as Mr. Sokol if you would prefer."

Father waved a hand. "No, no, that's perfectly all right, so long as he won't be calling you 'Anna' in my presence."

I almost questioned him on this, as he'd seemed to be open to the idea of Sokol's interest in me earlier, but perhaps he'd reconsidered the notion and found it to be idiotic, as I had.

"Mr. Hammond checked the keys and confirmed that one did fit the locks of both doors leading to the study."

"Both doors?"

"Yes, there are two doors into the study: one from the hall, and one from his bedroom, or into his bedroom, depending on how you look at it."

"Which is where Miss Kelthorpe said the gun was kept, though it was found in Mr. Jackson's desk."

"Yes. Not in his hand. He held only a pen, which again tells us it obviously wasn't suicide, and that he was caught in the middle of his work."

I nodded. "The evidence seems to suggest that the murderer retrieved the gun from Mr. Jackson's bedroom and then shoved it into the drawer when he was finished. He completely overlooked the fact that he might have saved himself a lot of trouble by leaving the gun in Mr. Jackson's hand, setting the scene to look like a suicide, as Miss Kelthorpe was quite willing to believe."

"Precisely."

"And you said one key opened both doors?"

"Yes," my father confirmed. "And according to the servants' statements, both doors were locked when they found Mr. Jackson's body."

"Both locked? So it appears Mr. Jackson was alone in the room? But we know it was not suicide. Why would the murderer try to make it appear as suicide by locking the doors, but not in any other manner?"

"A locked room mystery," my father murmured, and I thought it a good name for it. "It is a question worthy of Sokol. I was just copying out my notes for him before you returned. I shall add your information, as well."

I nodded distractedly. Just then a knock at the door interrupted us. It was Mother Grace informing me we'd be leaving for the theater in an hour, so I might want to begin getting dressed.

"Will you be joining us, Father?" I asked.

"No. I've already promised Mrs. Heritage I'll be enjoying her meal this evening and I'd hate to throw her off another night."

I agreed this was probably best and went to prepare myself for the pleasure of a night at the theater.

After much deliberation, I decided on a white evening gown with red rosebuds sewn diagonally across the front. I'd considered several darker ensembles, assuming that after the theater, I would be hard-pressed to find the time to change into something more suitable for my late night trip to the garden, so I'd need to pick something I could also wear on my excursion. In the end, however, I realized there was no way I'd be going in an evening dress to the garden; I'd just have to change quickly later tonight.

Upon our arrival to the theater house, we took a moment to find our seats in the boxes to the left of the stage, seats we were fortunate enough to obtain thanks to Mother Grace's patronage of the arts. She'd made it a point that we, as her children, should be exposed to all the best of New York City's theater life, and it was a highlight of my week when I was able to join them. If there was one thing I enjoyed more than writing or reading, it was the theater.

"Did you remember your notebook?" Sarah whispered to me as we waited for the curtains to rise.

"Yes," I said with a smile, pulling the small booklet along with a pencil from my reticule. I often found myself wishing to record the lines from the great Bard that stood out to me during a performance, every rendition being unique from the last.

"What was the last Shakespeare play we attended?" Mother Grace asked. "*Midsummer Night's Dream? King Lear?*"

"I believe it was *Hamlet*," I said. "Yes, the last note I have is '*My words fly up, my thoughts remain below: Words without thoughts never to heaven go.*'"

"Ah, yes. An excellent line," Mother Grace said with a nod.

The lights in the theater began to dim and I leaned forward in anticipation of the opening of the play.

As soon as the theater was dark, the lights flashed and the sound of thunder rumbled into my chest as three gnarled witches suddenly appeared on the stage, as if by magic.

"When shall we three meet again? In thunder, lightning, or in rain?" the first witch asked.

"When the hurlyburly's done, when the battle's lost and won," said the second witch.

"That will be ere the set of sun," said the third witch.

They continued and then the lightning and thunder came again and they were gone as suddenly as they'd appeared, replaced with several men in armor, one wearing a crown.

The king spoke first, pointing to a man who was bleeding. "What bloody man is that? He can report, as seemeth by his plight, of the revolt, the newest state."

A young man stepped forward into the spotlight, and my breath caught in my chest. His eyes and nose were adequately proportioned, but when he smiled, it was somewhat crooked, giving a jocund look to an otherwise solemn face. He was quite the most devilishly handsome man I'd ever seen.

"This is the sergeant, who, like a good and hardy soldier, fought against my captivity," he said, raising a hand. "Hail, brave friend! Say to the King the knowledge of the broil as thou didst leave it."

This meant he was playing the part of Malcolm, King Duncan's son, a role I had thought of in the past as quite...well, tedious and dull. I found this was not the case this time, however. I was quickly drawn into the plot, finding the calculated and yet almost witty way this particular actor delivered his lines to be the very definition of an excellent performer.

Shakespeare's words were difficult for even the most learned player, so I always found it a thrill when someone truly talented put breadth and depth behind them in a new and thought-provoking way.

"And often-times, to win us to our harm, the instruments of darkness tell us truths, win us with honest trifles, to betray us in deepest consequence," I wrote, and later, "A deed of dreadful note."

As the play continued, I recorded several lines in my notebook, but found I never did so while Malcolm was speaking. Indeed, when he was on the stage, I could hardly pull my eyes away, so entranced was I.

During the intermission, I was quick to flip through my program to identify the actor.

"Charles Rohlfs," I whispered to myself.

He had a young face, but I could not tell his age, and since the program only included his name and no further information, I was tempted to remain behind after the show to meet him in person.

I shook my head at myself. I was no better than Lenore.

The play began again, and I found myself waiting with bated breath for the scenes when he would return. I only recorded one other line by Lady Macduff, "When our actions do not, our fears do make us traitors," before he was finally back.

Scene Three in Act Four, a scene I usually found myself losing interest in given the rather long discussion between Malcolm and Macduff, was riveting, and I applauded most heartily as they left the stage.

Before I knew it, we'd come to the end, and I leaned forward as Malcolm ended the play with his lines: "This, and what needful else that calls upon us, by the grace of Grace, we will perform in measure, time, and place. So thanks to all at once, and to each one, whom we invite to see us crown'd at Scone."

Malcolm looked about the theater as he delivered this final line, and heat rose to my face as our eyes connected and held for two long heartbeats.

Then the connection was broken, the crowd was standing to applaud, and the actors were giving their final bows.

I blushed when he gave his bow, and then blew me a kiss in my box seat.

Well, perhaps not to me precisely, more of a kiss to the audience at large, but as far as I was concerned, I snatched that kiss out of the air and held it to my chest, tucking it into my little notebook for safe-keeping.

The ride home was full of the typical after-show dissection, and I was pleased to find I was not the only one who had noticed Mr. Rohlfs's stellar performance.

"Malcolm was marvelous, didn't you think? He brought an almost comedic wit to the part with that wonderfully expressive face!" Mother Grace said with a laugh at the memory, removing her gloves as we unfastened our coats in the foyer.

"Thank you for taking me," I said with a kiss to her cheek. "That was the most fun I've had at the theater in quite some time."

"You seemed most enamored of the play," Sarah said, but I thought I noticed a quirk to her mouth indicating she might have seen more upon my face while I watched than I'd thought I was divulging.

"It was wonderful. Almost as good as that time we went to see the murder mystery play," I said, hoping to distract her from the subject.

"Ah yes!" Mother Grace said, giving Father an affectionate kiss as we joined him in the parlor. "The clues sprinkled throughout the first act gave the answer away to such minds as you two possess, making the play entirely disagreeable for the rest of us."

She was right: we had declared we knew the murderer by intermission and were proven right by the end, which had by no means lessened the fun we'd had that evening, as far as my father and I were concerned.

"It is the clues hidden in plain sight that are the most difficult to find," Father said knowingly.

"Missing the forest for the trees, and such?" Sarah asked.

"Not quite," I said. "It is more missing the trees for the forest in this matter."

"Ah, good point," Father said with a nod. "For example, I had a case where the murderer had used a stocking, and had returned it to his wife's bureau drawer so that we could not be certain of the exact murder weapon."

My sister shuddered delicately, reminding me that Sarah was not one who appreciated discussions of violence of any sort, though somehow she'd enjoyed *Macbeth.*

A knock sounded at the door, causing us all to jump.

After a moment, Teagan entered the parlor from the foyer, his mouth pressed into a thin, disagreeable line. "Begging your pardon, Madam, but the police have come to speak with Mr. Green."

We all turned to Father, who took a deep breath before rising.

"If you will excuse me," he said to us.

All eyes followed him, but we didn't dare rise to accompany him.

Long moments later he returned and declared what I had feared.

"Miss Kelthorpe has been arrested on a charge of murder. I will be her defense."

13

Assignation

"The greatest mistake a girl can make is to marry in haste.... They do not study his instincts and ideals. They do not know the character of the man they intend to marry."

—Anna Katharine Green, quoted in "Life's Facts as Startling as Fiction," by Ruth Snyder

My father said good evening to us all and followed the policemen out. I excused myself and went to my bedroom, where I paced back and forth before coming to a decision, changing my clothes into something more comfortable, and descending the stairs.

"Where are you off to?" Mother Grace called, appearing from her bedroom in her dressing gown, having changed out of her theater attire.

"I..."

Mother Grace eyed me thoughtfully. There was no question that this woman was more than a second mother to me, as much a friend and confidant as any girl could hope to find in a mother figure. I was eternally grateful for my father's sense in picking such a suitable helpmate as a replacement for someone who could never truly be replaced.

"Never mind," she said. "Just be careful, will you? Take one of the footmen with you."

I nodded at the intelligence of the suggestion and gave her a hug before completing my descent. I found Lane and asked him to accompany me. He followed without hesitation, seemingly eager for a bit of action. No doubt he was one of those young boys who wished he'd been old enough to fight in the War, too young and too naïve to realize what a foolish wish that was.

He called a carriage for me and told the driver to take us to Washington Square. I climbed into the covered back seat and Lane joined the driver on the front rail. We were there in mere minutes, as it was not a long distance, and I was grateful to see the lamps were lit, so I would not be forced to do something so dangerous in utter darkness.

I thanked the driver and asked him to wait for me, turning to walk with Lane farther into the park, only to shriek and nearly fall to the ground in terror upon realizing a man stood at my shoulder.

"Dear God!" I cried, clutching at my coat lapels in an attempt to catch my breath.

"I did not mean to scare you," the slow, steady voice of Sokol responded, though if I was not mistaken there was a hint of laughter on his lips.

His mouth twitched in that almost-smile at the wheel of the carriage and I wished I could step on the man's booted foot so he would look at me.

"What on earth are you doing here?" I asked, still trying to hide my shaking hands by holding my coat closed, though the buttons worked perfectly.

"I was sent by your father. He was worried you would make the assignation alone following Miss Kelthorpe's arrest."

I shook my head. "He knows me too well. I brought Lane with me, however. I do not require your assistance."

Sokol looked toward Lane, who was eyeing him warily, as though unable to determine if he was a threat to his mistress or not.

"Go home, boy. I will return Miss Green when we are through."

Lane smiled widely, no doubt interpreting Sokol's statement in quite a different manner than it was meant, but as there was no way I could dispel the rumors already forming between his wide-set ears, I gave him a nod of assurance.

"Thank you, Lane. You may go."

He climbed back up with the driver and they were off at a trot that clattered against the cobblestones, drowning out any second thoughts I might have.

I turned to Sokol. "What gives you to think that I am easy with the idea of walking alone with you at night?"

"You would prefer me over Lane, would you not?" Sokol suggested to the falcon-head on his cane.

"My father approved of your coming? Knowing we would be alone together?"

"Yes," said Sokol, though naturally he could not say otherwise, and I would not know if it was true until I confronted my father over the matter. By then it would be far too late to question Lenore's secret lover.

"Very well, then. Let us proceed."

"By all means," Sokol said, with a wave of his hand, offering his arm to me like a true gentleman.

"I take it your rheumatism is not bothering you this evening?" I asked as I took his arm. It was surprisingly sturdy for someone who suffered from a debilitating disease.

"It comes and goes like waves upon the shore."

"How poetic," I said with a sidelong smile.

Sokol eyed the trees to his left, but did not answer.

I glanced at the trees. "Do you even know what we are about here?"

He nodded. "We are meeting Miss Kelthorpe's lover in her place, to ascertain whether he was at the home of Mr. Jackson yesterday afternoon at one o'clock, and happened to shoot him while he was there."

A small laugh escaped from me and Sokol's mouth twitched at the ground.

"I suppose that is the crux of it."

Not too far along, we came to a music stand, glowing white in the combined moonlight and gaslights. On the far side, a shadow moved.

My heart thumped and I was glad for Sokol's strengthening presence at my side.

"He is here," Sokol muttered softly.

I led the way, praying the shadow would not disappear into the night. Thankfully, he did not, but instead took a step into the light as we approached.

I knew him the moment I laid eyes on him.

His eyes were less outlined, and his ears seemed larger now he wasn't wearing a wig. By the glow of the yellow lamplight, I could see he was much younger than he'd appeared before, no more than nineteen.

He smiled crookedly as he caught sight of my face.

"Madam, I believe you must be following me," he said in a low, melodic tone, just as he'd done when he'd said, "Hail, brave friend!"

"Mr. Rohlfs," I breathed, suddenly irritated by Sokol's presence at my elbow.

"Good evening," he said politely, with a tip of his top hat, revealing black hair parted down the middle in the current fashion. "It's always a joy to see such a beautiful woman twice in one day."

I prayed the darkness was heavy enough he wouldn't be able to pick up on my reddening cheeks.

"Good evening, Mr. Rohlfs," I repeated, stronger this time. "I am pleased to see you again. Your performance tonight was...exhilarating."

I ignored the way I could see Sokol's brow furrowing at this statement out of the corner of my eye.

"Thank you. I do not believe I had the honor of catching sight of your gentleman friend at the playhouse this evening?" He glanced toward Sokol.

"No, no, he didn't attend with me," I said, eager to remove my elbow from Sokol's now. "I was with my mother and sister."

"Of course. I am sorry, I didn't catch your name."

"She didn't give it," Sokol said rudely.

I glared at him and offered my hand to Mr. Rohlfs.

"*Miss* Green," I said, emphasizing the "miss." "This is Mr. Sokol. He is merely here as my...guide tonight."

"I see, and what brings you both out here in the middle of the night?"

I took a deep breath. *Here goes.* "I am a friend of Miss Kelthorpe, and I am afraid I come with rather a dire message."

The actor startled at my words, telling me I'd not made a mistake in identifying this man as both the actor who'd played Malcolm and Lenore's lover.

"My dear Lenore? What has happened?"

Why did it sting so to hear him call her "dear Lenore?" The words of affection he'd sent her in his letters ran before my eyes, muddying my thoughts for a moment.

"I am afraid she has been arrested," Sokol said softly at my side.

"Arrested? Why?" Mr. Rohlfs declared. "Whatever for?"

"For the murder of her uncle," Sokol intoned.

The actor whipped his head toward the man, his face accusatory. "How absurd! Why would she be suspected?"

"Because of you," I said clearly. Mr. Rohlfs turned to me and I balked under the intensity of his look. "Her uncle would not have approved of your marriage, she lied about your existence in her life, and she knew how to fire the gun that killed him."

"That is all circumstantial," Mr. Rohlfs declared with a wave of his hand. "There is nothing in any of that. Why, the same might be said of me!"

"Precisely," said Sokol, studying the man's collar.

Mr. Rohlfs looked between the two of us. "You are quite serious? You think I killed her uncle?"

"Well," I asked abruptly, "did you?"

"No!" Mr. Rohlfs shouted so loudly it reverberated off the music stand and the surrounding trees, his actor's ability to project filling the quiet night air. "No," he repeated quietly.

"Were you at the house yesterday afternoon?" I asked.

Mr. Rohlfs hesitated just long enough for me to wonder if what he said was the truth. He was an actor, after all. "No," he said. "I have never once approached her uncle's home. Miss Kelthorpe made it quite clear I was never to expose our relationship to her uncle."

His choice of wording gave me pause. Had Lenore been keeping her actor lover at arm's length for a reason? Perhaps she didn't return his affection after all? The only letters I'd seen had been from him, so I had no idea of the ebullience of her response.

But then I recalled the fervor with which she'd expressed her affection for her "prince," and how I would "surely love him" upon meeting him.

She didn't know how much, indeed, I could understand her adoration of this young man. After all, how far was twenty-five from twenty really, when one did the math?

Perhaps Mr. Rohlfs was simply her prince in the sense that he seemed the perfect man to rescue her from her present situation?

Mr. Rohlfs rubbed his forehead with his hand, pushing his hat back on his head with the movement. Then he pulled it down in a decisive manner. "It does not matter now. What matters is that I am in love with Miss Kelthorpe, we are engaged, and I had intended to run away with her tonight to be married."

Again, a pang went through me that had no right to be there. I didn't know this man from Adam, no matter if I found him attractive.

"Are you certain you were not anywhere near Mr. Jackson's yesterday?" Sokol asked.

Mr. Rohlfs eyed the detective, who was studying the architecture of the music stand.

"I may be a poor actor, but neither of us care for money so much as to kill, especially one such as her uncle, who has been like a father to her."

"Many have killed for less," Sokol murmured, and I had to agree.

14

The Dream

“The other night I had a wonderful dream, which has impressed a story on my mind.... It is so passionate, so strong, so subtle, so dread, dark, and heart-rending, it ought to be written with fire and blood.”

—Anna Katharine Green, quoted in “An American Gaboriau,” by Mary R. P. Hatch

I sat at my desk, pen in hand, the ink dripping onto my clean parchment in a most irritating manner.

I looked down at the letter I was trying to write—and suddenly I wasn't the one sitting at the desk. Instead, I was the one standing behind myself, a gun pointed at my head. I was looking over my own shoulder, watching my hand write something that made me displeased. Anger welled up inside me.

I pulled the trigger.

Blam!

I was standing in the corner, watching the body at the desk fall with a heavy thud, thankful it wasn't my own, for it now appeared to be that of Lenore. And it wasn't myself standing behind the desk, gun in hand, but a man.

A faceless man in a suit. Something told me I knew who the man was, but try as I might, I couldn't get into a position where I could see his face.

I circled the still figures, who were holding their places like people in a Regency-era *tableau vivant,* enabling me to view them from all angles, without them moving or changing.

There was something odd about the way the man was holding the gun. I tried to focus on it.

But no, it wasn't the gun itself, it was the clock behind the man. The time was wrong. It showed twelve noon, not one o'clock.

My head spun. Why was the clock wrong?

It must have stopped. I crossed the room to correct the clock when suddenly I heard the gun go off behind me.

Blam!

Only this time, it had been aimed at me—

With a jolt, I sat up in bed, my chest aching from where I could have sworn the bullet had hit me.

The dream had felt so real. So immediate. I could still feel the bullet hitting me squarely in the chest, and at the same time the cold, heavy metal of the gun nestled in my hand. Could feel the trigger beneath my finger. Could feel the anger that had caused me to pull it gently but firmly.

I shuddered. I must think of something else.

Instead, I leapt from my bed to my writing desk, dipped a pen into the inkwell, and recorded the dream before it grew too cold for memory.

Afterward, I pulled out the poem I'd come home to write the night before, having returned around midnight too stimulated to find immediate sleep. I'd tossed and turned and then finally rose, a poem filling my heart with words too potent not to write down.

If I had known whose face I'd see
Above the hedge, beside the rose;
If I had known whose voice I'd hear
Make music where the wind-flower blows, —
I had not come; I had not come.
If I had known his deep 'I love.'
Could make her face so fair to see;
If I had known her shy 'And!'
Could make him stoop so tenderly, —
I had not come: I had not come.
But what knew I? The summer breeze
Stopped not to cry 'Beware! beware!'
The vine-wreaths drooping from the trees
Caught not my sleeve with soft 'Take care!'
And so I came, and so I came.
The roses that his hands have plucked,
Are sweet to me, are death to me;

Between them, as through living flames
I pass, I clutch them, crush them, see!
The bloom for her, the thorn for me.
The brooks leap up with many a song —
I once could sing, like them could sing;
They fall; 'tis like a sigh among
A world of joy and blossoming. —
Why did I come? Why did I come?
The blue sky burns like altar fires —
How sweet her eyes beneath her hair!
The green earth lights its fragrant pyres;
The wild birds rise and flush the air;
God looks and smiles, earth is so fair.
But ah! 'twixt me and you bright heaven
Two bended heads pass darkling by;
And loud above the bird and brook
I hear a low 'I love,' 'And I—'
And hide my face. Ah God! Why? Why?

When I finished reading it now, I sat back and considered what to title it. Then I leaned forward and added across the top, "Through the Trees."

Of course, it was not a true telling of what had happened last night, but sometimes a poem didn't need to be based on truth. Instead, it needed to capture a feeling.

These words had captured my feelings all right.

And now this dream.

I wondered what the day would hold.

As I dressed, I had to force myself to breathe deeply, as though the pressure of the dream wouldn't allow my lungs to work properly.

I descended the stairs to the dining room slowly, my thoughts still in another room many streets away. I was halfway through my eggs and toast when I realized my stepmother was asking me a question.

"I'm sorry, Mother Grace, were you speaking to me?"

Mother Grace smiled kindly. "It is no matter. I can see you are in the midst of formulating another masterful poem."

I blushed. "I'm afraid it was not a poem that I was thinking upon so deeply."

Mother Grace spread jam upon her toast as she said, "There's only one other person in this family who ever looks as concerned and concentrated at the same time, and that's your father." She cocked an eye toward me.

I blushed again and distracted myself with eating the egg that was cooling on my plate.

"He tells me you've taken it upon yourself to assist him in this new case. Lenore Kelthorpe, is it?"

"Yes," I said with a nod. I waited for my stepmother to tell me it was unladylike to pursue such things, and that I should turn my focus back to my poetry. But she did not.

"You've read Wilkie Collins's *Moonstone*, yes?"

I set down my fork. "I'm reading it right now, as it happens."

"How about Edgar Allan Poe's 'Purloined Letter' or 'The Goldbug?'"

"Yes..."

"Any Émile Gaboriau?"

"Yes!" I said excitedly. I'd recently read *File No. 113* and found it exceptionally riveting. Monsieur Lecoq's use of disguise, guile, and deduction had caused my heart to race and an inability to close the book until the wick had burned down to a nub that night.

Mother Grace nodded. "I wonder if you mightn't take notes while you assist your father, perhaps for your own mystery?"

I was taken aback. "But...I write poetry. I eschew prose. Poetry is my forte; story-telling is not possible to me, as much as I may enjoy reading mysteries."

"Who says a poetess may not try her hand at another form of writing? Your poems are often already in a long, narrative form. Think what you could do when allowed thousands of words, rather than just a choice hundred."

"But therein lies the daunting truth: the number of words I should be forced to write to express what could be suggested so readily in a few lines of verse." I paused, however, for even as I said the words, I thought, *But if I ever do write a story, it shall be one of intricate and complex plot. Like a mystery...*

"Nonsense, I believe more authors should approach writing by that route, for a poetess can bring a deliberateness to her choice of words and form, in a way that a prose writer might ultimately miss."

"But...mystery?" I said haltingly.

"What is wrong with mystery?"

I blushed. Suddenly I felt like I was on the other side of Sokol's argument against poetry.

"Nothing, Mother Grace. I quite enjoy a good mystery, as I just said. I love the puzzle, the riddle. A puzzle which absorbs one must be a relaxation. The puzzle of the plot and the rapid movement of the story should take the reader's minds somewhere else..."

"But?"

"Well...it's just... I write poetry."

"So you keep saying. I'm merely suggesting that perhaps you should try your hand at something new? You might be surprised with what comes out of your head, and your heart."

My thoughts flashed to the dream which had started this conversation, thanks to its distracting elements. I was grateful I'd been able to recall and record every little detail that morning, engraving it, as it were, onto my mind.

"I couldn't write about a real case," I said aloud.

"Naturally. But where do you think those authors get their ideas? I'm certain it's from the newspapers. And you have something better than a newspaper's second-hand, biased story available to you: first-hand experience, and a father who's the best lawyer in New York."

She was right. Truth was stranger than fiction. The facts and figures I had picked up simply by listening to my father's relating of his work day at the dinner table were enough, much less the times I'd sat in on inquests, listened to surgeon's reports, eavesdropped on conversations between my father and policemen, or learned about ballistics as I had done at this most recent inquest. It was like my entire life had been leading me to this point.

And then there was Sokol. Perhaps he'd be more willing to work with me if I was a mystery writer rather than a poetess. Perhaps he'd see the purpose of my interest more clearly.

"I can see you're already planning plots and picking your characters," Mother Grace said, drinking a sip of coffee. "Might I make one more suggestion?"

I pulled back from the precipice of idea and focused on my stepmother.

"Don't be afraid to incorporate a little poetry."

15

Interview

"[Anna Katharine Green's] father was a well-known lawyer... This may account for the skill with which the daughter has tied and cut Gordian knots. It unquestionably accounts for her nimble imagination, her skill in producing subtle hypotheses and her strength in handling the most intricate psychological problems."

—E.F. Harkins and C.H.L. Johnston, "Anna Katharine Green," ***Little Pilgrimages Among the Women Who Have Written Famous Books***

I had a lot to consider that morning as I joined my father in a trip down to the police station. He'd invited me along to offer a comforting presence to the unfortunate Lenore, who had spent her first night in the terrifying confines of the local jail. He said he intended to remove her from there as soon as possible, would go so far as to bring her home to stay with us if the police would not allow her the freedom to return to her own house.

"It's most unnecessary to keep her at the jail, and I argued as much last night," said Father, "but Detective Billings wouldn't listen to me. Stubborn as a hound that one."

I stifled a laugh. The poor man couldn't seem to escape comparison with a dog.

We entered the station and I marveled at how such a place could feel so warm and welcoming on the upper floor, when I knew the jails down below were cold, hard, and dreadful.

An officer led us to a back room, where we were seated to wait for Lenore. When she entered, I stood and went to her, my heart breaking for the care-worn pile of wrinkled clothing that had once been an enviable beauty only a couple days before. After helping Lenore to the table, we sat down, Lenore leaning on my shoulder like I was the mother she'd never known.

Like for so many young people, freedom had lost its shine after the loneliness of reality set in; perhaps protection wasn't such a bad thing after all.

"Miss Kelthorpe, I am so sorry. I will do everything in my power to get you out of here before we leave," Father said with genuine concern for the young woman.

It was clear he was extremely unhappy with the appearance of his client, and I knew he wouldn't hesitate to go to the chief himself if needed.

"Thank you, Mr. Green," Lenore murmured, clasping her hands together on the table before her. "Is there any chance of my getting something for my head? I've suffered from a headache all night."

"No doubt these cold rooms," my father said with a shake of his head.

"Here, I have some peppermint oil," I said, handing her the small vial I kept on my chatelaine so she could rub some on her temples.

"Thank you," said Lenore, gratefully anointing herself. When she had finished, she handed the vial back to me, straightened her shoulders and said, "I am ready to tell you anything you need to know."

I was glad to hear it, hopeful that the seriousness of the situation had been made apparent to her.

"Thank you, Miss Kelthorpe, that would be most helpful." My father opened his files and pulled out his fountain pen. "Let us begin with the day of the murder. Please tell me from the moment you awoke what you did and where you were."

"A simple matter, Mr. Green, for as I said, I was not allowed to leave the house. I was there from the time my feet touched the floor beside my bed to when I returned to bed after the longest day of my life."

"You did not leave for any reason? Perhaps to secretly send a note to your lover?"

Lenore blushed. "I did send a note to Charles, but I did not leave the house to do so. I sent it by way of my lady's maid, who is the only person aware of the truth."

"Your lady's maid, Miss...?"

"Isabella Murphy, though I call her Murphy."

And Murphy calls Lenore "mavourneen," I recalled. I wondered to what lengths the woman would go to protect her young charge. It came suddenly to me that perhaps there were more suspects in the house than it had at first appeared.

"You say Murphy is aware of your involvement with Mr. Rohlfs?"

"Yes," Lenore said firmly. "She sends and receives our correspondence, so that nothing addressed to or from myself will come to the notice of my uncle."

"And she sent a note for you the day of the murder? When?"

"Just afterward, before the arrival of the coroner."

"And what did the note say?"

"'My uncle has committed suicide. Please do not come.'"

I raised an eyebrow, but Father asked my question.

"Why didn't you want him to come? With your uncle dead, you no longer needed to hide his existence."

"I, well, I...," she stuttered, as though she had not considered this.

"We'll return to that later. For now, let us record the facts. Tell me the course of your day."

Lenore gathered herself. She'd woken at seven, as usual, breakfasted, returned to her room to embroider, read, and write letters, lunched, met with the cook about meals for the week in the front parlor, and then around one o'clock heard the gunshot and rushed to her uncle's study.

"Wait, so the cook was with you when you heard the shot?" my father asked excitedly.

"Yes."

"Why didn't you mention this at the inquest?"

Lenore looked at him blankly.

"Lenore, this proves you're innocent! You have an alibi," I said, squeezing her hand.

"I do?"

The naïveté of this young woman! Then again, what else could I expect from someone who'd lived such a monotonous existence, cooped up in her tower like Rapunzel. No wonder Lenore related with Cinderella.

"Yes," said Father. "If the cook will verify she was with you when you both heard the shot, then we can prove without a doubt that you are innocent." He stood. "If you will excuse me, Miss Kelthorpe. I believe I can get you sent home." He left the room with a bounce in his step.

"I'm sorry I didn't mention it before," said Lenore, shaking her head. "I suppose I haven't been thinking clearly ever since..."

"It's only natural," I said. "If you don't mind my asking, when you were with the cook, could you tell where the shot seemed to come from?"

"From my uncle's study," Lenore responded with a quirk of her eyebrow. "Where else might I have heard it from?"

I waived the question. "I merely wondered."

Father returned, his brow furrowed. "I'm afraid the great Detective Billings will not release you until we can confirm your statement."

Lenore's face took on the wearisome aspect of one who had expected no less after so much recent distress in her life. She nodded.

"Happily, he's agreed to go to your house as we speak to ask the cook. Let us continue, while he checks."

Lenore pressed her lips together and nodded again.

Father took up his pen once more, clearly agitated with the police's adherence to laws which he would otherwise use in court.

"Let us see... So then you ran to your uncle's study with the cook?"

"Yes."

"And when did you discover you no longer had the study key on you?"

"At the door, when I went to unlock it to check on my uncle."

"You had not noticed it missing before then?"

"No."

"Where did you normally keep it?"

Lenore reached down mechanically to where her chatelaine would normally have hung, if it had not been confiscated by the police upon her arrival the night before. "I kept all my house keys on me at all times."

"And at night?"

"Locked in my jewelry box, the key to which I wore about my neck."

"Even in bed?"

"Even in bed." Lenore nodded.

"And Murphy does not have a matching set?"

"No. She does not even have a key to my jewelry box. I must always hand it to her when I require she bring out a piece for me to wear."

Father nodded, his notes sprawling across a new page.

"Who else has keys to the study?"

"Only my uncle and Mr. Farwell."

"Why does Mr. Farwell have a key?"

"He has been working with my uncle on his manuscript for over a year, and has only recently received his own key, as a sign of my uncle's trust in him."

"He does not have keys to other rooms?"

"Only his own."

"He lives in the house?"

"Yes. He has the room next to my uncle's, no doubt so my uncle could hear Mr. Farwell's movements at night, should he ever cross the hall to my own door."

"Your door is across from your uncle's?"

"No, I meant across the long part of the hall. My room and personal salon are to the left of the main stairs as one comes to the second floor, while my uncle's room, adjoining study, and Mr. Farwell's room are to the right."

I nodded in agreement at this description, recalling from when I'd sat in Lenore's rooms before the inquest.

"Did Mr. Jackson have reason to worry his secretary may have an interest in you personally?"

If he was worried about such things, I wondered at his not having fired Mr. Farwell long before now.

Lenore blushed. "I, well, I…," she stuttered yet again. "Mr. Farwell does seem to have an interest in me, though I have never encouraged him, and am devoted to Mr. Rohlfs."

I recalled the secretary's looks of concern and open admiration for Lenore when she'd taken the stand. He'd been the first to spring to her side after her faint, and to help her to her feet once she'd roused. I'd assumed he was the author of the letters I'd discovered.

"I see," said Father. "So you entered the room and we'll skim over the first thing you saw, but can you tell me what happened next? Was it you who sent for the surgeon?"

She blushed. "I'm afraid I do not know who did that, as my reaction upon entering was to faint, much as I did at the inquest upon merely trying to relate the fact."

Father nodded. "It was only natural. Who was in the room with you?"

"All the staff, but when I came to, it was only Mr. Farwell."

"Mr. Farwell, again. Where were the others?"

"He said he'd sent them to call for the surgeon and to get me a glass of water."

"And they'd *all* gone?"

"Yes."

I understood where Father was going with this line of questioning. If Mr. Farwell had been left alone in the room for any length of time, there was no telling what he might have done with the place to himself. Perhaps he'd cleaned up any remaining clues that might lead them to his guilt. Then again, he might have done exactly as he'd said.

"Let us return to the day before," said my father. "Did you notice anything odd about your uncle? His behavior or carriage?"

Lenore shook her head, her curls not quite so buoyant as they'd been the first day I'd met her.

"Nor on the day of the murder?"

"Well, as I mentioned to Miss Green," she nodded to me, "he was distressed over her dismissal of him in regards to courtship. But otherwise, he seemed quite ordinary. I saw him at breakfast that morning, and he skipped lunch, as was often the case when he and Mr. Farwell were busy with his book, and the next time I saw him he was..."

"So you did not see him all day except at breakfast?"

"Yes, but as I said, this was not unusual."

"Did anyone see him?"

Lenore pondered, tilting her head slightly. "I should think the upstairs maid, Bridget, would have seen him when she brought up a tray for lunch. And, of course, Mr. Farwell was enclosed with him."

"Mr. Farwell was with you on the other side of the door after the gunshot?"

"Yes, for he was the one who unlocked the door."

"Why did he leave your uncle? Had someone come to call and he'd been excused?"

"I don't know. For that you'd have to ask him, or Boyle."

I wondered if Mr. Rohlfs mightn't have taken it upon himself to visit Mr. Jackson while Mr. Farwell left the room for some reason, and the interview had ended badly. But Lenore was right, that was a question for the butler or the secretary. I'd have to return to the house, sans Lenore, in order to obtain more information from the staff.

Father held up a piece of paper with a list of names. "So the household staff are as follows: one butler, Boyle; one private secretary, Farwell; one lady's maid, Murphy; one upstairs maid, Bridget Kelly; one cook..."

"Kate. I don't recall her last name, as it happens, for she's been Kate as long as I've known her."

"Which is how long?"

"Since I was a girl."

Father made a notation. "One cook, Kate; and one downstairs maid, the dismissed and now missing Emily O'Connell."

Lenore grimaced at the words.

"Please tell me precisely what occurred the night before the murder when you say Emily visited you."

Lenore tugged at her dress sleeves. "It was late, perhaps eleven o'clock at night, when I heard a knock at my door. I rose, robed, and answered it, finding Emily standing there, holding her head with a look of great pain upon her face. I let her in quickly and asked her what was the matter. She told me she had a headache and would I have something for it in the medicine cabinet. The maids are always coming to me complaining of headaches, so I told her to use peppermint oil for now and I would find her something in the light of morning to ease the pain. She didn't leave, however. Instead, she lowered her hand and smiled at me, a most unnerving smile." Lenore shuddered at the memory. "Then she proceeded to blackmail me."

"*Attempted* to blackmail you," Father clarified.

"Yes. As I said at the inquest, she did not succeed."

"What did she say, exactly?"

"She said, 'Miss Kelthorpe, I know about your uncle's will.' I said I knew about it, too, and what of it. And she said, 'I know it is about to change, and there is nothing you can do about it except pay me to discover how.'"

I watched Father's face, but he did not react, so practiced was he at receiving surprise information.

"I said, 'Nonsense. You know nothing. Be gone with you.' She smiled at me and I..." Lenore stopped.

"Yes?" Father coaxed.

"I'm afraid I back-handed her." Lenore bit her lip and lowered her eyes in shame, rubbing her right hand as though it still hurt from the slap.

"Had you ever hit her before?"

"No! Never! I've never hit any of the servants. In fact, as Miss Green can attest, I'm quite fond of all of them. But she dared—and that smile—" Lenore clenched her teeth angrily. "Oh, I could just—"

"Kill her?" Father interrupted.

Lenore gasped and covered her mouth. "No, no, never. Never that."

"Be careful with your reactions, for I'm afraid the jury will not view kindly on one who hits her servants."

"But she deserved it! She tried to blackmail me!"

"Yes, but in the jury's mind it is not a far step from a woman hitting her servants to shooting her uncle, especially if both are in reaction to someone denying you what you want."

"But Emily didn't deny me anything."

"She threatened you," I said. I reached out and took Lenore's hand. "She threatened you with the loss of your inheritance, and you slapped her."

"And dismissed her," Father added.

"But I didn't...she didn't...there was no threat. I haven't lost anything." Lenore looked at Father pleadingly. "Have I?"

"No...," Father said slowly. "As far as I am aware, you are still the one and only heir to Mr. Jackson's estate and fortune. But it is a sum that any would be hard-pressed to believe you would not kill for."

"I didn't. I swear I didn't. I am innocent!" Lenore cried, her face pale as tears began to fall down her cheeks.

"We must find Emily," I said, handing Lenore a handkerchief and squeezing her hand comfortingly. "If we can find her, then we can learn what she knew."

Father nodded. "A servant maid who has a grievance is a very valuable assistant to a detective. It's imperative we find her before Detective Billings."

16

Poetry

"Character added to loveliness gives us those rare specimens of womanly perfection which assure us that poetry and art are not solely in the minds of men."

—Anna Katharine Green, "Is Beauty a Blessing?"
The Ladies' Home Journal

I decided I would walk to Sokol's home rather than take a carriage, appreciating the fresh spring air and the chance to think over some of my father's notes, which I currently held tightly grasped along with a collection of poems I'd written. Along the way, I spoke some of the poems aloud, a habit that had formed after my family moved to Buffalo when I was a child.

Pearls

The wave that floods the trembling shore,
And desolates the strand,
In ebbing leaves, 'mid froth and wreck,
A shell upon the sand.
So troubles oft o'erwhelm the soul;
And shake the constant mind,
That in retreating leave a pearl
Of memory behind.

I considered the sweet melancholy of the lines, the rhythm and rhyme, and decided I quite liked that one, and would share it with Sokol as an example of my talent.

But when I was beckoned into the front parlor once more, and found him seated at his desk at work, the words slipped out into the ether, leaving behind nothing to share except anxiety that he would not like what I had written.

"Ah, Miss Green," he said, turning to admire the cuff of my dress sleeve, "how is Miss Kelthorpe faring?"

"I'm afraid the police cells did nothing to enhance her beauty, Mr. Sokol."

"Sokol, please," he corrected.

"Sokol," I said.

"And I was not inquiring as to how she fared in regards to her appearance, for I have yet to meet a man or woman who is improved by time in the cells, but I wondered if she was more open to sharing the truth of her tale in regards to her uncle's sudden demise."

I pursed my lips, for he had once again hit the nail on the head, so to speak, and landed directly upon the truth of the matter.

"You will be happy to hear she gave my father and me a detailed, genuine account of her actions the day of her uncle's death, and also of her encounter with the maid, Emily, the evening before. We also learned she has an alibi for when her uncle was shot."

Sokol raised an eyebrow. "Does she now?"

"Yes. She was meeting with the cook discussing the week's meals."

"Interesting." Sokol nodded to his fingertips. "And you are convinced she had no more to share?"

"Yes," I said, recalling the immediate responses of Lenore at this latest interview in comparison to what sometimes sounded calculated at the inquest. "You can read it all for yourself here." I handed him the collection of notes.

He turned and placed them on his desk without looking at them before motioning for me to take a seat in the Sheraton armless chair beside the fire. He joined me in an armchair across from me, where he proceeded to study the fireplace poker as though it was a fascinating piece he had never seen before.

"Tell me in your own words."

I did so, entering a sort of recitation mode similar to when I spoke my poems aloud, finding a rhythm in it I had not before. It occurred to me that should I follow Mother Grace's advice and try my hand at writing prose, there may be something to her idea of incorporating a poetic aspect to the lines of description and dialogue.

"Beautifully told," Sokol said, causing my cheeks to warm slightly at the compliment, quite aware that he was a man who did not give them freely. "It seems it is time for me to take a more active role in assisting you and your father. I shall find the missing maid."

I raised an eyebrow at his surety of manner.

"You doubt I will be capable when the police have been unable to find any trace of her?" he asked the poker sardonically.

"They have certainly not had any luck thus far," I said. "As my father and I were leaving the station, Detective Billings informed us that he was closing in on her location, which we both know means they haven't a clue."

Sokol tapped the side of his peaked nose. "Spot on, Miss Green, spot on. You have a most ingenious knack for noting human characteristics of dialogue."

"I believe writers and poets are merely students of human behavior. The thing which interests us most in human beings is their emotions, especially their hidden emotions. We know a good deal about what they do; but we don't know much about what they feel. We are always curious to get below the surface and to find out what is actually going on in their hearts."

"I suppose even a poetess must have some familiarity with the human psyche," Sokol said, his eyes glancing at my dress sleeve once more.

I couldn't be sure, but I thought he was trying to be witty rather than repulsive this time.

"And I suppose you consider yourself a master, if you think you can find a girl the police cannot?" I inquired, getting back to the issue at hand.

"Removing myself from the police force was the best decision God ever made for me," Sokol said, rubbing his crooked hands in remembrance. "It opened me to new avenues of inquiry, new *modus operandi.*"

"Such as?"

"For example, I've already received background information on our Mr. Rohlfs which the police have not yet obtained. Indeed, I don't believe Detective Billings would even be aware of Mr. Rohlfs's existence had your father not informed him. He *has* informed him since our little meeting in the park, has he not?"

I raised a brow. "It is his duty to keep the police informed of any evidence that should come to him, no matter the consequences."

"I doubt very much that there is any man in politics—local or national—that is as conscience-bound as your father," Sokol said, once more delivering the compliment in his peculiar manner where one was uncertain if it was truly a compliment at all.

"In short," Sokol proudly told the poker beside the fire, "I have had a communication from Boston in regard to the matter. I've a friend there in my own line of business, who sometimes assists me with a bit of information, when requested. It is enough for me to telegraph him the name of a person, for him to understand that I want to know everything he can gather in a reasonable length of time about that person."

"And you sent the name of Mr. Rohlfs to him?"

"Yes, in cipher."

"In cipher?"

"Yes, though you needn't be too impressed by this, as the information received was nothing which we did not already know. He is young, he is an actor, and he is in love with Miss Kelthorpe."

Clearly Sokol had missed the part of his statement that had surprised me. I had never met someone who used ciphers in their every day. It was like something straight out of "The Goldbug."

"For another example," he went on, oblivious, "as a policeman, I was often dismissed in servants' minds from the moment I entered the house. As a private citizen, and someone who can impersonate a multitude of characters, I'm much more likely to be welcomed with open arms into the kitchen, say, for a *tête-à-tête*."

"A multitude of characters? You mean disguises?"

"Yes. For example, it would not take much for me to transform into a hunched beggar woman seeking a handout."

I laughed aloud at this image. "A beggar woman? Why would you ever need to disguise yourself as a beggar woman?"

Sokol looked hurt, and I immediately regretted my outburst. "I suppose we shall just have to wait and see," he said to his hands.

I studied the hands he studied, realizing the long fingers were gnarled and oddly bent, the arthritis having done its part in forever shaping his limbs and joints.

"How long have you had rheumatoid arthritis?" I asked quietly.

He did not seem surprised by my question. "Long enough for acceptance, not long enough for peace."

I furrowed my brow. "Does it hurt?"

This did surprise him, for he lifted his eyes to mine for only a moment. "Always," he said, before waving a crippled hand in dismissal. "But enough of that. What matters is that I shall find the missing Emily, and we shall have our answer to what she thought she knew."

"Do you need my help?"

He shook his head. "I have others to hand, one of whom you met at the door, as it happens."

I recalled the barrel-chested man of middling height who'd let me in, whom I'd assumed to be a butler, though I now recalled I'd been admitted entrance by a maid on my previous visit.

"I call him Fobbs, as he is an excellent man for watching people."

I half-expected Sokol to wink at his play on the words "fob watch" but he merely looked toward the doorway leading to the hall, where no doubt Fobbs was awaiting orders.

"It's your turn now," he told the door, and it took me a moment to realize he was actually talking to me.

"My turn?"

"You said you would help me to see how poetry can change the most hardened of hearts, in exchange for our working together on your father's case."

I prayed the words of "Pearls" back into my mind. Instead, another took its place, but as it was another I liked, I decided it would have to do, and so I stood and delivered.

"At the Piano:

Play on! Play on! As softly glides

The low refrain, I seem, I seem

To float, to float on golden tides,

By sunlit isles, where life and dream
Are one, are one; and hope and bliss
Move hand in hand, and thrilling, kiss
'Neath bowery blooms,
In twilight glooms,
And love is life, and life is love.
Play on! Play on! As higher rise
The lifted strains, I seem, I seem
To mount, to mount through roseate skies,
Through drifted cloud and golden gleam,
To realms, to realms of thought and fire,
Where angels walk and souls aspire,
And sorrow comes but as the night
That brings a star for our delight.
Play on! Play on! The spirit fails,
The star grows dim, the glory pales,
The depths are roused — the depths, and oh!
The heart that wakes, the hopes that glow!
The depths are roused: their billows call
The soul from heights to slip and fall;
To slip and fall and faint and be
Made part of their immensity;
To slip from Heaven; to fall and find
In love the only perfect mind;
To slip and fall and faint and be
Lost, drowned within this melody, —
As life is lost and thought in thee.
Ah, sweet, art thou the star, the star
That draws my soul afar, afar?

Thy voice the silvery tide on which
I float to islands rare and rich?
Thy love the ocean, deep and strong,
In which my hopes and being long
To sink and faint and fail away?
I cannot know. I cannot say.
But play, play on."

I let my voice drift as I brought myself back to the room, surprised to find myself not seated at the piano.

Sokol was quietly studying my face. "You wrote that?"

"Are you surprised, Mr. Sokol?" I asked, the heat rising on my neck and cheeks under his intense attentions.

"No," he said, dropping his eyes, which finally allowed me to breathe. "No, I am not."

17

So It Begins

"She does not write unless vitally interested in her characters and plot."

— **"Anna Katharine Green and Her Work,"**
Current Literature

I set down *The Moonstone* and sighed. It had been without a doubt one of the best books I'd read in a long time, certainly much better than the dime novels Sarah recommended. Romance, suspense, mystery, and so many twists I knew I'd still be thinking about it for many years to come.

If only I could write like that. If only I could manufacture a plot with such intrigue...

I considered the plot of the mystery I was currently living, but the trick was, I had no doubt that Wilkie Collins had written

The Moonstone backward. It was the only way he could have come up with such a clever contrivance as the answer to the riddle had been. And all those clues and misleading bits of dialogue along the way. Right up until the end, I'd been convinced of one person's guilt, only to discover it was another's.

If I was going to listen to Mother Grace's advice and write a mystery, I'd first have to solve this one. Then I could begin at the end, with the knowledge of who the murderer was and how it had all been done, before beginning to drop clues along the way. I could plan the whole story before even putting pen to paper, to ensure each part worked in its proper place, and in the end obtain a harmonious whole.

Then again, perhaps if I began writing, the pieces would fall together naturally? Perhaps what was needed was a list of suspects and where they'd been at the time of the murder?

But no, that seemed too prosaic. Surely most prose writers didn't approach writing that way? Where was the fluidity and passion that came when I wrote poetry? And yet, even when writing a poem, I'd endlessly return and rework each line, each collection of words, until it became a cohesive piece that could never have been written any other way.

Back and forth my mind debated, the part of me that wanted to try my hand at a novel sounding increasingly more and more like Mother Grace, while the poetry side sounded more like Father.

Finally, I decided to instead begin with a letter, as my dream had done, to my dearest friend in the world, Mary Platt, now Mrs. Antipas Hatch, whom I had met upon my return from college nearly six years ago. Although she was my brother's wife's cousin, I often referred to her as "my cousin" for simplicity's sake, as she was as much family to me as Mother Grace.

I couldn't explain Sokol on the page, and I knew I shouldn't reveal facts about our current case in writing. So instead, I wrote to her about the play.

"We went to see the most wonderful performance of the Scottish play the other night. Oh, Mary, I wish you could have seen the young man who played Malcolm. He was deliciously clever and brought such heart to the role I could hardly take my eyes off him."

I blushed at the very thought, but if there was anyone in this world with whom I could be completely open and honest, it was Mary. I decided not to include the part where I discovered he was the lover of another young woman, though I folded up the poem I'd written, "Through the Trees," and decided to enclose it with my letter once I was finished. I would leave it up to her to decipher the meaning behind the words.

"Do you remember, Mary, how a critic once told me, 'Keep out of the magazines if you can.' If he had only known how hard I had tried to get into them! The girlish larks we indulged in, the costumes, quaint, ugly and curious, we dressed up in, the walks we took past the glaring brick yards, the outré characters we filched for our stories, the plans we sketched, the hopes we matured... Such dear memories, Mary. I wish you were here so we could indulge in our writing together as we once did."

I paused, mulling over these fond memories, recalling two female characters in particular we'd made up for a story we'd planned to write together, but which had never come to fruition. In fact, the two women might make for perfect characters in central roles of this new plot. I decided to ask Mary if she'd mind my using them, though I guessed she would advocate that I do as I pleased.

I was searching for another clean piece of paper when I discovered the letter I'd received from Emerson regarding my poetry. Before I could stop myself, my eyes ran over the words once more.

"The poems are well chosen and give me as you meant they should a good guess at your style and quality of your work: they clearly indicate a good degree attained in power of expression, and the specimens together show the variety and range of the thought. I think one is to be congratulated on every degree of success in this kind, because it opens a new world of resource and to which every experience glad or sad contributes new means and occasion. But it is quite another question whether it is to be made a profession—whether one may dare leave all other things behind, and write..."

Whether one may dare leave all other things behind and write.

A swell of surety filled me. I would write. I would do it. And what's more, I'd begin today—this very moment, by writing to Mary and telling her of my dream, and my decision to try my hand at a mystery novel.

Having admitted my ideas and plans to Mary, I felt more certain about attempting such a project, but I would wait until the story was finished, or at least mostly finished, before I would share it with others. Until then, I would keep it to myself.

A knock on the door interrupted my thoughts. It was the butler announcing the arrival of Miss Kelthorpe.

So my father had been successful in obtaining her release! I was happy to hear it, and hurried down the stairs to welcome the bedraggled newcomer.

Bedraggled wasn't the half of it. In only one day the bloom of youth had disappeared from Lenore's cheeks, and even out of the unflattering light of the jail she was not the beauty who'd welcomed me to her home just a few days prior.

I kissed Lenore's cheeks as she had done to me only the day before—so long ago now—at tea. "You must rest, my dear," I said.

Lenore merely nodded and allowed me to lead her to the guest bedroom that had been made up for her hoped-for arrival.

As I shut the door on the resting girl, I was not surprised to find Father beckoning me with a nod of his head toward his study.

He shut the study door behind me as I entered and took a seat.

He rubbed his hands together. "I seem to have brought the chill of the jail home with me," he said, reaching for lighting paper from atop the mantel to prepare the fire.

"Let me call a maid to do that, Father."

"Nonsense. I'm perfectly capable of doing it myself, and I wish to be alone with you, to discuss this matter which has now been brought beneath our own roof."

I nodded and clasped my hands upon my lap while I waited for my father. Eventually the fire took hold and he seated himself with the sighing groan of an old man, reminding me that he was in fact sixty-three, though he did not look it to me.

"I'm an old man," he said, and I nearly laughed at his ability to read my thoughts.

"Not at all, Father. And if you begin to speak of retiring yet again, I shall remind you that you've already tried it and found it wasn't to your liking."

He smiled at my kind reproach. "Perhaps I am merely wearied of Manhattan. What would you say to moving back to Buffalo?"

"I would say the Greens have lived in Buffalo, Haverstraw, Albany, Connecticut, and even Indiana, and yet we always manage to find ourselves back here, in your beloved Manhattan."

"We've also lived in Brooklyn Heights, where we were fortunate enough to have you join the family."

As well as a fifth child, I thought, though we were unfortunate to lose my mother and younger brother there, which tainted Brooklyn with sadness in my memories.

"For now," I said aloud, "let us rest our weary minds upon the issues at hand, rather than how we might run away from them."

Father's face soured. "You do not think I have moved you so often in your life in an attempt to run away from life's problems, do you?"

Part of me did, but I could never admit such a thought to that loving face.

"No, I know you've only ever wished the best for your family, and it is in hopes of finding those greater opportunities for us that we have circled the state of New York and its neighbors."

"I'd kindly remind you that you, yourself, attempted to leave by way of college in Vermont, only to find yourself back here with me once more."

I smiled. "Yes, Father."

He shifted in his seat with another sigh toward the fire before pulling out his pipe. Now I knew we'd get down to business.

"What do you make of Miss Kelthorpe?" he asked, packing his pipe with tobacco.

I considered. "When I first met her, while we were waiting in her rooms, she asked me only one question: if I knew the name of Mr. Jackson's sister."

Father paused in his packing and looked up. "That was her question?"

"Yes. Other than that, she simply sat embroidering in an attempt to avoid conversation."

"Embroidering has never stopped your stepmother from conversation," Father said with a fond smile.

I smiled in return. "No, it most certainly has not. It was Miss Kelthorpe's body language along with the embroidering—like when someone is clearly reading a book to avoid speaking, but forgets he must turn the pages occasionally to complete the facade."

Her father nodded and went back to preparing his pipe.

"Eliza," he said. "Mr. Jackson's surviving sister is named Eliza. I do not know her married name, or if she even has one. He only mentioned it to me once in passing, to say that Eliza must never be allowed to get her hands on his money."

"That's rather cruel."

"Perhaps she cannot be trusted." Father shrugged. "After all, Mr. Jackson did take in Miss Kelthorpe when his other sister died. Why didn't Eliza? Normally it is a woman's prerogative to raise a young orphan girl."

It was a good point, and worth considering.

"Do you believe Miss Kelthorpe is truthful?" Father took a couple pulls on his pipe with a match held to the bowl in order to light it.

I hesitated. "Do you?"

"Oh, you know I have no opinion. I gave up everything of that kind when I put the affair into your hands."

I smiled. Father was such a lawyer. "I do not believe she has been *entirely* truthful." The handsome face of Mr. Rohlfs fluttered before my eyes. "But I believe we have uncovered the truth of the matter regarding the secret lover."

"Ah," said Father, shaking the match out. "Therein lies the greatest difficulty when building a case. Every one is hiding something. The trick is to uncover *what.*"

I thought about my idea earlier to begin a list of suspects and their locations. Perhaps listing their lies and motives would also be beneficial.

"I suppose being a lawyer is not much different from being a detective."

Father chuckled at this, puffing on his pipe. "I suppose," he said. "In the end, we both fight for truth and justice, though our approach is decidedly different. While the detective is searching for clues to prove a man's guilt, I am searching for clues to prove a man's innocence."

"I thought all men were innocent until proven guilty."

"That's the idea," said Father. "But it is not the way things usually work out."

"How do you decide whether a man is telling you a truth or a lie?"

"His hands." He shook his empty one before him. "And his eyes." He pointed to his own. "And in the end, I trust."

"Trust the man?"

"Never trust men. I trust that God's will will win out."

I nodded. It sounded like something Father would say.

"Tell me," he continued, "how do you know when you've got something worth sharing after you've written a poem?"

The change in topic surprised me, and yet I thought I understood where he was going.

"I just...feel it."

He nodded as he took a pull on his pipe. "When a man—or woman—tells me the truth, I just feel it. It's the same way."

"And when they lie?"

"I assume everyone is lying to me, always, until I am proven otherwise."

I noted this statement in my mind, thinking it something a detective would say.

My detective.

As I looked at my father, I realized he would make a great detective in a book. The lawyer detective.

And suddenly I knew what I needed to do.

I stood. "If you will excuse me, Father, I've just had an idea."

He smiled. "Ah, the poet's fire is on the move."

I simply nodded and kissed his forehead. "Thank you, Father."

I rushed to my room and to my desk, pulling forward a piece of paper and my pen in one fluid motion. I dipped my pen in the inkwell and scratched hurriedly, before the words could leave my mind.

I had been a junior partner in the firm of Veeley, Carr & Raymond, attorneys and counsellors at law, for about a year, when one morning, there came into our office a young man whose whole appearance was so indicative of haste and agitation that I involuntarily rose at his approach and impetuously inquired:

"What is the matter? You have no bad news to tell, I hope."

"I have come to inform you that Mr. Leavenworth is dead; shot through the head by some unknown person while sitting at his library table."

18

Mr. Leavenworth

"It will require all my enthusiasm, study and power, and then I may fall short, but I believe I shall sometime try. Perhaps it is somewhat sensational, but I hope by characterization and earnestness to lift it to a higher ground."

—Anna Katharine Green, quoted in "An American Gaboriau," by Mary R. P. Hatch

The name "Leavenworth" was not a new one to me, for he had been a hero in one of the stories I'd concocted as a child of fourteen, but to find him the *victim* in this mystery surprised even me. Yet the words flowed as I continued to write and introduce my main character, the young lawyer Everett Raymond.

I could see him in my mind, though I decided to avoid too much description in order to make him an Everyman with whom the reader could identify, something my professors had taught me to do in college fiction-writing courses.

In truth, he was my father, young and just starting out in his career, and before long I learned that he was hopelessly in love with one of the main characters, who of course was also the one who seemed most likely to have killed Mr. Leavenworth. It would become Mr. Raymond's passion to prove her innocence, much as it had become mine for Lenore.

> *A sweet picture...the vision of a young flaxen-haired, blue-eyed coquette...standing in a wood-path, looking back over her shoulder at some one following—yet with such a dash of something not altogether saint-like in the corners of her meek eyes and baby-like lips, that it impressed me with the individuality of life.*

I decided for the time being to name the character Eleanore, close enough for me to keep the story straight. I would name the second woman Mary, in honor of Mary Hatch, since she'd helped me create the basis for these two characters when we were younger.

> *Sitting in the light of a solitary gas jet, whose faint glimmering just served to make visible the glancing satin and stainless marble of the gorgeous apartment, I beheld Miss Leavenworth. Pale as the sculptured image of the Psyche that towered above her from the mellow dusk of the bow-window near which she sat, beautiful as it, and almost as immobile.*

As I began to describe the two women, however, I found myself giving Mary the pale, blonde features, and making Eleanore darker, more like my coloring. It was not that I was trying to write myself into the story, for I soon realized there were elements of myself coming through in both young women. I wanted the dynamic between them to not only reflect my relationship with Lenore, whom I was still only just coming to know on a more personal level, but also that of mine with my sister, and my cousin Mary, and that of several dear school friends. I wanted them to be close, like sisters, but not quite, so I decided to make the girls cousins.

> *Eleanore Leavenworth must be painted by other hands than mine. I could sit half the day and dilate upon the subtle grace, the pale magnificence, the perfection of form and feature which make Mary Leavenworth the wonder of all who behold her; but Eleanore—I could as soon paint the beatings of my own heart. Beguiling, terrible, grand, pathetic, that face of faces flashed upon my gaze, and instantly the moonlight loveliness of her cousin faded from my memory, and I saw only Eleanore—only Eleanore from that moment on forever.*

I recalled how Lenore had decried the need for protection, though I wondered if her opinion on the matter had changed since her night in jail. It was a common theme in stories, I thought: a woman who needed protection. It was certainly common in the sorts of books Sarah preferred.

But I didn't want to read that sort of story, much less write it. I was more interested in a valiant young woman who wasn't afraid to do the protecting, rather than being protected.

The year after Louisa May Alcott's mystery novella *The Mysterious Key and What It Opened* was published, she'd released one of my particular favorites, *Little Women,* which was, in my opinion, filled with some of the most beautifully written characters ever created. My favorite, of course, had been Jo, the writer, the strong one in the family, the one who knew what she wanted and went out and got it, the protector.

In my head, Eleanore was Jo and Mary was Amy, the little sister who needed protecting. But then I realized: What if it was a matter of misunderstanding? What if Mary was the elder sister, who thought Eleanore was the one who needed protection, only to discover later in the novel that their roles were reversed?

I dipped my pen and scribbled a note to myself on a separate sheet of paper, reminding myself of this decision. Perhaps I shouldn't write linearly at all? Perhaps I should write the scenes that jumped forward, eager to be written, and then piece them back together once I knew more?

I nodded to myself. This made sense to me, though it was probably not the way a "real" author ever went about writing. But what did I care? This was my first attempt. I needed to give myself some grace. I'd learn along the way, and I knew this wouldn't be perfect from the first attempt. Authors had drafts upon drafts before publication... Didn't they?

I shook my head and bent back over my words. Just keep writing.

> *Eleanore Leavenworth, very pale, but with a resolute countenance, walked into the house and into the room, confronting Mary. "I have come," said she, lifting a face whose expression of mingled sweetness and power I could not but*

admire, even in that moment of apprehension, "to ask you without any excuse for my request, if you will allow me to accompany you this morning?"

I was pleased with the way the two women in my story were taking shape. Strong women, with a fierce determination lying behind their sensibilities. I knew there must be some amount of fainting and hand-holding for the book to be viewed as acceptable to the reading public, but I decided that such would only occur when and where the women themselves were aware of what they were doing.

I would still have them faint, but only when they were doing so in order to cover for someone or to distract from evidence. My women would be strong and brave, following that timeless Bible verse: "Greater love hath no one than this, that he lay down his life for his friends." My women would show a Biblical bravery, willing to die for the other to defend them, to protect them.

If I was going to write fiction rather than poetry, then one of my intentions with this book would be to write a mystery containing fully realized characters. Like *The Moonstone,* I wanted each character to have his or her own backstory, to the point that the reader wouldn't know whom to suspect, because they all would seem to have a motive for murdering Mr. Leavenworth. In that sense, I could hide the murderer like a needle in a haystack.

The very house in which the murder took place must be a character in its own right, reflecting nuances and details for the solving of the murder: telling and yet not too telling.

> *The gorgeous house, its elaborate furnishing, the little glimpses of yesterday's life, as seen in the open piano, with its sheet of music held in place by a lady's fan, occupying my attention fully as much as the aspect of the throng of incongruous and impatient people huddled about me.*

As I wrote, I tried to change the story in other subtle ways here and there to be sure it was not exactly the same as our current situation. Of course, not knowing who the murderer was in real life leant a certain air of confusion to the writing, but I pressed forward nonetheless.

Quickly I filled page after page with the opening scenes, including an inquest, where I could detail notes from the one I'd only just attended, but it was not long before I realized I would need more to fill in the blanks left where the servants should give their testimonies. Unlike in real life, I could not leave the reader locked in the room with the lady of the house, but must take them along, introducing them to the servants one by one, listing what they saw as they gave each of their statements.

I sat back and brushed the back of my pen against my chin.

It was only then that I noticed how black my fingertips had become. It had been a long time since I'd had the fingers of a writer to show at dinner.

The gong sounded below, and I realized I did not know if it was the dressing gong or the dinner one, and glanced at the mantel clock.

Six o'clock. It was the dressing gong. I hastily poured water from my pitcher into my washing bowl, and scrubbed at my fingers until I could be sure the ink that remained was permanent, and would not mar the inside of my gloves, nor my evening gown. Then I changed quickly, putting the finishing touches on my hair before realizing Lenore was most likely unable to dress herself, as she'd been accustomed to a lady's maid until this evening.

I made my way to Lenore's door and knocked, hearing a timid, "Enter," before turning the knob.

Within I found Lenore seated on the window seat, staring out into the darkening sky, seemingly lost to the approach of the evening meal.

"Lenore?" I asked.

The young woman turned, her eyes shining with tears, some of which had streaked her cheek.

"Good evening, Anna," she said with a sniffle, dabbing at her eyes and cheeks with the handkerchief clutched in her hand. "I'm afraid I won't be joining you for dinner this evening."

"Why not? I have come expressly to ensure that you are helped into an evening gown."

"I have nothing to wear."

"You must borrow one of mine, then," I said, crossing to help Lenore to her feet and guide her to my room before she could protest.

It became quickly clear that Lenore and I did not share the same outline of form, but finally a black gown was made suitable through the use of a few strategic pins, and we joined the remainder of the family downstairs before too long.

After introductions to Mother Grace and Sarah, the five of us enjoyed a happy meal of meaningless discourse upon such topics as the weather, theater, and the latest fashions, which seemed to put Lenore at her ease.

The entire time, however, I could hardly keep from shoveling food in order to enable the next course to come sooner. I could not wait to return to my desk, and knew I'd be up late into the night getting my thoughts down.

It occurred to me that I would need an actual detective. A professional, to work alongside my lawyer, thrust into the midst of the mystery. Although the Bulldog was not the only example available to me, I felt a strong impulse to try my hand at creating a female detective, something that would shock the world and its sensibilities, but which might win me the admiration of male and female readers alike.

I'd have to do it carefully and with great skill, something which I was not certain I possessed, given I'd only ever written poetry until now. But what better voice to give a female detective than that of a poetess? Perhaps, like Mother Grace had suggested, I might even incorporate some of my original poems.

Finally the meal ended, and I was honestly thrilled when Lenore excused herself from further activities and made her way to bed early for the night. This meant that I, too, could be pardoned for extracting myself.

I changed into my nightgown and promptly returned to my pages, losing myself in them until I became aware of daylight streaming in through my window announcing that I'd successfully written through the entire night.

19

Murphy

"You expected revelations, whispered hopes, and all manner of sweet confidences; and you see, instead, a cold, bitter woman, who for the first time in your presence feels inclined to be reserved and uncommunicative."

—***The Leavenworth Case***

I knew what I was working on had never been done before. Yes, there had been women writers who'd tried their hand at mystery, such as *The Mysterious Key,* and there were perhaps more of whom I was unaware, since they'd published under a pen name, even Alcott doing so as L.M. Alcott.

But I also knew I wasn't the only woman who enjoyed unraveling a mystery. Mr. Jackson himself had declared I was "one of *those* women fascinated by crime," which implied I was not alone in my interests. Perhaps more women should try their hand at writing mystery? Perhaps I'd start a wave of criminal romance authors, and go down in history as the first?

I tapped my pen. If I lost myself to daydreams I'd never get this book finished. My stack of pages lay to my right. The jubilation which had filled me through the night and forced my pen ever onward, however, faded swiftly.

I was not ready—could not be ready—to share this with anyone. It must be kept secret until it was complete. And for that, I would need more information.

Turning to my wardrobe, I selected a black ensemble that I felt comfortable wearing with ink-stained fingers, while continuing to meet the call for mourning out of deference for Lenore, and then dressed for the coming day. The first thing I had to do was speak with the servants of the Jackson household, in order to fill in the holes left in the inquest scenes.

I shook my head at myself. I shouldn't think of it in terms of my book, for a flesh-and-blood young lady was just a few doors down, wracked with grief and fear over what the future held, and it was for *her* sake that I must gather information. Not Mr. Leavenworth's.

After a few quick bites of eggs, sausage, oatmeal, and fruit before I left, I knocked at Lenore's door, to remind myself of my true purpose. Lenore answered and apologized for missing breakfast, claiming she wished to remain within for the day, as she suffered from a headache—no doubt from all the crying—which couldn't make me more delighted, though I naturally couldn't say so. Instead I asked if I might go by Lenore's home to pick up anything she required.

"Thank you, Anna!" she cried, reaching for a pen and paper to make a short list. "I don't know why I bothered," she said, handing it to me. "Murphy knows everything I need. Oh!" She reached for the keys on her chatelaine, which had been returned to her upon leaving the station. "She will need this."

Lenore handed me a small key, as to a cupboard.

"This is the key to the medicine cabinet. I have asked Murphy to send along some of my migraine pills."

"I'm certain we have everything you might need," I said, taking the list and the key. "We are fully stocked, and you need only ask if you should require anything."

"Thank you. These are special ones the doctor prescribed for me. I suffer from terrible migraines, so I usually require something stronger than peppermint oil."

Lenore gave me heartfelt words of gratitude, and then I was off.

It was not long before I was within the Jackson home once more, and was enabled, with the help of Lenore's list, to find her lady's maid open to conversation.

"Thank you for your assistance, Murphy," I said, seating myself on the edge of Lenore's bed while Murphy removed and folded garments—all in somber black—to place into a traveling trunk. "You must know that Miss Kelthorpe is lost without you."

"And I without her, Miss Green," the lady's maid replied in rounded Irish tones.

"It must be strange to find yourself without your mistress about."

"Indeed, it most certainly is, Miss Green. I have not been away from her side in ten years. I came when she was just a lass, and now she is a lady," Murphy said, tenderly tucking the long sleeves of a gown beneath the bodice.

"You must be quite fond of her."

Murphy looked up. "Indeed, I am, Miss Green, as I have every right to be."

"Naturally, naturally," I hastened to say. "You are really the only mother she's ever known."

Murphy smiled. "Yes, I suppose I am. It hurts something fierce to see her in such distress. It was hard enough when Mr. Jackson was found dead, but now to have Miss Kelthorpe suspected of the deed—why, I can hardly fathom it."

"Did you know Mr. Jackson before you became governess to Miss Kelthorpe?"

Murphy shook her head. "I was hired through an agency, the same that had found me my previous two positions."

"You have been governess to three young ladies, then?"

"Four," Murphy corrected. "One position was with two sisters. And that is not counting my brothers and sisters, whom I raised until they were old enough to find positions of their own."

"Were the others also orphans?"

"No, the other three were living with parents who required assistance, was all."

"Of course." I considered how best to ask my next question. "Were they as...protective as Mr. Jackson?"

"You mean, did they let their girls attend balls and parties and the like once they were old enough to enter society?"

I nodded.

Murphy slowly folded a dress before replying. "Mr. Jackson had his reasons for keeping Miss Kelthorpe contained, I am certain."

"Do you know what those reasons might have been?"

Murphy frowned at me. "I am sorry, miss, but I do not see why that might be anything you need know."

"I only wondered if perhaps Mr. Jackson had suffered in some way in India. That perhaps there was something that had happened there to cause him to become somewhat of a recluse upon his return to New York."

"I'm certain that if something had happened to Mr. Jackson in India, Mr. Farwell would be the one to know about it." Murphy focused on her folding. "As I said, I did not know Mr. Jackson before, and he has not confided in me regarding his background in any manner."

I nodded. "At least some good may come of all this, now she is the lady of the house."

Murphy stopped folding.

"What I mean to say is: she told me you were the one she trusted to deliver the correspondence between herself and Mr. Rohlfs."

Murphy relaxed.

"I understand Miss Kelthorpe sent you with a secret note just moments after Mr. Jackson's death."

Murphy nodded as she reached for another dress from the wardrobe. "Yes...and I am certain once my mistress is cleared of all doubts concerning her innocence, there will be joy once again in this house regarding their union."

"Mr. Rohlfs being a poor actor meant nothing to her?" I asked carefully. "There was no other man who might draw her affections?"

Murphy narrowed her eyes only slightly before responding. "If you mean Mr. Farwell, he showed plenty of interest in Miss Kelthorpe, but she never once returned his advances in any way. Most improper. He should have known better given his station."

So Mr. Farwell *did* love Lenore, as I'd suspected. Unrequited love—the worst kind when it came to motive.

"All that was keeping them from marriage was Mr. Jackson?"

"As far as I know."

"I merely wondered if my new friend might finally find happiness? I suppose money will be no object to her now she will inherit the entirety of Mr. Jackson's estate."

"I do not think money was in any way involved in her love for Mr. Rohlfs," said Murphy, straightening her shoulders as though offended by the idea. "If you had read but one of their letters, you would understand as I do the strength of their affection for one another."

As well as Mr. Rohlfs's proclivity for using the Bard's lines to woo his love, as I recall. But this was not what stood out to me about her statement. "So you not only delivered, but read their correspondence?"

Murphy's cheeks reddened slightly and she turned to grab Lenore's jewelry box.

"I am sure you were only looking out for her, as any governess would do for her charge," I encouraged.

Murphy turned and nodded, but kept her eyes on her packing.

"I am also sure you will be glad to hear that Miss Kelthorpe is certain to be cleared soon, as she has stated that she was with the cook when Mr. Jackson was killed."

Murphy's head shot up. "Indeed?"

"Yes."

Murphy sighed and clutched her breast. "Praise be to God!" she exclaimed, and crossed herself. "I knew she was not guilty!"

The way she said it made me wonder if she'd had her doubts until this moment.

"Yes, an alibi does wonders in proving innocence."

Murphy nodded in agreement. "I could not be certain where she was at the dreadful moment, as I myself was alone in this room doing the mending."

Alone, I noted. *And profoundly eager to supply her young charge with happiness.*

"I knew she was innocent," Murphy continued. "She had to be, even after she said she knew how to fire that horrid gun, though I had no notion she'd ever learned such a thing."

"Oh?" I cocked my head.

"Why she'd be interested I do not understand."

"At the inquest, she said she felt she needed to defend herself. Was it because she and Mr. Rohlfs intended to run away together? Did they plan to be wed out west, perhaps?"

Murphy shook her head. "I do not know. I only know she intended to run away with him, as I believe you know yourself."

I nodded. "Yes. I met with Mr. Rohlfs in Miss Kelthorpe's place to tell him of her arrest."

Murphy smiled slightly. "He is a handsome man, is he not?"

My heart skipped a beat as I thought how best to avoid answering the question, deciding a nod would do for now.

"My poor *mavourneen.* She was finally to know true happiness, only to have it dashed from her lips like a fairy drink."

The mention of a drink gave me a reason to excuse myself and make my way to speak with the cook, feeling that I had obtained enough from the lady's maid for the time being. If I had any further questions, I could ask them when I collected Lenore's things before returning home.

I wondered what a detective would ask in this situation, and was still considering this as I descended the basement stairs to the servants' dining hall. Seated at the table, helping herself to a bit of bread and cheese, was an old beggar woman like something out of an Irish fairy tale.

But what startled me all the more was when the woman turned, and in her features I beheld those of the one and only Sokol.

20

The Staff

"It will be observed that [Anna Katharine Green] does all that is necessary to cultivate an air of authenticity in what she writes."

—**T. Fisher Unwin,** ***Good Reading About Many Books Mostly by Their Authors***

"Welcome, Miss Green," said the cook. "Boyle told me you were here helping Murphy collect clothing for the mistress."

Her name was Kate, as I recalled, though I had difficulty keeping my face straight while marveling at the beggar woman at the table.

Sokol had taken an old, piteous rag and wrapped his entire head and upper half of his body in it, sticking curls of some sort to hang upon his forehead. He'd also done something to his nose to make it even more beak-like. But he was right: his naturally hunched back and tendency to avoid eye contact made him completely believable as a tramp. All he'd needed was the clothes.

"Don't mind her," Kate said. "I have a hard time turning away anyone in need. It's me weakness." She motioned me past the servants' table and back into the hall to the kitchen. "Now, tell me, what can I do fer ya?"

What can you do for me? I wondered, having difficulty regaining my train of thought.

"I was wondering if I might trouble you for a cup of tea," I finally said. "I only stopped by to collect a few items for Miss Kelthorpe, but I find myself feeling parched."

Kate smiled. "Of course, dearie, I always keep the kettle on for a good cup of scald, so I'll just be a minute. Why don't you have a seat, if you don't mind joining the less fortunate at the same table?" she finished with a whisper.

"Of course not," I said, eager to engage this particular beggar in conversation.

Kate hobbled her ample figure back into the kitchen to procure the tea things and I seated myself at the simple table.

"I'll have you know, I'd almost obtained everything I needed before your unnecessary interference," the tramp muttered into his hands.

"I'm certain you think you did," I said. "May I ask what facts that might include, so I needn't ask Kate to repeat herself?"

Sokol gave a sidelong glance toward the door to the kitchen. "Her name is Kate?" he asked his piece of bread.

I laughed.

"That was not necessary information," he murmured in response.

I shook my head. If her name wasn't necessary, I wondered what was.

"I *did* confirm, however, that she met with Miss Kelthorpe the day of the murder just before the shot was fired. They were in fact together at the time, so she indeed provides your friend with an alibi."

"Thank you. You needn't have gone to the trouble. Miss Kelthorpe stayed with us last night, which could only have been because Detective Billings had confirmed her alibi already."

Sokol clenched his jaw.

"And did you know they normally met right here to plan the meals, but this particular day Miss Kelthorpe asked...*Kate*...up to the parlor instead?"

This, I had to admit, was new, and I said as much, immediately noticing a slight straightening of Sokol's shoulders beneath the rag, which then dropped as soon as Kate returned with a tea tray.

"Here you go, dearie. And would you like some, too?" she asked in a slightly higher tone to the tramp, who merely shook her head and focused on the hunk of cheese in her hand.

"Something tells me you're here to ask me for more than tea," said Kate as she poured out for me.

I blushed and glanced at the tramp.

"The daughter of a great lawyer donnae come all this way just to pick up a few necessary items for a young lady persecuted by the law," added the cook knowingly, her Irish accent much thicker and more difficult to understand than Murphy's, which suddenly seemed elegant and graceful in comparison.

"You will be happy to hear she spent last night at our home, rather than in a jail cell," I said.

"Oh, I am glad. I figured as much after that detective came round asking me where she was when we heard the gunshot."

"May I ask why you didn't mention it at the inquest? Miss Kelthorpe might have avoided arrest then."

"It must'a clean slipped me mind is all," said Kate with a flush upon her cheeks. "So much had happened, and seeing Mr. Jackson's body like that, why we were all still a bit flustered. And then the coroner and the jury all looking at ya—it gave me the frights, it did. I was lucky to recall me name, much less what I was doing when I heard the shot. As I was just telling this kind lady, listening to me ramble on and on about me own problems, in the end, I was just that glad I could be of assistance to our dear Lenore—I mean, Miss Kelthorpe."

I smiled at the familiarity, which confirmed Lenore's closeness with the cook, at least, and implied she'd been honest about her relationships with the staff. "It is lucky for her that she was with you."

"It was nothing outta the ordinary. We always meet on Monday to discuss the week's preparations."

"And in the parlor?"

"Sometimes there, sometimes here. But it is a good thing we were up there this week as I don't think we would have heard the shot from down here. I never hear a thing when I'm in the kitchen."

"Too many banging pots?"

"And the walls down here are thick. It's like an oven in more ways than one, but then that's standard practice for houses in these parts."

I nodded. Our own kitchen was also on the ground floor, with a door that opened onto the back garden.

"Is there a door down here? Perhaps that you'd keep open?"

"Yes, just there, but I only keep it open when I'm baking, which usually requires a higher heat than cooking—bread and the like needs as much heat as you can stand to get it to rise properly. I build up the heat in the oven, then open the back door to the kitchen. No need to bake meself, I say!"

I nodded but didn't have the slightest notion how to start an oven, much less cook in it.

"I do wish the detective had asked me more about Emily, though. It bothered me something fierce what Miss Kelthorpe said about her."

"You mean about the blackmail?" I asked, recalling my catching the cook's shaking head at the inquest.

The cook shook her head again now. "She'd never blackmail. Not Emily. She's sound as a pound that one, a good Irish girl. As far I knew, she and Miss Kelthorpe were on the friendliest of terms, as are we all. She may have had her sins, did Emily, but blackmail was never one of them."

"May I ask what sins she did have?"

Kate took a long, slow sip of her tea. "I suppose I might as well tell ya, as it might be helpful to your da in looking for her."

I appreciated this.

"See her there now, she had 'notions.' Now I know for a fact that she and Mr. Farwell were, well...," she glanced at the tramp and apparently decided if anyone would know what she meant, it would be someone from that world, "…intimate," she finished in a whisper, as though to lessen the sting of it.

I still blushed at the idea, glancing at the tramp, too, but for quite a different reason from Kate. "For how long?"

"Oh, I haven't a rashers. They've been trying to keep it secret, but me old eyes can see the truth clear enough," the cook said, not actually answering the question put to her.

"So you think he might know where she is?"

"To be sure, to be sure. I think he might be the reason she disappeared. I have a difficult time understanding why she'd blackmail the mistress, unless it was for money so they could marry."

It seemed the house had contained two pairs of star-crossed lovers, I thought: Lenore and Mr. Rohlfs, and now Emily and Mr. Farwell. Although Mr. Farwell and Emily may not have been too far apart in the class of things, there was still a societal implication that one didn't run off with the staff of one's employer.

"Couldn't he have asked Mr. Jackson for money, if that was what they needed?"

"Mr. Farwell is not what I would call a strong-willed man." Kate considered her teacup. "I do not think Mr. Farwell would have ever risked asking Mr. Jackson for anything that might cost him his job. Asking his permission to marry a member of his staff would have been out of the question. So it might have meant Emily must ask for money in order that they begin their life anew elsewhere. That is the only reason I can think for Emily's actions."

"So you're not questioning the veracity of Miss Kelthorpe's statement?" I clarified.

"It must have been something greatly dear to Emily's heart to force her to take such steps," intoned a voice, and I turned to find the butler, Boyle, had joined us.

"You do not believe Emily would blackmail Miss Kelthorpe unless she had no other choice?" I repeated.

"I donnae believe anyone would blackmail another person without considering all other choices, would you, Miss Green?"

The butler had a point. Blackmail was a risky business.

"Do you have any idea where Emily may be hiding?"

Boyle shook his head. "You might ask Mr. Farwell."

Kate nodded her head and waved a hand. "I already informed Miss Green in all, Boyle."

I nodded. "That does remind me of another fact I wished to put to you, however, Boyle," I said, turning to him. "I was wondering if anyone visited the house the day of the murder, at any time?"

"No. As I said at the inquest, the only people in this house, that I was aware of, were the normal members of the household."

If he'd said as much at the inquest, I wondered why my father hadn't mentioned it. Perhaps he'd merely forgotten that I had missed the first hour.

"Thank you. As I was unable to hear that information first-hand, I merely wanted to confirm it. It puts rather a strain on the remaining household, as it means the murderer must be one of them."

Boyle nodded solemnly. "It is a fact which worries us all most decidedly, Miss Green."

21

Sound Theory

"With her, action speaks louder than words."

— **"Anna Katharine Green and Her Work,"**
Current Literature

I excused myself after finishing my tea, and returned upstairs to see if I might catch the remaining housemaid for a couple questions while I was here.

Unfortunately, it seemed she was not within the house, and I had just given up on locating the girl when I turned with a start to find Sokol standing behind me, returned to his normal appearance.

"Good morning, Miss Green. Boyle said I might find you here."

I held a hand to my heart. "You must stop doing that!" I cried. "You're going to stop my heart one of these days."

"Perhaps that is my intention," Sokol said deeply.

I wondered what exactly he'd meant by those words, but was distracted by another fact.

"May I ask whether you expect to work entirely by yourself; or whether, if a suitable coadjutor were provided, you would disdain her assistance and slight her advice?"

"Whatever do you mean?"

"Dressing up like a beggar woman when I was capable of obtaining the same information without disguise."

Sokol considered the wall sconce. "You are a woman, Miss Green."

"Yes I am," I said, straightening my jacket top, "and as such, I was also able to discuss matters quite openly with Murphy to obtain further information on Miss Kelthorpe. She has even given me a possible lead—"

"Wait," Sokol interrupted, "does she know this? Was it done intentionally and with sinister motive, or unconsciously and in plain good faith?"

I sighed. "In good faith, I should say."

Sokol remained silent for a moment. "It is not that a word from you now and then would not be welcome. I am not an egotist."

I bit my tongue from responding.

"I am open to suggestions: as, for instance, if you could conveniently inform me of all you have yourself seen and heard in regard to this matter, as you have done previously at my residence, I should be most happy to listen."

Would he now?

"But I am almost afraid to trust you to make investigations on your own. You are not used to the business, and will lose time, to say nothing of running upon false scents, and using up your strength on unprofitable details—"

"Like the cook's name?" I interrupted.

"It was not important," Sokol repeated.

"Mr. Sokol," I said purposefully, "we cannot continue to work together if you will not trust me to do my own investigations. It does us no good competing when there are certain people better questioned by a lady, and others by a gentleman. It wastes time and effort better spent chasing down new leads. You must allow me to find out what I can in my own way, while you search with your ciphers and disguises."

Sokol studied the sconce with a clear look of irritation. "In other words, you are to play the hound, and I the mole; just so, I know what belongs to a lady."

I decided that was the best answer I could hope to receive. "Speaking of your disguise, did you ring after discarding it or simply hide the rags in the hall closet?"

Sokol's mouth twitched. "I knocked. Boyle answered. And I am here. You simply weren't listening."

"It is a most quiet house," I said musingly.

The cook couldn't hear things from the basement, before the inquest I hadn't heard Sokol exploring the rooms, and now I hadn't heard him return. And yet everyone in the house had heard the gunshot.

"May I ask you to amuse me with a little experiment, one you mustn't tell to my father?" I asked suddenly.

Sokol raised a brow at a lamp near me. "If you promise not to tell your father about *my* little experiment."

I smiled at his reticence to share about his disguise. "I promise." I looked about me. "I would like to ascertain where one might hear a gunshot in this house, but as I believe shooting another gun might bring the police, perhaps we might use the dinner gong in its place?"

"I assume you'd rather not ask Boyle for permission first?"

"Decidedly not, as that would ruin the experiment." I walked out into the main hall and removed the dinner gong and mallet carefully from its place where it hung between two poles. It was not large, but it was assuredly loud enough to be heard throughout the house when it was rung.

"We must first test the most difficult place from which to hear it, so as not to give away our intentions," I said, carrying it with me up the stairs.

Sokol followed slowly, his cane tapping behind me upon each step.

"Where do you intend to try first, then?" he asked.

I stopped at the top of the stairs. I glanced to the left, toward Lenore's rooms, and then to the right, to Mr. Farwell's room and the late Mr. Jackson's rooms.

"The study, of course."

"That was where Mr. Jackson was shot."

I turned and gave Sokol a small and, I hoped, mysterious smile. "Precisely."

Sokol's mouth twitched and he nodded his approval to the bannister.

I led the way to the study and knocked before entering, I knew not why, but perhaps merely out of respect to the dead man's work. There was no answer, so I tried the knob. It was locked.

"This makes things more difficult," I muttered.

Suddenly, there was a key in the lock, turning and unlocking the door from within.

I stepped back in surprise when Sokol opened the door from inside.

"How on earth—"

Sokol studied the doorknob in his hand.

"As I said, this key," he held it aloft, "opens both study doors—this one and the one from the bedroom. As Mr. Farwell and Mr. Jackson both appear to have their copies, we must assume that this key belongs to Miss Kelthorpe, and is her missing one."

I decided it would be inappropriate to hit Sokol over the head with the gong. "You have the most irritating way of proving your theories, Sokol." I took a steadying breath. "But, I admit, effective."

I passed through the doorway and looked about the study. It was my first time in the room where the murder had occurred and I was surprised and horrified to find myself almost swooning when I looked at the chair, and the dark, dried splotches marking where the dead man had sat...a clean piece of paper already laid out for him, a pen in his hand...just writing, working...never knowing that someone was sneaking up behind him...with a gun...about to—

"Miss Green?"

I leapt into the air, and almost hit the gong too early, but at least the blood was rushing back into my head again.

Sokol stood at my shoulder, his hand behind me, as though prepared to catch me if I'd fallen.

The blood rushing to my head filled my cheeks with embarrassment.

"Are you all right, Miss Green?" Sokol asked, and I was surprised to hear genuine concern in his voice, but then again it might have simply been worry that he'd almost had to touch me.

"Yes, I'm fine," I said, forcing myself to look over at the fireplace instead, calming myself by cataloguing the items on the mantel: matches, a vase full of lighting paper, an ornate gold clock, a couple of baroque wooden carvings, a pair of silver candlesticks. Another painting that looked to be an original Turner hung above the mantel, this one with colors of iron and fire.

Once finished there, I took in the rest of the room, noting two windows, the door leading to Mr. Jackson's bedroom, two overstuffed armchairs with antimacassars draped across the backs, a tea table between them, a small table with a cigar box beside one of the chairs, and a cabinet along the wall with an open door revealing wine glasses and a decanter within. I crossed to this and set down the gong and mallet quietly upon one of the chairs so I could pick up the decanter.

"I did not figure you for a woman of drink," Sokol said.

I turned quickly, my eyes skimming over him as he stood beside the desk and chair, where I could still make out dark patches that might be—I stopped the thought and turned back to the cabinet.

"Most certainly I am not. I merely wondered why the door was open and..." I lifted the decanter, removed the stopper, and took a sniff, wrinkling my nose. "I wondered what was his drink of choice. Sherry, it seems, like my father."

Sokol crossed and leaned in to smell, as well. "Yes, sherry."

His head was quite close to mine as he leaned over the decanter, so close that I was able to see the graying hairs upon the top of his head. Most likely he was unaware of their existence, given their location, and I smiled at this.

When he raised his face, I was still smiling and although he did not meet my gaze, he frowned at the decanter.

"Why are you smiling?"

"No reason. Why do you think the door was open?"

"Why do I think the door to the sherry cabinet was open? Is that a trick question?"

I shrugged. "Naturally, it was open because someone wanted a drink, but if so," I motioned about the room with the decanter before replacing the stopper, "where is the wine glass from which Mr. Jackson took his last sip?"

"You mean sherry glass." Sokol sniffed, which I took to mean I'd noticed something once again that he had missed. "Perhaps it's simply a case of one of the staff helping themselves to the dead man's sherry. Besides, Mr. Jackson was shot, not—" But he stopped himself.

"You were about to say, 'not poisoned,' yes? But we do not know that for certain, do we?" I asked pointedly, placing the decanter back in the cabinet and returning the door to the position in which I'd found it.

He rubbed the top of his cane. "Correct. A detail I shall take up with the coroner."

I shook my head. "He'll never follow the theory without probable cause."

"You sound like your father," Sokol said, though he didn't seem to think that was a bad thing.

I smiled, deciding it was a compliment. "Shall we move forward with my gong theory?" I picked up the gong and mallet again and stood in the center of the room.

Sokol moved to each door and closed them securely before turning to me and nodding.

I hit the gong soundly with the mallet.

The noise reverberated throughout the room so loudly I couldn't believe no one came running to us.

"Have we any idea where everyone is currently stationed?" Sokol asked the gong quietly.

"No," I admitted, "but given everyone immediately ran to the study upon hearing the gunshot, I have difficulty believing no one heard that."

"Try again."

I nodded and did so, the sound pealing and echoing off the walls and around the room.

Sokol crossed to the door leading to Mr. Jackson's bedroom. He opened the door, but went through and closed the door to the hall from that room. He returned and motioned to me, and I hit the gong again.

The noise was not quite so contained, this time, but still, no one rushed up to see what we were doing.

Sokol rubbed the top of his cane and opened the door of the study leading to the hall.

"But we know for certain that door was closed," I said.

"After the murderer left," said Sokol.

I nodded and hit the gong again. Every time, my eyes closed in reaction to the *bong.*

Still no one came.

This surprised me greatly. I'd been certain that at least with the door—*both* doors—to the study open, *someone* should have heard the sound.

Sokol stood by the desk, considering.

Then, he closed both doors to the study once more, crossed to one of the windows, the one beside the sherry cabinet, and, using both hands, pried it up and open. Immediately the murmuring rumble of the city streets met our ears and I was impressed with the thickness of the windows that could drown out such noise.

"Try again," Sokol said quietly.

I struck the gong.

Within minutes, there were footsteps on the stairs beyond the study door.

A hand turned the knob and in marched Boyle followed by the upstairs maid and Murphy.

Boyle's look of surprise found me holding his gong and it was clear he wanted to know why I'd taken it, but it was Murphy who asked the question.

"May I ask the meaning of this?"

"Where were you all just now, when you heard the gong?" I asked.

"In my pantry, Miss Green," Boyle said first, "polishing the silver."

"Is that where you were when the shot was heard?"

"Yes, miss."

"I was in Miss Kelthorpe's room, completing the packing," said Murphy. "And before you ask, as I said before, I was in her salon, mending when Mr. Jackson was shot."

"I believe you told me you were in her bedroom, Murphy?" I corrected with a tilt of my head in question.

The woman straightened at this. "Inner or outer room, it donnae matter." Her Irish lilt was more pronounced in those few words than they'd ever been. "I was in my mistress's chambers when the shot was fired."

I glanced at Sokol, who was studying the world outside the window, but he nodded.

"And you?" I asked the maid, whom I recalled was named something like Bridget Kelly.

"I was upstairs, begging your pardon, miss," she said softly—with another slight Irish accent—bobbing, her eyes studying her hands as they rubbed back and forth. "I was asked by the detective to box up Emily's things for him."

"So you were upstairs in the servants' quarters?"

"Yes, miss."

"And where were you the day of Mr. Jackson's death?"

"I was cleaning, miss."

"Yes, but where?"

"Um..." The upstairs maid seemed flustered, her eyes running across everyone in the room. "I was..."

"Weren't you cleaning in the kitchen, Bridget?" Murphy suggested, and I almost glared at her for leading the witness.

"Oh, yes, yes." The maid nodded emphatically, breathing heavily, relieved someone remembered what she'd been doing.

"How can you know where Bridget was working when you said you were mending upstairs?" I asked Murphy.

"That's what she's always doing after luncheon."

"But Kate the cook was upstairs."

Bridget nodded. "Mondays, Kate meets with the missus to discuss meal plans while I finishes the clean-up."

I studied Bridget. "Then how did you hear the gunshot?"

Bridget's eyes widened. "I..."

"Kate claimed she cannot hear anything when she's in the kitchen," I said.

"Surely with the back door open..." Again, Murphy seemed to have all the answers.

Bridget looked to Murphy and then nodded. "Yes, yes, that's right. The back door was open so I must've heard it that way."

She most certainly "must've," I thought.

I glanced to Sokol, who was surveying the group. "Is Mr. Farwell not at home today?" he asked the room at large.

Boyle cleared his throat. "I believe he is in his room, sir."

Sokol was already moving toward the door.

He left and could be heard knocking upon a door down the hall. There was no answer.

I excused myself from the others, who were still looking perplexed, and joined Sokol outside Mr. Farwell's door.

After a more resounding knock, finally, the door opened to reveal the somewhat disheveled appearance of Mr. Farwell, masked in a cloud that smelled distinctly reminiscent of the sherry in the decanter.

"What?" he asked irritatedly.

22

Mr. Farwell

"They thought me a good machine and nothing more."

—***The Leavenworth Case***

"Pardon me, Mr. Farwell, but were you not awakened by a sound just now?" Sokol asked the man's vest pocket.

Mr. Farwell's bloodshot eyes looked from Sokol to me and back. "No. It's not luncheon, is it? Have I slept the morning away? I merely meant to take a short nap."

"You were asleep, Mr. Farwell?" I asked.

He glanced at me and back to Sokol again. "May I ask what you two are doing in this house?"

"We are here on behalf of Miss Kelthorpe, to determine the murderer of her uncle," said Sokol.

Mr. Farwell brightened. "Has Miss Kelthorpe been released already?"

"Yes, she is currently safely ensconced in my home," I said, but still Mr. Farwell kept his bleary focus on Sokol rather than me.

As it was clear Mr. Farwell did not wish to speak with me, I decided this was an example where one of us was better than both when it came to questioning, so I excused myself, leaving Sokol to his own methods, as he no doubt preferred anyway.

I returned to the study and asked the servants if they would please return to their locations one more time, and come as soon as they heard the gong.

With a few shuffling nods and looks of disquiet, they finally left to do as I'd asked.

Once more, I closed both doors to the study, leaving only the window open before hitting the gong, but this time beside the desk, making sure to avoid looking directly at the chair.

No one returned. It was only when I hit the gong beside the window that the servants returned, as well as Sokol and Mr. Farwell.

"May I ask, Miss Green, why you are hitting the dinner gong out the window?" Mr. Farwell asked, his irritation clear.

"*Out* the window? An interesting way of putting it," I said, hoping to catch Sokol's eye, but he was engaged in holding a close and confidential confab with his fingertips, and did not appear to notice. I hoped his fingertips, at least, would recognize the importance of the secretary's choice of words. "Tell me, Mr. Farwell: Were you and Mr. Jackson in the habit of opening this window while you were working?"

He glanced at the window, and then at the open door on the sherry cabinet beside it before answering. "If it became too warm in the room, we might open it momentarily, but not for long, given Mr. Jackson's irritation with any noise interrupting his thoughts."

"He preferred to work in quiet?"

"Yes, Miss Green." He waved his hand about the room. "As you no doubt have noticed, if you've been standing here hitting that gong repeatedly, no sound comes in or goes out of this room."

"What about the dinner gong? Could you hear it when it was struck downstairs?"

"No. Boyle or one of the maids always came to inform us of its ringing."

"I see."

"And now, Miss Green," Mr. Farwell said, crossing to the window and closing it with a *bang*, "if you don't mind, I have work to do."

"Actually, we do mind, Mr. Farwell," interrupted Sokol, apparently done consulting his fingertips.

"Pardon me?"

"Pardon us, Mr. Farwell, but as I already informed you, we are here to determine the murderer of Mr. Jackson, and so we must ask you some questions."

I handed the gong and mallet back to Boyle and dismissed the servants, closing the door behind them so the three of us could continue our conversation in private.

"Please, have a seat, Mr. Farwell," Sokol said, with a wave toward one of the armchairs. "Miss Green," he said, motioning for me to sit in the remaining armchair.

I looked about for a seat for him, but other than the chair behind the desk with its odious qualities, there was nowhere for him to perch. He seemed quite at ease today upon his cane, however, and stood with all the imperiousness his battered stature could command.

The young secretary rubbed his eyes warily as he took his seat. As I had noted at the inquest, he lacked any distinctive quality of face or form agreeable or otherwise—his pale, regular features, dark, well-smoothed hair and simple whiskers, all belonging to a recognized type and very commonplace. Indeed, there was nothing remarkable about the man, any more than there is about a thousand others you meet every day on Broadway.

I tucked the description away for later use in my novel. It was his normalcy that made him forgettable, and this, I realized, was something of import. A man who was considered forgettable was most likely often overlooked, and a man who was often overlooked could be jealous or even enraged by this. Everyone in the world wanted to be noticed, some might say loved.

He seemed just the right type for a secretary, though he'd have made an ideal footman, for footmen were not meant to be noticed when they were in the room. As this thought crossed my mind, I considered in which class I'd place a personal secretary. They were rather unique, neither born of meaningful families nor of low enough stock to be considered servant-class. He was somewhere in the middle. Stuck in the middle. Stuck forever in the role of secretary to rich men who embodied the American dream, men who had acquired wealth, homes on Fifth Avenue, and beautiful heirs to whom they'd leave their fortunes.

"So tell me: What business did you have in this room today?" Sokol began, resting his hands together on the top of his cane so that he might better admire his long, crooked fingers.

Mr. Farwell glanced toward the sherry cabinet again, and I wondered if Sokol had noticed, though I had the distinct impression that even when his eyes were not upon his subject, he was noticing everything. Perhaps that was why he avoided eye contact in the first place? To lull his suspects into a false sense of security before surprising them with his knowledge? Maybe I still had something to learn from this man, after all.

Mr. Farwell cleared his throat. "I thought I might finish the work I was employed to complete."

"The manuscript?" Sokol's eyebrows rose.

"Yes. Mr. Jackson hired me to take his dictation for his book. I still have the dictation from that final night to complete."

"I take it you write first in short-hand?"

"Yes, and then return later to write out long-hand and edit. As I have the time now...endless time...," he murmured. "After writing out our last session, I can read through the entire manuscript for any last editing remarks and complete it."

"How can you finish a memoir when the author is dead?"

Mr. Farwell shrugged. "I cannot. I would complete it with a postscript written by my own hand. A farewell letter to an impressive man."

"I know very little about Mr. Jackson's past, only that this was to be a memoir of his time in India," said Sokol. "Did he have any enemies?"

"From India, you mean?"

"From anywhere, but India in particular. Perhaps he stole a large diamond protected by a Hindu god?" Sokol's eyes drifted to my hand as his mouth twitched. I almost laughed at his referencing *The Moonstone,* and recalled how I'd attempted the same joke with Mr. Jackson not so long ago.

"A Hindu—sir, what are you on about?" Clearly Mr. Farwell was not as familiar with this piece of literature.

I also didn't think it meant anything if Mr. Farwell didn't know of Mr. Jackson bringing any secreted items back with him. Why would his employer confide in him about such a thing? It would be better to search the house, but I knew if something had turned up of that ilk, Sokol would have found it.

"I merely meant, through the course of your writing of his memoir, did anything come to light through his dictation, or perhaps his correspondence, that might give us a clue as to who might have wanted him dead?"

Mr. Farwell shook his head. "No, nothing of that sort."

I couldn't help feeling that Mr. Farwell seemed determined to be unhelpful. But was he really the sort of man who might murder his employer? Not in a passion—for this man was plain as oatmeal, and couldn't have an ounce of passion within his breast. For money? Did he have debts? For his job?

Perhaps for love? Forbidden love? I recalled Murphy's statement that Mr. Farwell had shown inappropriate interest in Lenore. The rumor regarding Mr. Farwell and Emily might have been just that—a rumor. Murphy could have been wrong about Lenore's indifference; after all, there must be things Lenore kept from her. If Lenore had returned his love secretly, and Mr. Jackson didn't approve...

It was just as possible that the secretary was guilty for the same reasons the police had suspected Lenore. He also had a key to the study door, and, after all, how could you tell one person's key from another? He also knew where the gun was kept and admitted to knowing how to fire and clean it.

Since in the end, all the evidence was circumstantial, either of them or neither of them might be guilty.

"Where were you at one o'clock the day of the murder?" Sokol asked.

"I was running to the study with all the others, having heard the shot," Mr. Farwell said, his fingers tapping on the arm of the chair.

"You know I meant before the shot."

"If I'd known, I'd have answered. I was in my room."

"Why? Weren't you and Mr. Jackson working that day?"

"Yes. In fact," Mr. Farwell's fingers tapped quicker, as though the very thought of the work caused his fingers to fly across an imaginary paper taking short-hand, "that final day Mr. Jackson was quite excited about a particular adventure, and we worked through lunch."

"You did not stop for lunch? Was that normal?"

I appreciated Sokol's thoroughness in his questioning. The way he repeated responses and followed up on them for clarification, sometimes asking the same question in a different way, so as to catch the witness in an untruth. It was quite a sophisticated manner of approaching the witness, allowing them to correct themselves if need be, without pointing out that they'd done so, all the while taking note if they did. It was something I'd seen Father do in court, but never a detective. I decided I'd have my female detective do the same in my book.

"Yes," Mr. Farwell replied. "We often missed lunch when Mr. Jackson was in the midst of a memory which he thought to be engaging."

"But these adventures were not always so engaging to you?"

Mr. Farwell shrugged again and his fingers paused on the armchair. "Sometimes yes, I suppose."

"And the day of his murder?"

Mr. Farwell rubbed his chin thoughtfully. "I do not particularly recall. I should have to look at my notes. What followed has removed his sordid tale from my mind."

So he *did* have an opinion.

"On that day, did one of the maids still attempt to bring you lunch, even if you ended up not eating it?"

"Perhaps someone knocked, but I honestly don't remember precisely."

"Come, now, Mr. Farwell," Sokol said with a certain look in his eye toward the fireplace mantel. "It was not so long ago."

Mr. Farwell rubbed his pinky finger. "I suppose Bridget might have brought us something and we declined the offer, saying we were much too busy to stop just now."

"You suppose?"

"Yes."

Sokol passed on to a more important question. "Was Bridget the maid who usually brought the food?"

"Yes."

"Not Emily?"

"No."

"Did you know Emily well at all?"

I watched Mr. Farwell's face closely.

"No," he said perfunctorily.

I bit back a scoff. Sokol did an admirable job, however.

"Mr. Farwell, I'm afraid we have heard otherwise."

"From whom?" he asked with something similar to a snarl.

I was surprised by this reaction. I hadn't thought the man capable of any passion whatsoever.

"It does not matter. Were you secretly involved with Emily?" Sokol asked clearly and succinctly.

Mr. Farwell rubbed at his pinky again. "Perhaps."

"We are all adults here, Mr. Farwell. Were you and Emily lovers?"

The secretary glanced at me and then at the door, then back to Sokol.

"I do not see what that has to do with Mr. Jackson's death."

"It may be nothing, it may be something. For instance, if she was your lover, do you know where she is now?"

"No."

"Why do you think she blackmailed Miss Kelthorpe?"

Mr. Farwell hesitated. "I do not know."

Sokol paused just long enough for me to know he was considering the best way forward. Should he press Mr. Farwell and insist on hearing what he knew? Or should he let him go, and circle back to the question at another time?

"So you said you were in your room when the shot was fired. How came you to be there?"

Apparently, he'd decided on the latter.

"I left to collect my notes from the previous day, for Mr. Jackson could not recall a certain fact. I kept all such papers in my room, so that I might organize and edit when Mr. Jackson did not require my assistance in the study."

"Did you close the door behind you?"

"What?"

"Did you close the study door behind you when you left?"

Mr. Farwell glanced at the door to the hall. "Yes, I suppose I did. You know, I cannot recall exactly." Again those nervously drumming fingers.

"Did you lock it?"

"What?"

Sokol cleared his throat and pulled his cane toward himself. "I know you heard my question, Mr. Farwell. Did you lock it?" Sokol repeated slowly.

I watched the secretary's face as he avoided Sokol's penetrating stare, which was for once looking straight into the secretary's eyes.

"N-n-no," he stammered in reply.

"You did not lock it?" Sokol's eyes were on the secretary's fingers now, which were as still as his face in the light of Sokol's attentions.

"No. I do not think so," Mr. Farwell repeated.

And so we had our "locked room mystery," as Father had called it. Why had the murderer locked the door to the hall after watching Mr. Farwell leave? Or why did Mr. Farwell insist on lying about a fact that didn't seem to point to him as the murderer?

I now knew where each of the staff claimed to be at the time of the murder. I may not be a detective, but I know a good detective's methodology. It was time to make a list.

23

The Funeral

"I endeavored to put away all further consideration of the affair till I had acquired more facts upon which to base the theory."

—***The Leavenworth Case***

I left with Lenore's packed things and returned straight home by cab. Upon arrival, I asked the butler to deliver the trunk to Lenore's second floor bedroom and told him I'd be missing luncheon, then I went directly to my room and my desk.

My list had already begun forming in my mind over the course of the carriage ride.

Taking a piece of paper, I jotted down each suspect and their location at one o'clock the day we'd heard that fateful gunshot.

1. Lenore—meeting with Kate in the parlor
2. Mr. Farwell—grabbing notes from his room
3. Murphy—mending in Lenore's chambers
4. Boyle—polishing silver in the butler's pantry
5. Kate—meeting with Lenore in the parlor
6. Bridget—cleaning in the kitchen

I added a large question mark after this notation. It certainly hadn't seemed to me that the maid knew where she was. The fact remained, however, that when Lenore had been trying to open the door of Mr. Jackson's study after the shot, she'd said all of them were present: herself, Mr. Farwell, Murphy, Boyle, Kate, and Bridget. That meant they must have all been somewhere in the house where they could hear it.

Many people on that list didn't have an alibi. In fact, no one did, except for Lenore and Kate, who could vouch for each other in the parlor. Murphy had seemed to know where Bridget was, but I wondered why, if she'd known for a fact Bridget was in the kitchen because she herself had been there, she didn't simply say so, thereby providing an alibi for the both of them.

I then added a seventh suspect to my list.

7. Mr. Rohlfs—unknown

Part of me hated seeing Mr. Rohlfs's name on there, but I knew he must be included. I hadn't been able to fully believe him when he'd said he wasn't near the house that day. He had as much reason to kill Mr. Jackson as any of them.

The next thing to do was to make a list of the motives held by each person—

"Emily!" I cried aloud, realizing I'd forgotten another very important suspect we had yet to locate. I wondered if Sokol had any developments on that line of inquiry.

"Emily?" a soft voice came from my doorway.

I turned in my seat to find Lenore standing there, enwreathed in black like a somber knell, reminiscent of her namesake.

"Lenore. I'm glad to see you up. Are you feeling any better?"

The young woman's eyes were puffy and red, as though she'd spent the morning crying. I quickly pulled a clean sheet over my list, hiding it from Lenore's sight, but I needn't have worried. Lenore remained standing in the doorway, her eyes devoid of light and life, seemingly lost in a world of grief.

"Lenore? Dear." I crossed to her and took her hands. They were cold.

At my touch, Lenore shook awake and looked up at me.

"I had hoped… I was wondering if you would…would…" She took a steadying breath, but not a very deep one. "Would you do me the honor of accompanying me," she tried again, "to…to the funeral?"

I nearly gasped. The funeral was today!

I funneled my surprise into my hands, gripping Lenore's in support.

"Of course. Let me just get my hat."

Thankful I was already dressed in mourning black, I tried to let go of Lenore's hand for only a moment to turn for my toque, but Lenore continued to hold on.

"I'm sorry…I just…," Lenore stuttered, and I worried she was about to break down into wracking sobs right there in my bedroom.

Not one for violent displays of emotions, I continued to hold Lenore's hand as I crossed to my closet, grabbed a mourning toque with a veil, and then led Lenore out of my room and downstairs, never once letting go.

At the base of the stairs, I was grateful to see Father was already planning on attending in a mourning jacket, tie, and top hat. The three of us donned our overcoats and entered a cab to make our slow, clip-clopping way to the cemetery.

As we pulled in through the gates and traveled farther amongst the graves beneath a darkened sky, it began to rain, softly at first, then a bit harder. I was glad my father had come prepared, opening a large umbrella over Lenore as she alighted. To my surprise, another umbrella opened over me as I stepped out.

Of course, it was Sokol, who studied the handle as though it might tell him the reason for the rain.

I knew why it was raining: because God was sad.

He seemed to be the only one who was sad about Mr. Jackson's death, however, as we approached the graveside and found we were joined solely by the staff of the household. No one else in the whole of New York City had come to the funeral of Mr. Howard Jackson. Not even those people I'd been thinking about the other day, the ones who brought a picnic lunch to a hanging. Perhaps a funeral was not as intriguing.

The pastor led Lenore, still grasping my father's elbow as though she might faint if she let go, to the head of the grave.

I was grateful for the comforting, yet once again surprising, strength I found in Sokol's arm. I pressed as closely to him as I dared, attempting to keep my hoop-skirts under the umbrella as much as possible. Sokol seemed intent on keeping me more covered than himself, his gloved left hand getting quite wet while testing the quickly dampening grass about us with the tip of his cane.

The two of us stood at Lenore's side; the girl reached out and hooked her arm through mine, providing additional support.

I gave Lenore a comforting smile from beneath my veil, but I didn't think Lenore saw it. She was focused entirely upon the coffin.

It was metal, perhaps iron, but I couldn't be certain, not being fully knowledgeable in the casket business. It shone dimly in the gray light, the rain sliding casually off the rounded lid and down the sides, giving the casket itself the appearance that it was crying.

There was something right about rain at a funeral.

The servants lined themselves across from Lenore, and I could see that none of them were crying. They were stony-faced, silent, and somber, but not sad. They seemed merely to have come to support the young lady who was now in charge of their collective fate, no doubt grateful they'd always enjoyed a closer relationship with her than others in service.

It occurred to me that here was something outside the capabilities of every human in the world: no one could protect someone from death.

It was inescapable. No matter how careful a parent might be, eventually, their child would experience death. It was all around us. It was part of life. Without death, there would be no clinging to life, no enjoyment of it. We must have death to appreciate life. And therefore, it was neither something a parent could keep from their child, nor something they should. Instead, they must raise their child to understand that grief was a part of life. A necessary part. A final part.

Perhaps it was this finality that made murder the most interesting of crimes. It is the only irreparable one. Robbery, forgery, kidnapping—none of these is absolutely irretrievable. But a life that is taken can never be restored. There is complete finality about such a crime. And as the motive must be correspondingly overwhelming, it is, therefore, of the most vital interest.

The pastor began his speech and I lost myself in the familiar words.

How many funerals had I attended? I could not remember the one that mattered most: my mother's. She had died when I was but a girl of three, along with my younger brother. The cholera epidemic had taken them.

They had left behind a disheartened family of five. Mother Grace had blown in like a fresh breeze off the sea, just as salty and ready to breathe life back into the Green family. We'd been happy ever since.

But it had all started with a funeral.

I decided then and there I would not include the funeral in my book.

The pastor ended quickly, perhaps because of the rain, perhaps because of the lack of attendees, or perhaps because there wasn't much to say about a man who'd been as much of a recluse as was possible for a wealthy New Yorker. Mr. Jackson's will hadn't even requested a reception to follow his burial, perhaps acknowledging the fact that no one was likely to attend—perhaps he'd wanted it that way.

Lenore removed her arm from mine and used a handkerchief to dab her eyes as she turned to receive the staff. Each person took the time to hold her hand and say something comforting, even in the rain.

When it came to the secretary's turn, however, I couldn't help but notice his hold lasted several minutes, rather than several seconds, and Lenore did not appear displeased by this, though naturally it was difficult to tell with her face tear-stained and red.

It occurred to me that there should have been another young man in attendance to hold her hand and offer support for as long as she required. Perhaps he had a performance.

A light hand at my elbow drew my attention away from the chief mourner and to my umbrella protector.

"A little bird told me you intend to try your hand at writing a detective novel," Sokol whispered quietly, studying the black puffed sleeves of my overcoat.

I raised an eyebrow, one hand still on his arm. "Oh?"

"Your father," Sokol explained, unnecessarily.

Obviously Mother Grace had mentioned our discussion to him, but why he'd felt the need to share the news with Sokol was beyond me.

"Is it true?" Sokol asked my sleeve.

"Yes," I said simply.

"Please," Sokol said, handing me the umbrella handle to hold while he reached inside his coat and pulled out a beautiful black notebook, "ACG" engraved in gold in the bottom corner. "Your father told me your middle name is Catherine," he said, again as though I'd asked the question.

"Yes. For my mother, though she spelled it Katharine with a *K*." Not for the first time it occurred to me that I would prefer my middle name spelled like my mother's, in honor of the woman whom I barely remembered.

"Consider this my token toward that great endeavor. I have no doubt that a poetess like yourself can bring a literary air to the dime novel detective story."

I almost argued with him that Wilkie Collins and Émile Gaboriau had already done precisely that, though British and French, respectively. But this was not the place for a discussion of mystery fiction.

"Thank you," was all I said instead.

Sokol took the umbrella handle back and I clutched the notebook firmly against my chest to keep it from getting drenched.

I didn't want to admit how much the gift meant to me just yet, but I knew it would be something to be greatly treasured.

24

Lovers

"But, as is very apt to be the case in an affair like this, love and admiration soon got the better of worldly wisdom."

—***The Leavenworth Case***

"Miss Kelthorpe," our butler said as we removed our soaked coats in the foyer upon our return, "a Mr. Rohlfs is awaiting you in the front parlor."

"Mr. Rohlfs!" Lenore cried, her face going from grief to joy in an instant.

Mr. Rohlfs? I repeated in my mind. *The actor, here, in my own home?*

Lenore maintained decorum long enough to enter the room, but upon seeing her fiancé, she crossed the room in two strides and they embraced.

I turned away and busied myself with removing my hat.

Father cleared his throat as he entered the front parlor, and the two lovers pulled apart in embarrassment.

Lenore's face was full of color, but for the first time in days it was the blush of happiness, and not the red of anguish or grief.

"Welcome, Mr. Rohlfs," Father said, shaking his hand and introducing himself. "I see you've met my wife and eldest daughter." He waved to where Mother Grace and Sarah were seated, playing hostess while Mr. Rohlfs no doubt distractedly awaited the arrival of his betrothed.

"We had the pleasure of making Mr. Rohlfs's acquaintance the other evening upon the stage," Mother Grace told Father.

"Oh?" he said.

"He was the one we were discussing upon our return. The one with the delightfully expressive face," Mother Grace said with a smile of admiration toward Mr. Rohlfs.

His cheeks reddened slightly at the praise. "You are too kind, Mrs. Green," he said.

Humble and *handsome,* I thought.

"Ah, then you already know my younger daughter, as well," said Father, "though I believe you also had the pleasure of speaking with her the other night."

Sarah turned and raised her brows at me, but Mother Grace leaned in and whispered, "Don't worry. She was accompanied."

Mr. Rohlfs nodded and gave a slight bow to me. "Wonderful to see you again, *Miss* Green." He emphasized the "miss" as I had done, and winked.

I blushed like a silly schoolgirl. How old would I have to be before I could get this silly rush of heat to my cheeks and neck under control? It was most exasperating.

"Thank you for saving my love," Mr. Rohlfs said passionately, holding Lenore's hand in his and even raising it to his lips to kiss. "She matters more to me than words can say."

I clutched the notebook from Sokol harder to my chest. I wasn't certain what to make of the gift, and was determined not to think too highly of it. But it was difficult not to read into it when a Regency romance was playing itself out in my front parlor. He had given it to me like it meant something, and I was honored, touched even. Sokol's thoughtful gift had me reconsidering everything he'd ever said to me. Was there more to this man than met the eye? Was there more to his feelings toward me than simple admiration? Was there more to *my* feelings?

The first parts of my novel called to me from my room upstairs, but I knew it would be impolite to excuse myself. Instead, I set down the notebook on a side table and made myself comfortable in a chair before the fire where I could dry my damp skirts. My stepmother and sister had seated themselves across from the settee which the lovers had claimed for themselves, unable to part their hands from one another even in the presence of others.

Clearly I had been wrong about the secretary. If he had hopes of winning Lenore's heart, he would have to do something extreme to distract her from Mr. Rohlfs.

Perhaps killing her uncle had been that attempt at distraction.

"I'm afraid Miss Kelthorpe is not saved yet," said Father. "To do that, we must catch the true murderer."

"Thank you for working so diligently to catch the man, then," said Mr. Rohlfs, "and for enabling my Lenore to eat at a dinner table rather than inside a cell. I could not stand the thought of her languishing in there and would have sprung her myself if you had not done the job for me."

"It was nothing," Father said, waving a hand. "But you both should know, this is only the beginning."

"Even with the testimony of the cook stating that I was with her when the shot was heard?" Lenore asked with a furrowed brow.

"I'm afraid Detective Billings believed that was only enough to let you go for now. He has entrusted you to my care under the assumption that I will return you for your court hearing in a week or two."

"A week or two?" Mr. Rohlfs asked. "I thought we might leave the state as soon as possible, go out west and start a fresh life together." His hand squeezed Lenore's.

"I'm afraid that's just not possible until this business is through. There will be at least a week before the preliminary hearing, and then a couple more weeks till the indictment, followed by months before the trial itself. At each stage along the way it is possible we might prove Miss Kelthorpe's innocence, but finding the real murderer would go a long way to enabling a smoother road."

"If we caught the murderer, would she be free? *Exeunt* stage left?" Mr. Rohlfs asked.

"Yes," said Father with a smile. "You could get married at the church on your way home."

Mr. Rohlfs beamed at Lenore.

"Anything I can do to help, please let me know. I intend to marry this woman." He clutched Lenore's hand in his.

"You must hear how the two met, James," Mother Grace put in. "It's really quite romantic." She smiled at Lenore.

Lenore giggled like the tinkling of bells. "It was such a splendid happenstance. My uncle was asked to speak at a hotel and he took me with him. I do not know why I was invited this particular time, but I'm so glad I was because it was there that I met Charles one night after his show." She blessed the man with a doe-eyed look of admiration.

"Yes," said Mr. Rohlfs. "After that, we met secretly whenever we could, as Lenore was eager to keep our growing attachment from her uncle. Unfortunately, he did come across us one evening out in the hotel garden, and I'm afraid we exchanged words."

"Oh?" Father asked, his fingers coming together to peak before his mouth.

Mr. Rohlfs's face reddened slightly. "Yes. Only words, mind, but Mr. Jackson made it quite clear that he had no intention of allowing his niece to marry an actor."

"Afterward, my uncle took me to our private rooms and told me perfunctorily that if I continued the relationship I would no longer be his heir," Lenore said, but then straightened her shoulders. "He blustered on and on about how this was why he'd not wanted to bring me in the first place. That I knew nothing of the world and its deceits. Naturally, I told him I would end the relationship, though I had no intention of doing so. It was then that I asked Murphy to be our go-between, and we worked out a way to mark our letters to and from one another through her."

"What mark was that?"

"A box around the stamp," said Mr. Rohlfs.

"Simple, yet clever," said Father.

"How long ago did you begin this secret affair?" Mother Grace asked.

"It's been three months," said Lenore. "Three glorious months of the most beautiful love letters." She smiled and squeezed Mr. Rohlfs's hand.

"Do you have any of these letters still in your possession?" Father asked.

Yes, I answered in my head.

Lenore blushed and looked away from Mr. Rohlfs. "Yes," she mumbled.

Mr. Rohlfs looked surprised. "I thought we agreed you would burn them after reading?"

"I just couldn't bring myself to do it. Your words were so beautiful!"

Mr. Rohlfs shook his head, but his smile said he was pleased Lenore had been unable to part with his words of affection.

"Did Murphy send them to you with your things?" Father asked.

"Yes," Lenore said, clearly surprised Father had thought of it.

I was surprised, too. Murphy must have sneaked them under some clothing after I'd left the room.

"May I see them?"

Lenore hesitated.

"As your lawyer, I must be the holder of all evidence for and against you. It is of the utmost importance if we are to gain your freedom."

Lenore nodded and stood. "I'll be but a moment, my love," she said, and kissed his hand before letting go.

Mother Grace and Sarah excused themselves then, so I did the same, intending to return, but leaving the two men for a moment, should they desire a private word between them.

I followed Lenore upstairs to deliver my notebook to my room, stopping long enough at my desk to jot down "Idea: secret marriage" on the first page. Then I returned with Lenore, now burdened by a stack of letters.

Father took the letters, promising to keep them private, and Lenore rejoined Mr. Rohlfs on the settee.

"Now," Father said, leaning forward toward them, his hands clasped together upon his knees, "is there anything else you two would like to tell me?"

The lovers exchanged a look.

"Like what, Mr. Green?" Mr. Rohlfs said. "Is there something you think we're keeping from you?"

Father shook his head. "No, but I am giving you the option to be upfront with me before I uncover something highly detrimental."

"Isn't the fact that we both clearly have a motive for killing Mr. Jackson enough?" asked Mr. Rohlfs.

I admired him for getting straight to the heart of the issue.

"There's also means and opportunity on the table," said Father. "Are you certain, Miss Kelthorpe, that you did not leave the house at any time on the day of the murder?"

"Yes, Mr. Green," said Lenore, her eyes wide.

"And are you certain, Mr. Rohlfs, that you were not at the house the day of the murder?"

Mr. Rohlfs was not so quick in his response, and Lenore turned to him.

"You weren't, were you, Charles?" she asked, worry creeping into her voice like a cold at the back of her throat.

"I...well...yes..." The word fell from his lips. "Yes, I'm afraid I did come to the house. But only for a moment! I was turned away at the door!" He spoke hurriedly as the fear and hurt masked Lenore's face just as quickly. "It didn't feel right running away together without him knowing we'd much rather have done it with his permission."

Lenore drew her hands away. She stood and turned in a rustle of petticoats, her arms trembling and entire posture bespeaking that manner of utmost displeasure.

"I'm so sorry, Lenore. I was just so finished with the lies. I know he thought we were too young, and didn't approve of my profession, but I thought... I thought I might be able to convince him. And I might have...with time...if he'd not... I'm so sorry, my love," Mr. Rohlfs said, coming to where she stood at the bay window, the gray light of the rain outside cloaking her features. "Please, say something. Please, forgive me."

"Charles," she said softly, turning to him slowly. "You needn't protect me from the truth. I can handle it. Please answer me in complete honesty: Did you kill my uncle?"

"No! No, I swear it!" He got on his knees and held her hands before him. "I swear it: I never touched him, never saw him that day. It was just poor timing. How could I have known that day would be the day—"

"You swear?" Lenore said.

"Yes. Yes, I swear."

Lenore looked to Father. "There. You have the honest answer of a worthy man, Mr. Green. Is that enough to prove his innocence?"

Father raised a brow. "It is enough for now."

"That is all?" Mr. Rohlfs asked, but his question was to Lenore, as he regained his feet and stood looking down into her eyes once more, rather than up.

"That is all you need say for me to believe your innocence," said Lenore, reaching up to rest her palm against his cheek. "You are all I need, my prince."

25

Lists and Outlines

"All is closely related, no word is written that has not its specific use in the makeup of my work. I proceed as one might to solve some abstruse problem, by clearly defined lines and deliberately planned steps."

—Anna Katharine Green, quoted in "An American Gaboriau," by Mary R. P. Hatch

"Father, why did you tell Sokol about my writing?" I asked later, closing the door to Father's study behind me.

Mr. Rohlfs had left and Lenore had retired to her room until dinner was called.

Father raised an eyebrow. "Do you mind?"

I thought about it a minute. "No, I suppose not, though I do not intend to share anything until it is complete."

Father nodded. "Did Sokol say something?"

I shook my head. "He gave me a notebook."

"That was thoughtful."

"Yes...," I said slowly, still uncertain as to my father's exact motives concerning his friend.

"I expect you will have many notes when we are through with this case," Father said.

I agreed. "Do you believe Mr. Rohlfs, Father?"

Father stared at the fire, which this time was already made, no doubt due to the chilling rain outside.

"I believe him as much as I believe Miss Kelthorpe," he said, ever the lawyer.

I crossed my arms. "Come now, Father. You can be honest with me."

Father leaned back in his chair and looked at the ceiling, much as Sokol would do.

"It seems to me to be a man's murder, not that I'm saying a woman wouldn't shoot someone, but it seems to me much more likely that a man pulled the trigger, and then attempted to clean the gun. In my experience, women do not think to clean the gun."

"In *your* experience?" I asked with a cock of my head.

"I'm simply saying it seems less likely."

I took note of this. "That leaves Mr. Rohlfs, Mr. Farwell, and the butler, Boyle," I counted off on my fingers. "Those are the only men in the house the day of the murder."

"That we know of."

I conceded the point.

"It is also possible that two people were working together. Mr. Rohlfs and Miss Kelthorpe, for one, or Mr. Farwell or Boyle with the missing maid, or anyone else."

"Then we haven't eliminated anyone?"

"No one is completely devoid of suspicion until we have the murderer in hand," said Father, and again I made note of this.

Already I was thinking of things I needed to write down in my new notebook—observations people had made, descriptions of characters, conversations worth recording—before they were forgotten.

"You look like you need to get back to your writing," my father said, knowing me too well.

I thanked him with a kiss on the forehead and returned to my room.

Once there, however, I didn't immediately get to writing. First, I wanted to complete my list of suspicion for everyone in the house on the day Mr. Jackson was shot. This time, I did it all in my notebook, feeling everything involved in this case made for excellent story fodder.

I began by re-listing what I'd done separately, so I'd have an organized account of who had the opportunity to murder Mr. Jackson. When I came to Mr. Rohlfs, I reluctantly changed my note from "unknown" to "stopped by to speak with Mr. Jackson; swears he did not see him." Emily still remained as "unknown." For all I knew, when we found her, we'd find our murderer.

Next, it was time to add motives to my list of suspicious characters.

1. Lenore—inherits everything, engaged to someone her uncle did not approve
2. Mr. Farwell—perhaps Mr. Jackson was going to fire him for having a relationship with Emily, or for secretly being in love with Lenore?
3. Murphy—she'd do anything to protect Lenore
4. Boyle—unknown
5. Kate—unknown
6. Bridget—unknown
7. Mr. Rohlfs—engagement to Lenore was against Mr. Jackson's wishes
8. Emily—she was attempting to blackmail Lenore

I sat back with a heavy sigh. It didn't seem like much now that I'd written it all out. Maybe this hadn't been so helpful after all.

I picked up my pen and turned to my novel, only to find I'd lost all the words that had been spinning about my head all day, and in their place was a weariness that reminded me I hadn't slept the evening before. This was not going to be like writing poetry, I realized. I couldn't just wait for the inspiration to come to me, for my muse to respond and breathe the words into my ear the way she'd done before. This was going to be more like writing a dissertation for a college course, or collecting notes for one of Father's cases. I'd need to be methodical.

I might also definitely have to work backwards.

My dream of the night before came to me suddenly in a flash of remembrance. I'd seen the killer's face, and yet I could not put my finger on who it had been. It was like my mind was trying to fill in the space for me, a cyclone of features tumbling one after the other in my mind's eye, making me light-headed.

And tired. So very tired.

After attempting several continuations of my work, I finally gave up and removed my chatelaine, outer skirts, bustle, stepped out of my hoop-skirts, and loosened my corset before lying down on my bed, telling myself repeatedly to awaken in one hour so that I might begin writing as soon as my brain felt capable. Perhaps I would dream again, and this time, the murderer's face would become clear…

When next my eyes opened, however, the first thing I noticed was that the room was full of the soft pink light of early morning. I'd slept through to the next day.

So much for telling my mind to awaken me after only an hour.

Frustrated, I threw myself off my bed, pouring water from a pitcher into the glass I kept by my bedside. A note lay there from Mother Grace saying she'd come to check on me when I didn't come down for dinner, but she'd not wanted to disturb me. I tightened my corset and dressed, choosing a third black gown, the last I had available for this season. I could always wear something from last season, but only if I wasn't to be seen in public, and since I wasn't certain what the day might hold, I thought it better to prepare for visitors.

While dressing, my mind woke to the point that by the time I seated myself once more at my desk, I was ready to pick up where I'd left off in my notebook. I'd just do a little work before breakfast…

I thought I might begin by making a list of things I'd noticed in *The Moonstone,* things I liked. Then I could do the same for other mysteries I'd enjoyed. I decided that if I liked those twists and ingredients, perhaps I might use them to my own effect in my own mystery story.

After writing "Parts I Liked" at the top of a clean page near the back, in order to keep it separate from my notes on the Jackson case, I paused and considered. My favorite part had been most definitely the use of disguise, which had also been used in *File No. 113,* by Gaboriau—in fact had been crucial. So I wrote "Disguise—victim, murderer, detective."

A smile came to my lips as I recalled Sokol's beggar woman disguise. Whether it had been of much use to him or not, I couldn't tell, and I made a mental note again to ask him about his search for Emily. He'd appeared to be quite sure of himself and his abilities in finding her, and I knew he'd let me know first thing when his search uncovered her, wherever she was hiding.

I hoped Sokol would not only find her, but be able to uncover the truth in regards to the blackmail. If she really had attempted to blackmail Lenore, what information had she been about to reveal? Had she somehow come across a letter from Mr. Rohlfs to Lenore? Perhaps while cleaning Lenore's chambers, she might have stumbled across the collection I myself had discovered quite easily. If Emily had read any of those—

But there I stopped. It was almost assured the girl could not read. Even if she had been able to piece together the letters, had it been enough to help her realize she could blackmail Lenore with the information, for fear of her uncle writing her out of his will?

I dipped my pen and added a second notation to my list: "Changed will." It was such a powerful motive, one worthy of my plot.

But to have a changed will, I would need to alter who benefited from the will.

I considered my characters. So far, I had created six central characters, each built upon descriptions I'd written in my variety of notebooks over the years. Of course, I'd thought originally that they were waiting for a poem, but now I knew I'd been saving them for the opportune moment to release them into a story.

First, there was the narrator, the young lawyer whom I'd discovered waiting in my father's study a couple days ago, who'd given me the first words of the book.

Perhaps second I might include the dead man, Mr. Leavenworth, a tea magnate writing his memoirs of his days in India, found shot through the head in his study.

Third, there was the personal secretary, Mr. Harwell, a man easily forgotten for his humdrum personality.

Then there were the nieces: Mary and Eleanore. Between the two of them, I'd funneled parts of myself, Lenore, and my friend, Mary Hatch.

And sixth, the missing maid, a poor Irish girl who'd disappeared the night of the murder leaving behind nought but a candlestick.

I intended to fill the home of Mr. Leavenworth further still with the necessary staff, but I had not yet compiled my notes from my interviews with the real ones.

The real ones.

I set down my pen. What was I doing?

Why was I wasting time writing fiction when my father needed my help on a real case?

Even so, the story called to me, beckoned to me, would not let me go. I felt entwined with its narrative as much as I did with the mystery in which I was currently living.

I looked at my list again and the last bullet: "Changed will." In the book, I would say that Mr. Leavenworth intended to leave the entirety of his estate to one of the girls, thereby giving a motive to either one: Mary, for the threat of losing her inheritance, and Eleanore, to lay the blame at Mary's feet, forcing the estate to go to Eleanore instead. Or perhaps vice versa, though in my head Mary was the one with golden hair and beauty so stunning every man dropped at her feet, while Eleanore was the intelligent brunette. A classic dichotomy, I knew, but then, why mess with something that worked?

What I was most excited about, however, was the chance to bring something never seen before in fiction: a female detective. In what I'd written thus far, Mary was forced into solving the case in order to prove her own innocence, as well as that of her cousin Eleanore. Indeed, so far all the evidence seemed to point to either Eleanore or Mary as the murderer.

But then I recalled what my father had said about women never cleaning guns. I wrote the note down at the beginning of the notebook. Perhaps this would be the fact that would tip the case away from the ladies and point more directly toward one of the men in the house?

Again I stopped.

What a muddled mess. How would I ever make head or tails of it all, getting every clue to lie flat in its place, rather than bumping out at odd angles, confusing the matter, and thereby the reader?

I flipped back to my list from books with a sigh. Methodical. I must be methodical.

Another aspect of the mysteries I'd read leapt to mind: "Red herrings." It was a term I'd recently come across, and one that seemed most apt for describing those clues that led the detective in the wrong direction, like a dog following a false scent.

Perhaps I could use some of the evidence I'd sprinkled into the book so far to mislead the reader, and the detective. It was certainly misleading me in real life. My lists of the night before only told me it was indeed an "inside job," something else I could add to my list of mystery ingredients. It was clear the murderer was someone who knew where Mr. Jackson kept his gun. The whole house knew, so every one of them was suspect.

Thinking of Lenore drew my mind back to the young pair of lovers who'd made themselves at home in my front parlor. I was surprised the light of their love had not scattered the rain clouds outside, its power seemed so great.

"Secret lovers" was a common theme in mysteries, in fact I'd heard stories like *The Moonstone* and *The Mysterious Key* called "criminal romances" as a way of describing that type of story. Love could drive a person to do a lot of things, even something that had never once occurred to them. But when something or someone stood in the way of true love, people tended to get hurt.

The same was true of money. If the lovers had known Mr. Jackson would write Lenore out of his will if he caught them, mightn't they have felt that was two strikes against him, and therefore, he needed to die to remove the obstacle?

If that was the case here, though, then it did not bode well for the missing maid, Emily. If only we could find her before it was too late, before the detective had his grand reveal at the denouement, when he would announce the twist that everyone had missed.

"The twist," I wrote in my notebook. This was the part of the book I was most worried about. What would be the twist?

I worried that I, myself, would not find out until the very end.

26

Reading Aloud

"The chain was complete; the links were fastened; but one link was of a different size and material from the rest; and in this argued a break in the chain."

—*The Leavenworth Case*

My stomach growled, reminding me I hadn't eaten in far too long. I joined the others at the breakfast table, but though my body was busy mechanically bringing a scone with jam and cream to my mouth, my mind was elsewhere. I did come out of my reverie long enough to hear my stepmother remark that she was pleased to see Lenore looking positively cheerful in comparison to days past.

Lenore blushed happily. "Mr. Rohlfs has offered to take me for a stroll through Washington Square today."

"Oh?" I asked, with a glance toward Father.

I was surprised to hear Lenore was allowed to leave our house for pleasure when she still had an impending court date to attend. I didn't think the Bulldog would approve.

"I shall accompany them as chaperone and guardian," said Father from the head of the table. "You needn't worry."

I should have known I needn't question my father. He always had everything straight in his mind. It was that very aspect which I wished to play with in my book when it came to my lawyer character. I intended to write Everett Raymond as someone who thought he had everything figured out, only to be repeatedly shown he did not. It also made him an excellent foil for my intrepid young female detective.

I wondered briefly if I should offer to go as chaperone, but then I imagined following behind the two lovers, affectionately linking arms and gazing with adoration into each other's eyes...

I excused myself soon after and returned to my desk, the words flowing more easily again now that I had lists and notes to inspire me.

As I completed my one hundredth page, I sat back and considered the notebook next to the pile. With a nod of decision, I stood, gathering the notebook and pages into a satchel I'd been gifted by my father for college, and walked straight out the door and down to Sokol's before I could change my mind.

I almost didn't make it. At his front door, a wave of indecision nearly crushed me, but when the door opened and I was beckoned into the front parlor, and I saw Sokol laid out once again on the couch, bandages wrapping his hands *and* feet this time, I wondered why I was so fearful of the opinion of a man forced to spend his days on a couch in utter pain.

"Miss Green?" he said in surprise. "I'm afraid once again I will be unable to rise to greet you." He waved his bandaged limbs instead.

"Your feet, too?" I asked, taking my usual seat and setting my satchel with its precious cargo against the chair legs.

"Rheumatism does not pick a favorite spot to enjoy, I'm afraid," he said with a wry twist of his mouth toward his feet. A wracking cough stopped him from saying more for a moment, and I nearly called for a servant before he stopped and wheezed, pointing to a pitcher and glass beside him. "Would you...be...so kind?"

I leapt to my feet and filled the glass, only to realize he could not hold it himself with his hands bandaged. I lifted the glass to his lips myself, trembling slightly at the intimate nature of the gesture. I was close enough to see the dark stubble of growth upon his cheek, to count the lines encircling his eyes, to see the gray hairs hiding within his hairline.

My heart thumped loud enough for him to hear. I nervously lowered my gaze.

"I was not aware rheumatism could affect the lungs as well," I said after he waved the glass away with a thankful look at it, rather than me.

"This is just a cold," he told the glass. "My reward for attending a funeral in the rain."

I replaced the glass on the table and returned to my chair.

"Speaking of funerals, I was surprised it had not been postponed so the coroner could order a postmortem," I said. I hadn't felt it was necessary to ask Sokol this in the middle of the rain and his lovely gift, but the question had been bothering me ever since.

"To check for the possibility of poisoning," Sokol said, nodding at my satchel.

"Yes."

"I'm afraid Mr. Hammond did not care for the idea when I presented it to him. He said there was insufficient evidence to support the necessity of an autopsy. He declared it imprudent to worry about poisoning when it seemed clear to him that the man died from a shot to the head."

"Yes, but..."

"I agree with you completely, Miss Green," said Sokol. "Trust me. Unfortunately, there are some battles we cannot win."

My shoulders slumped. Just as I'd feared. I prayed we weren't missing crucial evidence. If Mr. Jackson had been poisoned, it might have dulled his senses, which would change the supposition that he had not reacted to the sound of someone approaching from behind him.

"So, what have you for me today?" Sokol asked, waving to my bag. "I believe I've been a part of all the most recent interviews."

I shook my head. "When we returned home we found Mr. Rohlfs waiting for Miss Kelthorpe." I related to him what had transpired as he considered his bandages. When I finished, I took a deep breath, straightening my skirts before admitting, "But that's not what I brought you." I reached down and drew my bag into my lap.

I withdrew the notebook first and Sokol smiled at it.

"I've filled several pages with my notes on the case, and with ideas for my novel. Would you care to glance over my list of opportunities and motives?"

"Acting like a detective already," Sokol said, admiring the rug as he had before. "Please, read it out to me."

I did so, and he nodded along with each note, reminding me that really all of the staff had the same motive as Murphy.

"They all seem fond of Miss Kelthorpe, and willing to provide a level of protection that we must consider when it comes to the murder of Mr. Jackson, a man who did not show them the same willing affection."

I agreed and noted so in my list.

"Now, regarding your novel: do you think this list will be of assistance in the writing of it?" Sokol asked.

"I believe it already has," I said, pulling out the one hundred pages in response.

"You've written all that in just a few days?"

I nodded and blushed.

"What is the book about?"

"Miss Kelthorpe. This case."

"No, no, tell it to me in one sentence, like you would a publisher."

I clutched the pages. How could I sum up in one sentence something that was taking more words from me than all my poems put together?

"It's about circumstantial evidence, and how it can be misused to the benefit of one person, while to the detriment of another."

"Well put."

"Miss Kelthorpe is in essence the main character. A young lawyer comes to her aid when her uncle is shot, and he is immediately overcome with love for her, and thereby a need to defend her, though the evidence piles up against her in endless waves."

Sokol scoffed, which turned into a cough, though this one did not last long.

Perhaps I shouldn't have brought my book to Sokol so soon. My first instinct had been to wait until it was finished. This was my first attempt at a novel. Maybe I should've let my stepmother read it first...but no, she wouldn't tell me honestly if it was any good, she'd just encourage me no matter what. I couldn't read it to Father until I was certain it was something worth sharing, as I knew his editing instincts would kick in on the first line, and all I'd hear from then on would be, "Semi-colon, dear, you want a semi-colon here." He meant the best, but he couldn't help sharing the critical eye with which he'd been blessed.

I began replacing my pages in my bag. "I came too soon. I should finish the book before sharing it."

"Perhaps, but I'd like to hear it nonetheless. Unless it is just a romance. I thought you were going to try your hand at writing mystery." He looked at the notebook like it had lied to him.

I wondered if he regretted gifting it to me now. "I believe the two are inextricably intertwined. In every great mystery there is a romance, sometimes doomed, sometimes not."

"This one sounds doomed from the beginning, if it is based on our real case."

"What makes you say that?"

"The general public will not be interested in a mystery novel about a person who is believed innocent. They much prefer the guilty."

"The mystery will end upon discovery of the guilty person."

"If you've picked a murderer for your book, is it the same person you've chosen for the Jackson case?"

I flushed and glanced at my notebook. I could not admit to him that for neither case had I "picked a murderer," as he'd put it.

"Circumstantial evidence is evidence that is not definite," he went on. "It requires an inference, and by its very nature, can usually be used against more than one person. Whom are the two you've chosen to circle in your book?"

"I will simply say that through the story I will show how circumstantial evidence can be used in a person's defense or prosecution depending on how one looks at it."

Sokol shook his head at his hands. "You've been spending too much time with your father."

"Nonsense. I could never spend too much time with such a brilliant man."

Sokol gave me an acquiescing nod. "So Miss Kelthorpe is one of the innocent victims of circumstantial evidence?"

"In the guise of the character Eleanore. Mary, her cousin, is also painted guilty, as well as the missing maid, the private secretary, and a mysterious visitor."

Sokol scoffed again. "Have you created nothing out of your imagination? Have you taken all from life?"

I glared at him at the suggestion. "You will just have to read the book and see."

"Very well, read it to me." He settled himself comfortably in his place on the couch. "If it's bad, you needn't read it at all."

I could tell he meant the remark to be an attempt at humor, but it filled me with a terror that could be more easily understood than described.

I began, and I must say I was pleased, despite my fears, with the beginning of the book, this being my first time hearing it read aloud. It was quick off the mark, jumping directly into the inquest, much as I had done. I'd gone back and inserted interviews with the servants, changing their names for anonymity as I'd done with the other characters, though I'd kept them all Irish for believability.

As I read the ballistics report, I glanced up more than once to see Sokol's reaction, but he only continued to study his bandaged hands, even though the information and words were almost exactly what he had shared with us that first night at dinner.

After reading two or three chapters I looked up to notice with alarm that Sokol's eyes were closed, and, thinking that possibly he might have fallen asleep through sheer lack of interest, I stopped. There was a pause of perhaps half a minute—then, without opening his eyes he said the one word, "More!"

So I read on.

27

Detective Gryce

"[Anna Katharine Green's] circumstances, moreover, though stranger than fiction, are not stranger than truth."

—**T. Fisher Unwin,** ***Good Reading About Many Books Mostly by Their Authors***

I set down the final sheet, and waited for Sokol to notice.

He opened his eyes and glanced in my direction, noticing my lack of page in hand, before asking, "That is all?"

"That is all for now. Naturally, there is much more to be written, but I would have your remarks on what is completed."

"You've only just reached the end of the inquest."

"Yes."

"So much detail in so many pages, placed right there in front of the reader."

"Yes, much as it happens in real life."

"Even the surgeon's report in all its gory and graphic detail. Do you not think it might be a bit much for most lady readers?"

I shrugged. "It's no worse than what's put in the scandal sheets and papers."

"Perhaps." He studied his feet. "And the names: You cannot name everyone in your book using names so close to real people. Lenore is Eleanore? Mr. Farwell is Mr. Harwell? It's not...hidden enough. You must hide the truth while bringing the truth forward."

"'Hide the truth while bringing the truth forward'—what on earth are you talking about, Sokol?" My irritation at his critiques was rising.

"I mean: what is your point in writing this story?"

"It's not so much a story as a real account of a real mystery occurring right now in this moment."

"At least you hear it, too. It needs to be a story. No one wants to read about a real mystery they can read about in the paper."

"But in real life we do not know who is the murderer."

"You may have to simply pick one. Go with your instincts. Who do you think is most likely the murderer—in your story? Remember, even if you're wrong, in the end, it doesn't matter because it's a *story*."

I bit my lip, the heat in my cheeks and neck nearly choking me. I'd asked for his opinion but...I was finding it much more difficult to hear his critique than I'd thought. I clearly cared far too much about what Sokol thought of my writing. This was worse than having my father tear into my poetry. This story was precious to me, and delicate. I felt like he was attacking my child.

"And you will need a male detective."

My breath caught in my chest like I'd been punched. I frowned.

"You know it's true," Sokol said, waving his bandaged hands toward me, seemingly unaware of the hatred rising in my breast at his remarks. "You are unable to defend Miss Kelthorpe in court in real life because you're a woman. Why would it be different in fiction?"

"I'm not suggesting Mary will defend Eleanore in court."

"But you're clearly setting her up to be your detective alongside your narrator. A beautiful woman and a lawyer—sound familiar?"

My fury stopped for a moment at his indirect compliment, but it was not enough to stop the rage that was about to boil out my ears.

"Was there *anything* about what I read that you liked?"

"Yes," he said. "The fact that you're using your own name as the author."

I felt like he'd slapped me in the face. *That* was all he liked.

"*That* was all you liked? You appreciate my lack of a *nom de plume*?!"

"Yes. I've never read a mystery written by a woman, and given that the beginning of the novel includes such details at the inquest, including ballistics and a surgeon's report, I do not think most people will believe it was written by a woman. Even if you use your real name."

"It's not like that anymore. Everyone knows the Brontë sisters and Jane Austen wrote their books, even though they published under pseudonyms originally."

"They weren't writing a detective novel."

I stood abruptly, clutching my pages. "This was a mistake. I have to go," I said, and excused myself before he could stop me.

* * *

I slammed the front door behind me and rushed up the stairs, my long skirts almost tripping me. I shut the door to my room firmly and threw the satchel with my pages and notebook on my bed.

I wanted to scream. Wanted to hit something. Wanted to—

I reached into my satchel and pulled out the notebook. I looked at the fire.

Thankfully, something stayed my hand. The part of me that remembered the notebook may have been given to me by That Man, but the notes inside were all mine.

I needed them if I was going to prove him wrong.

A soft knock at my door called me to my senses. "Yes?"

"It's your father," his low voice answered. "May I come in?"

I turned the knob and opened the door for him. "Of course."

He entered and looked around, taking in the manuscript pages that were spilling out of the satchel upon my bed, then pointing to the notebook still in my hand.

"Did I come in time?"

I smiled ruefully at him. "In time to stop me from making a giant mistake?" I shook the notebook and smacked it down on my desk, seating myself before it. "Yes." I sighed and covered my face in my hands. Through my fingers I said, "I shared the first part of my manuscript with Sokol."

"I take it he did not like it?" Father asked.

"I thought he did like it..." I pulled my hands down. "Until he opened his mouth." The anger began rising again but I resisted the temptation to feed the flames.

Father pulled a chair from the corner over to my desk, resting a hand over mine as he sat. "Anna, I think you should take a break from this case."

My eyes shot up to him. "What?"

"Now, hear me out," Father said defensively. "I'm not saying you should stop considering the case. In fact, I beg you to continue considering it, in the event that I've missed something. We're only ten days away from the preliminary hearing, and all this might be over then if we put up a good fight. It would definitely be over if we could get a confession out of the true murderer."

"Over before it's even begun."

"Precisely. I do need your help." He patted my hand. "But I think you might help me best by writing."

I raised a brow at him.

"I want you to spend the next ten days writing your book. Your mystery. From morning till night, I want you to pour your heart out onto those pages. I want you to forget this case except for where it's inspiring your pen. Do not let the facts here hinder you. Just write. Write the story that's in here." He pointed to my chest. "And not the one that's here." He touched my forehead.

I took a deep breath and smiled. "You're right, Father." I nodded.

Father squeezed my hand and kissed my forehead. "I always am, dearest."

He stood, walking to my bed and pulling my first hundred pages out from my satchel and bringing them over to lay on my desk.

"You might find there are parts of this worth keeping," he said. "But sometimes, the best foot forward knows what it's doing going forward, not backward."

I sighed. "If I must make the detective a man, I'd like him to be more like you, and less like every detective I've ever met in real life."

"You mean dashingly handsome and intelligent?"

I gave him a courteous laugh. "I do not want a bulldog detective who only gets answers by beating people into giving them. I want a detective like Poe's Dupin or Gaboriau's Lecoq, but, of course, less French."

"Perhaps you should look further back, then, to the inspiration for both of those detectives."

"Oh?"

"The man's name was Vidocq, though I cannot recall his first name at the moment. He was a French criminal who became the first private detective back at the beginning of this century. He wrote a collection of memoirs, a bit of hyperbole really, but quite an interesting read for police and lawyers alike. I have an English translation in my office somewhere. He inspired both of those literary detectives, as well as characters like Jean Valjean and Javert in Victor Hugo's *Les Misérables.* Vidocq is really the reason we have the investigating detective at all, and not just the...um, 'bulldog' as you put it."

I smiled. "I would love to read it if you find your copy."

"I will bring it to you when I find it." He put a hand on my shoulder. "No matter what you end up writing, I know it will be perfectly your own. Good luck."

"You, too," I said.

I picked up my pen as the door closed behind him.

But all I could hear was Sokol.

"You cannot have a female detective," he said.

"I do not like your names," he said.

"I only like your name," he said.

I growled internally.

The audacity of the man. So Sokol didn't believe a female detective would work? Fine. Then I'd create a new detective.

I smiled to myself as I dipped my pen.

I'd base the new detective on a certain someone who already believed himself the greatest detective alive. I'd name him...

"Ebenezer," I said aloud with a chuckle. "Like Scrooge."

And a last name to match...something like...Grump or Grizzled or Grouch or...

"Gryce. Ebenezer Gryce."

It was perfect. I could see him already.

> *Mr. Gryce smiled darkly at the doorknob. "It has a dreadful look!" I exclaimed. Mr. Gryce immediately frowned at the doorknob. And here let me say that Mr. Gryce, the detective, was not the thin, wiry individual with the piercing eye you are doubtless expecting to see. On the contrary, Mr. Gryce was a portly, comfortable personage with an eye that never pierced, that did not even rest on you. If it rested anywhere,*

it was always on some insignificant object in the vicinity, some vase, inkstand, book, or button. These things he would seem to take into his confidence, make the repositories of his conclusions; but as for you—you might as well be the steeple on Trinity Church, for all connection you ever appeared to have with him or his thoughts. At present, then, Mr. Gryce was, as I have already suggested, on intimate terms with the doorknob.

I leaned back and laughed to myself with glee. That would teach him.

28

Running Out of Time

"Her books are read and re-read, and with keener zest upon the subsequent reading than upon the first, when her remarkable constructive skill does not stand in the way of appreciating the many touches indicative of a truly comprehensive and artistic mind."

— **"Anna Katharine Green and Her Work,"**
Current Literature

The next ten days leading up to the preliminary hearing might have been long and arduous if I hadn't been busy writing from nine in the morning until five at night, only stopping for lunch and tea.

I wished with all my heart that the murder of Mr. Jackson could be as simple as the murder of Mr. Leavenworth.

Not that it was exactly simple, of course, with the amount of red herrings I'd sprinkled about—they were awfully fun to throw in here and there—but because I knew now how I intended to end the novel. I yearned to be as certain in real life.

I was also finding that my favorite part of the description was not the people, but the rooms. I kept coming back to the idea that a room should inform the reader about the person living there. When I thought about the stark nature of Sokol's rooms in comparison to the ornate, elaborate, and expensive furnishings I'd noted at Mr. Jackson's, the difference between the two men seemed self-evident.

To that end, I'd gone to great pains to describe each room in my novel, especially the ones my characters needed to spend time in, in order that they might better understand the person they would encounter in that scene.

> *It was a pleasant apartment, as I have already said; square, sunny, and well furnished. On the floor was a crimson carpet, on the walls several pictures, at the windows, cheerful curtains of white, tastefully ornamented with ferns and autumn leaves; in one corner an old melodeon, and in the center of the room a table draped with a bright cloth, on which were various little knick-knacks which, without being rich or expensive, were both pretty and, to a certain extent, ornamental.*
>
> *But it was not these things, which I had seen repeated in many other country homes, that especially attracted my attention, or drew me forward in the slow march which I now undertook around the room. It was the something underlying*

> *all these, the evidences which I found, or sought to find, not only in the general aspect of the room, but in each trivial object I encountered, of the character, disposition, and history of the woman with whom I now had to deal. It was for this reason I studied the daguerreotypes on the mantelpiece, the books on the shelf—*

Ah, the books. I would need to remark on the books this woman had on display in her house. I considered the un-dusted books I'd noted at Mr. Jackson's. Had I seen any books at Sokol's?

Yes, though I'd not reflected upon them while there. Now that I thought of it, however, they told me plenty about how he approached literature, and should have warned me about how he would most likely perceive my own attempt. His walls had held tomes of Shakespeare, Homer's *Odyssey*, *Beowulf*, Plato's *Republic*, Augustine's *On Christian Doctrine*. Why had I ever thought he'd be capable of holding and sharing intellectual thoughts on something as "common" as mystery?

And yet, he'd made that reference to *The Moonstone* when we'd interviewed Mr. Farwell…

The same went for poetry. If he preferred the long form of epic poetry, I needed to share with him some of my pieces more in keeping with that style, rather than my short, evocative ones.

I turned to collect some poetry for the next time I went to his house, but stopped myself. I would not return to him until he apologized for his hurtful critiques. Until then, back to my writing.

With every passing day, as I wove a more thorough quilt of evidence for the murder of Mr. Leavenworth, my father was hard at work, determined to get the charge of murder against Lenore dropped at the hearing, not even going to trial.

In the meantime, Lenore's reputation was being scandalized in the papers, as reporters were wont to do. It was a good thing Mr. Rohlfs didn't care what the papers said, and that Lenore already had his heart in her hands.

All the while, I wrote. I wrote with a good hope in my heart, never cutting, never looking back, but forever looking forward. Sometimes thoughts would come to me, even in the middle of the night, and I'd write them down in my notebook, which I kept at my bedside just in case. When the dawn caressed my face, I'd leap from my bed, my mind already awhirl with the words necessary for the next scene.

The night before the preliminary hearing finally came. I was seated at a dinner which included my brothers and their wives, which was typical on a Sunday. My brother Sidney asked me how the book was coming along, though perhaps not in the best manner of putting it.

"I hear you've taken a rather morbid fascination with Father's current case," he said, raising a glass to me as though to diminish the hurt in his words.

"It's not morbid fascination," Father said defensively.

"It's all right, Father," I said. Little did he know, they had been the same words used by Mr. Jackson. If I could defend myself against him, I could do so against my older brother. I turned to face Sidney across the candlelit table. "Why do you call it a 'morbid fascination?' Have you never followed a case in the paper with avid curiosity?"

"Yes, but men do that. It is unseemly to have one's younger sister doing the same."

"There is a rather general impression, I think," Father said from the head of the table, "that men are more interested in this sort of thing than women are, but this is not my experience."

I set down my fork. I wanted to hear everything he said.

"I believe that women are often more keen than men in sensing the solution of mysteries. Women have more subtle intuitions than men have—a fact which would make them valuable in actual detective work."

I bit back the thought on the edge of my lips: *Why was it when a man made great deductions using logic, it was just that, but when a woman did it, it was considered "a woman's intuition" and given almost magical properties?*

"Father, are you really suggesting Anna take up detecting?" Sidney asked, scoffing only so much as he dared toward our father.

"No, no, not at all. Yet I am proud and pleased she is writing a mystery novel. I have a feeling it will be her finest feat yet." He raised a glass to me in salute and I blushed.

"You must admit, James," Mother Grace said, "you have not always been fully supportive of the idea."

I looked back at my father.

"It is true. Until recently, I had been more inclined to believe poetry was Anna's forte, but I have no doubt the prowess she's brought to our discussions of my cases shall be evident in her pages."

I blushed again.

"And this 'morbid fascination' of which you speak," Father continued saying to Sidney, "isn't actually morbid. It is perfectly natural and legitimate. The people involved in these cases are like us." He waved toward where Lenore sat, sitting in on a conversation that was probably not the best to have while she was with us. Too late now. "That someone should commit murder, for instance, seems as strange as the idea that we should do it ourselves. It is this strangeness that interests us."

I nodded in agreement. Father was hitting the nail right on the head.

"It is as if a member of our own family should suddenly betray an unexpected and terrible trait," I said. "That they should do something so grotesquely horrible that we cannot reconcile it with what we know of them. Crime novels must touch our imagination by showing people, like ourselves, but incredibly transformed by some overwhelming motive."

"In the end, I suppose you will just have to hold off judgment until you read the book," Mother Grace said to Sidney.

I smiled. "Yes, I look forward to reading it to all of you, but you must wait until it is complete." I would *not* be making the same mistake I'd made before, sharing it too early with Sokol. "I must admit, it is leagues more fun creating a mystery than living in one." I was nearing the end of my first draft and I could feel the denouement approaching. "In my writing, I am able to ensure all the correct clues are provided, if not hidden masterfully, while in real life, it seems sometimes the clues are simply landed upon by luck, rather than talent."

"Perhaps, then," Mother Grace said, spearing some asparagus, "in your book, the detective must stumble upon a clue here and there, to make it more believable."

"That is my hope."

That night—or rather the next morning, for once again I'd written through the darkest hours by gaslight—I finished it.

My first draft of my first novel.

I held it before me like a newborn baby. Not to lessen the pain and discomfort my mother had gone through, but I wondered if giving birth felt anything like this. This absolute pride.

I shook my hand, the pain in the muscles along my fingers and up to my elbow lessening as I did so. How I'd managed to write so much without losing all feeling there, only God knew. I did not know how many words my manuscript contained, but it was certainly a great many.

I couldn't wait to share it with my family.

With great relief, I dressed for breakfast. My stepmother and sister tried to speak lightly to take our minds off the coming hearing as we ate.

Afterward, I joined my father and Lenore in the foyer, Lenore looking radiant in black. Father nervously checked his case for all his papers one final time.

A knock at the door made us all look up sharply.

Teagan answered the door to find a messenger holding a letter. Father took it, a look of deepest concern upon his face.

I peeked over the edge and when I saw Sokol's name, my first thought was that he'd died, and my heart sank into the heels of my boots. But no, the letter wasn't edged in black.

Father's eyes rose to meet mine, excited, jubilant, even.

"He found her! And just in time!"

"Found who?" I asked.

"Emily, the missing maid. Emily O'Connell."

29

Mrs. Fairbanks

"I did not consult my knowledge, sir, in regard to the subject: only my feelings."

—*The Leavenworth Case*

Father's face went first up with glee and then down with frustration. He looked from Lenore to his case to me.

I nodded. "I'll go, Father. You two go to the hearing."

He nodded perfunctorily. "Thank you." He handed me the letter and grabbed his case. "Miss Kelthorpe?" he said, offering his arm. "Send me a letter as soon as you get to her, and again once you've learned everything you can," he told me.

"I will. Now go, or you will be late."

Once they'd left, I asked Teagan to call me a cab whilst I finished pinning on my hat, switching to a travel one rather than the more ornate one I'd picked out for the hearing.

I looked down at the letter, skimming the words to find my destination: Greenwich, Connecticut. Sokol had kindly included the next train north for Father, and it was only once I was seated on that train that I wondered how Sokol would react to finding I had come in answer to the letter, rather than my father.

I removed my notebook, which I'd thankfully grabbed before leaving, thinking I'd take notes on the hearing. This was much better. I'd completely forgotten the missing maid, the one who had tried to blackmail Lenore before disappearing. How could she be forgotten when she'd been at the forefront of my mind whenever I had considered my notes from those first few days?

As soon as I returned home, I'd have to add another ten thousand words or so just to tell the maid's story. The book was getting longer by the minute, I thought despairingly, knowing full well a publisher was more likely to ask me to cut words than to add them.

This miserable thought kept me company the rest of the way to Connecticut, where I took a cab from the train station to the address in Sokol's letter. Fobbs, Sokol's assistant, helped me alight. I was glad that Sokol and I would not be alone together, though Fobbs's dour countenance was as serious as a stopped pocket watch.

I looked up at the house. It was Colonial, quite classic in architecture, a simple seaside abode for the upper-classes, and therefore the last place on earth I'd have thought we'd find Emily.

At the gate stood Sokol. He did not look pleased with the landscaping done about the place, and appeared particularly put out by the large rose bush to his right.

"Good day, Sokol," I said.

"Miss Green," he returned stiffly. "I see your father could not make the trip?"

"The hearing is this morning," I said succinctly.

Sokol nodded to Fobbs behind me, as though he'd said as much to him before my arrival.

As we approached the front door, I almost inquired as to whose home this was, and how Emily came to be found here, but I figured it was better to trust that Sokol and Fobbs knew what they were about.

Sokol knocked and the door was answered after a respectful time by a middle-aged woman.

"Yes?" she asked, opening the door just enough to take in our motley crew.

"Mrs. Fairbanks?" Sokol inquired, removing his hat and speaking to it solemnly. "I am Mr. Sokol. I sent you a letter this morning concerning a visit with your lovely daughter in regards to her employment with Mr. Jackson?"

"Her daughter?" I whispered to Fobbs.

"Yes. This is Mrs. Eliza Fairbanks."

"How is she—"

"Oh...yes...," the woman said slowly, though she seemed puzzled by the three of us.

"May I present Miss Green, a young lady of great assistance to myself, as well as to her father, the lawyer I was telling you about. It appears he was unable to join us today, but I have no doubt she will be capable of answering any and all of your questions."

I blushed at the words. Perhaps he was not as upset as I'd imagined he'd be at finding I'd come.

"And this is Mr.—"

"I'm terribly sorry, Mr. Sokol. I know you have come a long way, but...you see...you will be unable to speak with my daughter today..." She drifted off into the handkerchief she raised to her mouth, tears choking her words.

I closed my eyes. *No, no.*

"She... I cannot..."

"What seems to be the trouble, Mrs. Fairbanks?" Sokol asked soothingly. "We are here to help."

"I fear you cannot. She will not wake..."

"Mrs. Fairbanks," Sokol said sternly. "May we please enter? Mr. Fobbs here has some medical training, you see. Might he take a look?"

"Oh! Yes, please!" she cried, flinging the door open with a sudden motion.

The three of us followed her inside quickly. I only had a moment to notice the flush of lovely color as it burst upon us. Blue curtains, blue carpets, blue walls. It was like a glimpse of heavenly azure in a spot where only darkness and gloom were to be expected.

We followed Mrs. Fairbanks up the stairs to where she paused on the landing, silhouetted against the sun as it streamed in through a bay window, the sea at her back, crying softly into her handkerchief. She looked like something out of a portrait painting, wearing a beautiful bustled gown of sea-foam green, trimmed with white lace that ran down her arms and up her neck.

"I cannot... Please... That room..." She waved toward the door down the hall on the right.

I entered the room reverently, unsure what would meet my gaze.

Emily appeared merely to be sleeping, so restful and reposed was she.

"Is she...?"

"Yes," Sokol said heavily, taking a seat in an empty chair as though the weight of the news had sapped all his strength.

Fobbs nodded from where he stood over the girl's body, his fingers pressed against her neck.

I closed my eyes again before opening them slowly, and turning to tell Mrs. Fairbanks in the hall.

"I...I'm afraid...," I began, but she did not make me finish.

"I cannot...," she muttered, the handkerchief returning to her face.

"Come, let's have a seat downstairs," I said comfortingly, taking Mrs. Fairbanks by the arm.

She nodded and led me back to the front room, where she lowered herself into an overstuffed chair without grace or dignity, only a heavy amount of grief. I took a seat across from her.

"Mrs. Fairbanks," I began, "perhaps you might tell me what happened before we arrived?"

She took a deep, steadying breath, clutching her handkerchief on her lap. "I took up her breakfast tray... Ever since she returned home, I've allowed her to sleep late in the morning. I know she hasn't had a good night's sleep since she went into service. I thought it would be a nice treat for her, while she was home, for her to sleep late and have her breakfast in bed. It was my custom to do this, you see. I would take it to her room and eat with her there, if she'd let me stay. But this morning..." She squeezed the handkerchief as though it might give her the strength to say the words. "This morning...she..."

I reached out and touched her hand. She didn't have to say it.

Mrs. Fairbanks nodded. "I have been unable to bring myself to send for the coroner. To do so would be to admit..." Tears stopped her once more.

I stood and poured her a glass of water from a nearby pitcher, handing it to her as a means of helping her focus on something else.

Emily's mother stifled her sobs and looked up, taking the glass with a nod of thanks. After a couple sips, she continued, "When I received the letter this morning requesting to speak with her, I thought I would ask her about it once she woke. She told me someone would be coming for her from Mr. Jackson, that she expected to hear from him quite soon. She said everything would be taken care of, and she'd want for nothing in the future."

"'Want for nothing?' I don't understand. The police have been looking for her."

"The police? Whatever for?"

"In the paper..." I looked about.

"We do not receive the paper." Mrs. Fairbanks shook her head then straightened. "If this has to do with Mr. Jackson's death, she was home—we were together the day he died, so I know she had nothing to do with it."

"So you know nothing of what caused her to leave her work?" Sokol asked.

Mrs. Fairbanks and I looked up to find Sokol descending the stairs with Fobbs at his side. They joined us in the parlor, Sokol taking great interest in the glass in Mrs. Fairbanks's hands as he took his seat. Fobbs stood in the corner like a grandfather clock, immovable, yet just as watchful.

"Well, yes," said Mrs. Fairbanks. "She chose to leave. She came home because someone had offered to straighten things out, to speak with Mr. Jackson in regards to her future. She said it was all taken care of."

"What was all taken care of? I don't understand," I said. "Emily was dismissed on account of blackmail."

"Blackmail!" Mrs. Fairbanks cried, sorrow stepping aside for fear in an instant. "She blackmailed someone?"

"Miss Kelthorpe," I said.

Mrs. Fairbanks shook her head. "No. She'd never do that. She'd have no cause. She didn't need money—" She stopped herself.

"Because she'd 'want for nothing?'" I asked. Perhaps Lenore had lied and Emily *had* succeeded in blackmailing her. Perhaps Lenore had promised Emily money if she'd simply leave? In which case, I still desperately wanted to know what information Emily had blackmailed Lenore with. "Was that because she'd been successful and she was about to live off the payments from—"

"No. She wouldn't. She didn't need to."

"You keep saying that, but I don't understand."

Mrs. Fairbanks looked about her well-placed home.

"Mrs. Fairbanks, I must ask: How came your daughter to be in service?" Sokol asked quietly.

Emily's mother glanced at me, and then around her parlor again. "I...I... Oh!" she cried, the tears coming again. "The truth is..."

"Mrs. Fairbanks," I said again, "what is the truth?"

"I am Mr. Jackson's sister."

30

Emily

"I declare, now that the thing is worked up, I begin to feel almost sorry we have succeeded so well."

—*The Leavenworth Case*

Eliza! Of course, I knew I'd heard that name before!

"You are Mr. Jackson's sister?" I repeated, glancing at Sokol.

"I am very much astonished," Sokol said to his fingertips, looking up long enough to give me an actual wink in a slow, diabolical way, which in another mood would have aroused my fiercest anger.

"Yes. He hasn't spoken to me in years, but ever since the birth of my second daughter he has provided for us." She gave a sweep of the hand clutching the handkerchief about the room. "Her father was an actor, who…left us."

This must be the reason for Mr. Jackson's intense dislike of all actors. But Mrs. Fairbanks had said something else that interested me.

"Second daughter?"

"Yes…I'm afraid I…" Mrs. Fairbanks blushed prettily and took a sip of water before replying. "Emily is my second daughter. My first was…"

I knew it before she said it.

"…Lenore."

I took in the deep breath I hadn't realized I'd been holding. "I thought Mr. Jackson had two sisters."

Mrs. Fairbanks shook her head. "Just me." Her shoulders sagged. "I've never been capable of living up to his expectations. I made a mistake. I fell in love with a man who left me and my daughter when she was only three years old. Even though she was born out of wedlock—which he never forgave me for—he said my sins needn't be visited upon the girl. He took her in, adopted her as his own."

"But Emily…"

"Yes, when I revealed to him that not only had my lover left me with my firstborn, but also pregnant with a second, he made it quite clear he would only take one of my children. He said he had no need for an infant, but Lenore…Lenore he would raise as his own, giving her everything she required and more." Mrs. Fairbanks played with the glass in her hands. "About a year later, he said he'd had a change of heart, and decided he would pay for Emily's expenses, within reason, but he would not take her in, neither would he leave her anything after his death. He said that by that time, she would most likely no longer require his assistance anyway, since he intended to find her a good husband who would provide for her."

"But then he died."

"Yes." Mrs. Fairbanks looked about her home. "That is the real reason why I have been taking up the breakfast tray to Emily. I dismissed all the servants but the cook when my brother died, and I intend to sell this place and move into something more suitable for just Emily and me—"

She suddenly stopped, realizing what she'd just said. There would be no new home for her and Emily. She was on her own now. Completely and forever on her own.

I attempted to distract her from the pain. "And Lenore? If Lenore is your daughter, and Emily is your daughter, that means they're—"

"Sisters, yes." Mrs. Fairbanks shook her head. "Emily knew the truth, but I do not think Lenore knew. As far as I know, Mr. Jackson only ever told her she was his orphaned niece. He never revealed her true backstory. It was not necessary. She was far more likely to make a suitable match without her unfortunate parentage."

"Surely, Mr. Jackson would still consider it beneath his niece to go into service for him."

"He did not know Emily was his niece. He knew her name, of course, but the likelihood of his realizing that the servant Emily beneath his own roof was the same Emily that was my daughter...well, it was highly unlikely."

I nodded.

"I told her to use a different name when she entered service. I thought she'd go to Manhattan and find an employer nearby. I did not know she intended to work for Mr. Jackson himself."

I shook my head sadly. The poor girl. "She must have hoped to build a relationship with him, and then reveal herself. If she knew Lenore was her sister, do you think she went there in hopes of having her on her side to help win over Mr. Jackson?" But then there was the blackmail... "Or do you think she did it in order to learn information so she might blackmail him into putting her in his will? Perhaps with threats to reveal the truth about Lenore's lineage to the papers?"

Mrs. Fairbanks studied her handkerchief before looking up and answering, "No. I refuse to believe my daughter was capable of blackmail or libel of any kind. I do not care if Lenore says otherwise."

"Do you dislike Miss Kelthorpe?" Sokol asked his cane quietly.

Mrs. Fairbanks shook her head. "It is not her fault that my brother loved her and chose her to be his heir. But I do wish...I wished... It is unfair that one of my daughters should live to find a future filled with happiness, while my other daughter was lowered to the point of having to serve in the very household that might have been her own someday. If only my brother could have found it in his heart to forgive me..." She sniffed. "My only solace is that Emily died happy."

"What makes you say that?" Sokol asked her glass with interest.

"Yesterday she received a letter from someone that made her face glow at the sight of it. Unfortunately, I did not see who it was from, and she immediately requested I leave her alone to read it." Mrs. Fairbanks shook her head. "I'm a terrible mother."

I reached out and took Mrs. Fairbanks's hand. "You must not blame yourself for her death."

"I just don't understand," Emily's mother said. "She was so happy when I left her. Why would she take her own life?"

I cocked my head. "Why do you believe she did so?"

Mrs. Fairbanks shook her head sadly. "What else am I to think? No one has come to call, there is only myself and the cook in the house. I have eaten everything Emily has, and Emily was too young to die of natural causes. She must have poisoned herself somehow."

I could not believe it. "I have been working with my father on Mr. Jackson's case," I said soothingly. "We wish to be of help to you. If you will allow us, it is possible we will be able to uncover something that will tell us what really happened to Emily."

Mrs. Fairbanks considered and then nodded.

Sokol, Fobbs, and I climbed the stairs once more to Emily's room.

"I have never seen someone so grieved by a death," I whispered as I stepped through the doorway once more.

"Then you have not been around death often enough," Sokol said softly, standing at the bedside of the dead girl. He sighed. "Now then, let's see what she has yet to tell us. We'll begin by looking for that letter."

Fobbs and I turned about in tiny circles, for there were not many places to search. Although the downstairs of the house had been furnished in the highest style, it was clear the personal rooms were kept sparse and in simpler decor, most likely to save money. I wondered why Mr. Jackson had provided his sister with a home and style of living that he knew she could never afford after his death.

It was cruel of him, and the notion flitted across my mind that perhaps the world was all the better for his death.

I swept the thought away, however, unwilling to think something so unchristian.

Beside the bed, there was a small table, upon which stood an oil lamp and a stack of dime novels—some romance, some mystery. In the corner was a chest of drawers with a bowl and pitcher and a drinking glass.

I pointed to this last item. "That glass. It appears there is some sort of residue in the bottom."

Sokol nodded, keeping his back to me. "Fobbs and I believe the girl drank something last night that caused her not to wake this morning. We will ask the coroner to request a sampling of it."

So he'd noticed the glass, too. Was there nothing his wandering eye didn't catch?

His back straightened and he turned to survey the room. "If I were a letter...where would I be?"

"It depends on what sort of news the letter held," I said.

"Enlighten us," Sokol said, and he genuinely seemed to wish to know my thoughts.

"Well, if it was a love letter, she would most likely have placed it beneath her pillow."

I walked to the bedside. "Forgive me," I whispered before reaching my hand beneath the dead girl's pillow and running it every which way. "Nothing. Did you check the drawers? Sometimes a girl has a hidden box." I recalled Lenore's collection.

"I doubt it was a lover's letter," said Fobbs in a low tone. "Why would she kill herself upon receiving such a one?"

"If it was a lover's last letter," I said. "Perhaps Mr. Farwell wrote to end things between them after hearing how she'd blackmailed Miss Kelthorpe?"

Fobbs rocked the dresser in the corner as he pulled out the drawers in an untidy manner. I wished he'd show some respect. When he reached in and began removing the girl's underthings, I quickly offered to take over. Hidden at the back of the drawer was what I sought.

I pulled forth a small bundle of letters tied together with a red ribbon. After removing the topmost letter, I read aloud:

"My dearest darling,

"I think of you most every day. When I pass you in the hall, your smile gives me the courage to go on. One day I will no longer need the old man and his long-winded stories. We will be free to write our own. Together.

"Love,

"Your future husband

"P.S.—Burn after reading this."

The postscript reminded me of a conversation between Mr. Rohlfs and Lenore in my front parlor.

"I thought we agreed you would burn them after reading?"

"I just couldn't bring myself to do it. Your words were so beautiful!"

What if...

I looked about the room.

"What are you looking for?"

"A place to burn..." I looked at the fire grate. "In there?"

Fobbs grabbed the poker and began searching through the ashes.

"Or perhaps..."

I got down on my hands and knees and looked under the bed. "Ah!" I cried in triumph, pulling forth a chamber pot.

Sokol smiled wryly.

"Don't worry, there is nothing in it but ash," I said, standing to my feet and holding it out for Sokol and Fobbs to see. Inside, there was only ash and the remains of a match.

"I suppose—" I was interrupted by Sokol breaking into a vigorous round of coughs, forcing him to fall back into a chair in the corner.

"I'll get him a drink," said Fobbs, leaving quickly for the kitchen.

I went to Sokol's side. "You still have a cold? It has not left you yet?"

Sokol shook his head. He took a small breath, as though fearing a large one would only bring about more coughing. "When it comes to my health, nothing leaves me easily," he wheezed.

My brow furrowed. "You should not have come."

He looked at the body in the bed. "I had to."

I followed his gaze. She was so young. Her life terminated before it had even truly begun. Beneath those silenced lips lay the truth of why murder was the most interesting theme for a mystery story. The act involved two persons; they alone held the explanation. And one of them has been silenced forever. That lifeless body, with its lips sealed on the great secret, had become an object of thrilling interest. I felt that I *must* know what those silent lips would tell if only they could speak.

"You're thinking about how to use this in your story, aren't you?" Sokol asked quietly.

I turned on him. "Yes," I said shortly, embarrassed. "Perhaps. What if I am?"

Sokol studied the body. "I only ask that you do her justice. Bring her killer to justice, at least on the page."

"What is this? The words of defeat? Not the great Mr. Sokol!"

He shook his head and coughed once more, but only a short one, as though his lungs were determined to have the last word.

"I have not given up hope, but it is clear the letter which might have told us the truth has been burned." He pointed his cane to the chamber pot.

"Don't give up so easily," I said with a smile, reaching in and pulling out a small bit of charred paper which had luckily blown up and stuck itself against the edge of the pot.

Sokol looked like he might just kiss that chamber pot.

I set it down and held out the paper carefully before the light of the window. Between the char marks I could only make out six letters: "dr-am -f m-".

"'Dream of me,' perhaps?" I suggested.

Sokol nodded. "It is possible the powder itself came within the letter disguised as a love potion."

He, too, had noticed the sort of reading material Emily had enjoyed.

My eyes alighted once more on the stack of dime novels beside the bed. I crossed to the novels and lifted them one by one: "The Dead Letter: An American Romance" by Seeley Regester,

"Winifred Winthrop, or, the Lady of Atherton Hall" by Clara Augusta, and "Who Wins?: Or the Secret of Monkswood Waste" by May Agnes Fleming.

Ever since the War, the dime novel's sensational stories had been extremely popular amongst the reading public. Not for me, of course, as I preferred the longer novel format for my reading pleasure. Within the dime novel would be nothing much more than romance and melodramatic adventure, the romance usually taking place between two people divided by class—the serving girl and the rich man—a modern-day Cinderella story that always ended in marriage and happily ever after.

It was stories like these that had probably given Emily the idea to blackmail Lenore as well.

I pulled out my notebook and placed the charred bit of paper carefully between two pages.

Sokol's mouth twitched at the notebook. "Although I have heard that sometimes women take their own lives when happy rather than melancholy, I do wonder why she would do such a thing? And why now?"

"The letter must have been from her lover."

"Ah yes, the secret lover."

"Not quite so secret, as we know who he is."

Sokol raised a brow at the notebook.

I flushed with pleasure at recalling something before he did. "The cook and the butler declared Mr. Farwell and Emily to have been lovers, even if Mr. Farwell never admitted it to us when we spoke with him."

"I thought you believed Mr. Farwell to have affections for Miss Kelthorpe?"

"Yes, and perhaps it was the admittance of this in the letter that drove Emily to take her life?"

"Why would Mr. Farwell send her a letter he knew would drive her to suicide, as well as the means to do it?"

A knock at the door interrupted us. Fobbs held a glass of water in one hand, with an elderly gentleman behind him.

"Coroner Richards," he announced.

31

The Note

"A web seemed tangled about my feet."

—***The Leavenworth Case***

Sokol stood stiffly as Fobbs introduced us to the coroner, who then crossed to Emily to begin his examination.

"No doctor?" I asked.

"Not today," the old man croaked. "He's tending to a birth across town. I told him not to bother, as she's dead already."

I pressed my lips into a line, but had to admit he was right.

"I'm glad I told him so. This is clearly a case of poisoning. The blue lips are unmistakable."

"We have evidence suggesting it was a powder mixed with water and taken in that glass," Sokol said, pointing to the glass on top of the chest of drawers.

"Ah. Suicide, then."

"No, it's not," Sokol and I said at the same time.

The coroner studied us, raising a bushy white eyebrow that connected to make one large shelf above his eyes. "What makes you think otherwise?"

"There's no note," I said, deciding the quickest answer would be best.

"No note?"

"Yes. A victim of suicide always leaves a note."

"Then what is that?" the coroner asked, pointing to the note I'd pulled from the stack of love letters tied in ribbon.

"These are letters from a secret lover," I said, showing them to the coroner.

He dismissed them with a wave of his hand. "Seems quite obvious to me what happened here."

As I held the letter in my hand, it occurred to me that I should compare it with the note we'd found in the chamber pot. I moved to the dresser and laid open my notebook next to the letter.

"Can you tell if they're the same?" Sokol asked, just over my shoulder.

My heart leapt inside my chest at his nearness, but thankfully I didn't react physically.

"You almost made me lose our most important clue," I hissed.

"Careful," he said, for my breath had indeed made the small bit of paper slide a bit up the page. He reached out his crooked fingers and closed my notebook once more over the clue, his hand upon mine.

I pulled my hand and my notebook away quickly, taking a step back from the dresser.

"Those few words were too small to really tell. It's possible it was written by the same hand, but perhaps not. I really couldn't say for certain."

Sokol nodded while leaning heavily on his cane. "I don't understand."

I didn't either. I looked at the chamber pot full of ashes, at the dead girl on the bed, at the empty glass, and back at the note. Then I returned to the peaceful repose on Emily's face.

"I have a request to make of you, Mr. Richards," Sokol asked the old man's black bag.

"Yes?"

"I need you to hold off on announcing that this was suicide."

The coroner raised his bushy white eyebrow. "Do you know something I do not?"

"Only circumstantial evidence at the moment, but if given time, I believe we could find you the hard evidence you require. We believe this death is connected with the death of a Mr. Jackson in Manhattan."

The coroner's eyebrow rose even further. "Indeed?"

Judging from common experience, we had every reason to fear that an immediate stop would be put to all our investigative proceedings if the coroner felt it was his duty to inform the public with due haste. Happily, Mr. Richards proved to be a sensible man. He had only to hear a true story of the whole affair to recognize at once its importance and the necessity of the most cautious action in the matter. He expressed himself willing to enter into Sokol's plans, offering to conduct the necessary formalities of calling a jury and instituting an inquest in such a way as to give us time for the investigations we proposed to make.

Leaving Fobbs behind to help the coroner sort matters, Sokol and I traveled to the train station, Sokol walking with more lively steps than he'd displayed as yet, his rheumatism and despair apparently forgotten.

We took a seat, much relieved, though still carrying the heavy burden of unrequited justice. It was while we waited for the train that I realized regretfully that I'd never sent a letter to my father upon my arrival, and that he certainly needed to hear this news before our return to Manhattan. I excused myself to do so, but Sokol stopped me.

"There is no reason for haste," he said.

"But I must tell my father—"

"You may tell him of Emily and Mrs. Fairbanks, but not of Mr. Farwell's possible involvement."

My brow furrowed. "And why not? We know he was Emily's lover, and he clearly sent her poison with an intention of tying off loose ends."

Sokol shook his head at his cane from where he sat, resting the rheumatic feet which had carried him through the rather full preceding hours. "There's something still not right here."

I sighed but agreed only to send my father the necessary information, and hurried to the post office inside the station. Upon my return, I found Sokol busily engaged in counting his own fingers with a troubled expression upon his countenance, which may or may not have been the result of that arduous employment. At my approach, satisfied perhaps that he possessed no more than the requisite number, he dropped his hands. I sat beside him on the bench, a proper amount of distance between us, and waited for him to speak.

He did not. Neither did he say anything once we were on the train, not even looking up when I bought a simple sandwich from the lunch cart.

As he clearly refused to share his thoughts with me, I decided I'd spend the time writing, so I asked the porter for some paper and a pen. When he brought it, Sokol still didn't seem to notice anything beyond the passing scenery outside the window, so I went to work writing the missing maid scenes that would need to be added to my book.

I soon realized this was going to be more difficult than I'd thought, squeezing a new scene into a book already laced tightly. I sat back to consider and found Sokol staring at me, though he quickly looked away when our eyes met.

"Have you decided to join me in this train car after all?" I asked.

"I hear you have a new draft of your manuscript," he said in response.

I flushed. "Yes, but don't worry: I won't suffer you to hear it again."

Sokol looked at the pen in my hands as though he'd just bitten into a rather sour plum. "Miss Green, I am sorry my remarks forced you to begin again, but I am thrilled they did not stop you from writing."

"I did not start over completely from scratch," I said stiffly.

"Oh, your father gave me to believe—"

"My father has been nothing but supportive of my writing."

"Has he read it?"

I took a deep breath, calming my racing heart. I would not let him rile me into anger again.

"No. He has not. Not yet."

"I gave my critique only so that your story might be made all the better for it."

My cheeks grew hot. "Your words did not feel that way."

Sokol looked up into my eyes. That penetrating stare. I hated that stare. I would not let him draw me into it.

"Miss Green, I do apologize if my words hurt you. I did not mean—"

"It's all right." I was the one to break my eyes away this time. "I admit, some of your comments did change the story I wrote. But I also ignored some of them, as well."

"And that is your right as the author."

"I'm glad you see it that way," I said.

"Did you change the detective?"

I gave him a sidelong glance. "Yes. Yes, I did."

He nodded at the falcon head of his cane. "I'm afraid the world is just not ready for a female detective. It may be someday, but not today."

I absolutely, thoroughly, unequivocally hated to admit it, but I knew he was right. Someday I'd create the perfect female detective, perhaps an old spinster, with experience behind her to give her wit and fortitude. Or maybe a young girl, like the stories Mary and I had planned out when we were younger.

"I would be honored if you would allow me to hear this newest manuscript," Sokol said, his eyes connecting with mine again, as though he wanted to send a telegraph signal from his eyes to my heart about the seriousness of his words.

I faltered. I wanted him to hear it, to hear how I'd fixed it and made it better, how I'd taken to heart my father's comment about making it my own story, breathing creative life into it, rather than sticking to the facts of the real case. Just as Sokol had recommended after my first reading.

"I'll read it to you after we have closed this case," I finally said.

He shook his head. "I need you to read it to me now."

I scoffed at the demand.

"I meant: I would like you to read it to me tomorrow morning. Please."

"Why?"

He sighed and splayed his crooked fingers before him. "I think I've pushed myself as far as I can go on this case. Physically, I mean. Now it's time to sit and think. The rest will come together without my having to move a muscle."

I raised a brow at him. "You really think so?"

"I do, and I seriously do believe that reading your mystery novel will help. In reading an ordinary novel, the reader simply lets the current of the story flow through their minds. But when they read a detective story, they are all the time figuring on the solution of the mystery, trying to guess how it is coming out. We do the same thing when we follow a criminal case in the papers. I'm hoping that, as your story is based on the real case, perhaps it will remind me of some fact we've overlooked."

I shook my head; maybe he wouldn't be pleased I'd changed it. "I'm afraid it's only loosely based. I've taken some liberties—"

"Like what?"

"Like picking the murderer—just as you told me to do."

Sokol's mouth twitched. "May I ask whom you picked?"

I paused. "Are you certain you want me to tell you?"

"Yes. If you feel there are enough clues leading you to a certain person, even unconsciously, you may be on the right track."

I took a breath. "All right. The murderer in the book is the secret husband of Mary, Mr. Clavering."

Sokol steepled his fingers and considered them. "That is a very pleasing belief. I honor you for entertaining it, Miss Green. I was under the impression you were too fond of Mr. Rohlfs to pick him as the murderer."

I blushed so profusely I almost asked him to open a window. "It's not... He's not... I just... I don't really think he..."

"I do not believe Mr. Rohlfs is our murderer. At least, not alone. For one thing: what purpose could he have for killing Emily?"

"But... I do not think Mr. Rohlfs is the murderer in real life, only in my book—I mean, his fictional version in my book." I heaved a sigh. It was all getting incredibly confusing. "In real life, I hold that it must be Mr. Farwell." Who was still Mr. Harwell in the book, as I had refused to change the names of the characters because Sokol disliked them. It was one of his comments which I'd decided to ignore.

"Why would Farwell send a poisonous dream potion to his lover?" he asked his fingers.

"She was more than his lover. According to that letter, he claimed to be her future husband. So perhaps he'd switched affections to Miss Kelthorpe and didn't know how else to escape the commitment of an engagement?" I proposed.

"Then why kill Mr. Jackson? We are going around in circles."

"Maybe the person who killed Mr. Jackson is different than the person who killed Emily. Maybe they're not connected..." I trailed off. I didn't need Sokol's look to tell me what I already knew: the two had to be connected. It would be too strong of a coincidence for them not to be.

"It could be as simple as someone overhearing something they shouldn't have. Let's say Emily did just that," said Sokol. "She overheard Mr. Farwell proposing to Miss Kelthorpe, perhaps? She gets angry, and approaches Miss Kelthorpe with a demand that she decline Mr. Farwell's offer."

"Then why would Miss Kelthorpe say Emily attempted to blackmail her?"

"What other way would you describe Emily demanding she give up Mr. Farwell?"

"But Miss Kelthorpe loves Mr. Rohlfs."

"Are you quite certain?"

I considered, my heart skipping a beat it shouldn't have at the prospect that maybe Mr. Rohlfs was in love with Lenore, but it was not returned. Which would leave him available.

But deep down, I knew this wasn't true. I remembered the way they'd held each other, the solemn and affectionate way they'd gazed into each other's eyes whenever I'd come across them together in the front parlor, Mother Grace studiously working on her embroidery in the corner to give them some affected privacy. Lenore was as in love with Mr. Rohlfs as he was with her. They'd agreed to be married, and the only thing stopping them was her court date.

I started tapping my cheek with my pencil to hide the shaking of my hands.

"It's impossible to know a woman's heart," I said, taking a page out of my father's book.

"Precisely. So let's say Miss Kelthorpe accepted Mr. Farwell. They go to Mr. Jackson to tell him 'the good news.'"

"And he refuses to accept the engagement."

"He threatens to remove her from his will," Sokol nodded.

"So she drops the matter. But Mr. Farwell has another plan in mind."

"He kills Mr. Jackson."

"And Miss Kelthorpe finds out it was him after the fact." I sucked in a breath and pointed my pencil at Sokol. "Which would explain her grief. She did not think Mr. Farwell would go so far."

"It also explains the drunkenness of Mr. Farwell."

"But his plan isn't complete. Emily has disappeared. Only she knows the reason Mr. Farwell would kill Mr. Jackson."

"So he sends her a letter which declares he has given up Miss Kelthorpe and wants to marry Emily. He has sent her a special potion in celebration, to help her dream of their future life together."

"Mr. Farwell...," I breathed.

32

The Manuscript

"Few authors wait to have a story to tell."

— **"Anna Katharine Green and Her Work,"**
Current Literature

"Given the fondness the cook has for Miss Kelthorpe, the judge was unwilling to believe the cook's alibi was truth," my father said in frustration over breakfast the next morning. "He said the fact that Miss Kelthorpe is the only one who stands to inherit, and thereby benefit from Mr. Jackson's death, is too great a motive. I think he honestly just likes the idea of a rich man's inheritance going to line the pockets of the state rather than the rightful heir."

I had arrived home late the night before, too tired to speak with my father or to hear about their trip to court. Things had clearly not gone as well as he'd hoped, and now Lenore would have to wait yet another three weeks for the indictment scheduled.

"Why must justice crawl so slowly?" I asked with a shake of my head.

It was just like in my book. I was making it as difficult as possible for Mr. Raymond to prove Eleanore's innocence, but I really didn't have to make up much, since what followed only upheld my most cherished belief: "Truth is stranger than fiction."

We needed to find the real murderer quickly. But then, it had taken my Detective Gryce an entire manuscript to find his murderer.

"I'm going to Sokol's this morning. I hope that's all right, Father."

"I thought you and Sokol had an argument?" Father asked.

"We did. We've moved past it."

Father nodded but searched my face as though he wondered if there mightn't be something else I wanted to tell him.

"Anything else you want to tell me?" he asked.

I shook my head. "No, Father."

He squinted his eyes an instant but then nodded. "I'm happy to hear you two are partners again. I have a feeling that together nothing will stop you."

"Except the murderer of Mr. Jackson…and Emily." My mind recalled the still body on the bed. So young. Silenced forever.

Father waved my remark away. "It has only been a couple weeks. Give it time. It is very rare for a murderer to escape detection. No matter how carefully a crime may be planned, or covered up, the criminal almost invariably forgets some significant detail. Curiously enough, Nature herself seems to be in league with circumstances to convict him. She puts a little muddy spot in his path so that he leaves a footprint. Or she blows a curtain aside at the instant that a passer-by can catch a glimpse of his face. Or she twists the current of a stream so that some evidence of his guilt floats to the surface. Crime is contrary to Nature. And Nature often seems bent on punishing it."

I nodded. Father was right. I gave him a comforting kiss on the forehead before I left, then headed to the foyer, pulling on my gloves as I went.

"I'm so sorry, my love," I overheard a man say.

"Perhaps if we make it to Canada, no one will follow us?" Lenore suggested.

Lenore had excused herself from breakfast upon hearing Mr. Rohlfs had come to call. Apparently they'd adjourned to the front parlor for a stolen moment alone.

"We can't," said Mr. Rohlfs, and I could hear the defeat in his voice. "You know we can't. They would find us."

"But I am innocent!" Lenore cried.

"I know that, and if I could think of a way to make the judge see the truth, I'd do it in a heartbeat."

As I pinned on my hat, I could hear him gathering Lenore into his arms, her sobs quieting as she no doubt nestled her blonde head into his strong shoulder.

"I love you. Do you love me?" he asked.

I could not make out Lenore's response, but I heard him say in return, "Then that's enough for me for now. Someday, we'll be together, and all this will be like some terrible nightmare."

I shook my head at the line, no doubt from some play he'd once performed. I wondered if actors were capable of delivering anything new, or if the entirety of his mind was filled with lines from plays, making it all the more difficult to say anything unique.

I was worried about the same thing with my book. What if Sokol thought it was too familiar a story? Too similar to books he'd read before.

I laughed at myself. There was no way he'd find my writing too similar to Plato or Shakespeare. As I shut the front door behind me, I prayed that Sokol was also right and my manuscript would bring something to light for us.

This time, when I arrived, I found Sokol lying on the couch, a book in his hands.

I looked twice at the book before realizing I hadn't been mistaken.

"Is that Wilkie Collins's *The Woman in White*?" I asked incredulously.

"I thought it might be helpful if I was more familiar with mystery fiction before offering you my expertise again." He waved a bent hand toward a stack of novels at his side.

I recognized a collection of Poe's works, Charles Dickens's *Bleak House*, two of Emile Gaboriau's novels, even the memoirs of Vidocq, the criminal-turned-detective my father had been telling me about.

Perhaps Sokol would recognize any tropes in my writing after all.

I handed the manuscript to Sokol, stating that while he read the beginning, I would add the missing maid parts, bringing it to him later once it was finished.

He didn't argue, but placed *The Woman in White* on the table beside him, adjusting a hot water bottle upon his aching feet. He took my manuscript pages in his crippled hands while I seated myself at the desk.

"*The Leavenworth Case*," he read, and I realized it was the first time I'd heard the title of my book aloud. "*A Lawyer's Story*." He put his finger on the subtitle. "So, *not* a criminal romance?"

"I've attempted to stay true to myself, to what I would prefer to read. Less romance, and more of a focus on the investigative side of things: ballistics, physical clues, witness testimonies, the sorts of things my father relies upon."

"So no romance at all?"

"Oh, no, there's certainly romance, but...it's not the central part of the mystery."

Sokol nodded and I turned to the desk.

"Before we begin," Sokol said, causing me to turn back to face him. "I want you to know that my thoughts are simply that: thoughts."

I took a deep breath and nodded, fully knowledgeable that he would give me his true opinion. This time, however, I was ready for it.

"I would appreciate it if you would share your own thoughts in return," he went on.

I laughed lightly. "You don't want to hear what I really think of your thoughts."

He glanced over to me and back to the pages. "I promise, I do."

Then his eyes began moving back and forth and I knew he was reading, so I turned back to the desk and picked up a fountain pen.

I was glad I'd given myself something to do while he read, or else I knew I'd be standing over him bouncing from foot to foot and asking, "Well? Well?" Instead, all that could be heard was the scratching of my pen and the steady crinkling of pages being turned over from one pile into the next upon Sokol's lap.

"The women in your book are much more demure than you are."

I spun in my chair, pen still in hand. "What?"

"I was just remarking that the women in your book are much more demure than you are," Sokol said in his low, steady voice. He kept his eyes focused on the page before him.

"I have to write what readers want. If I wrote a book with a woman who said everything that came to her mind, no one would read it."

"I would. It would be a nice change. I cannot stand the way women think they must suppress their emotions. Men, too, for that matter. How can we claim to be Americans when we insist on hiding our inner thoughts like characters in a Jane Austen romance?"

"I never did care for Austen's idea of propriety. Her stories rely entirely on the fact that a man and a woman should not tell each other what they are really thinking and feeling. Strip away that element, and her books would be as short as poems."

"What would the world be like, I wonder, if men and women were able to share their true thoughts with one another?" he muttered softly to his aching feet.

I blushed as I quickly ran through the words I'd just shared with him, wondering if any of them might reveal what I was attempting to keep tucked down in the depths of my heart. Really, I was no better than Elizabeth Bennet or Anne Elliot.

"Your lawyer character never has a problem sharing his thoughts, however," Sokol continued.

Had I gone too far, been too open in my manuscript? Sokol might say he wanted to know my thoughts, but I knew he didn't mean it. No one ever *really* wanted to know what another person was thinking. There was a reason why God had given us mouthpieces that opened *and* closed. Sometimes it was better to close one's mouth against the torrent of words that would only admit one's prejudices, pride, greed, meanness, and all the other sins that eventually brought people to my father for his assistance.

"That's the way with characters," I said. "One minute they're doing your bidding, playing the part of the docile female, and the next they're revealing your innermost thoughts to the reader, perhaps more so than you'd originally intended. Raymond may be a man, but I admit, he's stolen words right out of my heart."

"Then I'll be sure to pay more attention to what he says," Sokol said.

I flushed yet again and turned my focus back to my writing, taking deep, quiet breaths to slow the beating of my heart.

The clock ticked on the mantel as time melted away. I scratched at my writing while Sokol continued to read. Sometimes I'd realize I was simply sitting there listening to the sound of the pages turning, and then I'd shake my head at myself and get back to writing. Other times I was so lost in my writing I'd lose track of—

"There's a problem."

"What?" I asked, coming to stand beside Sokol as he held my precious manuscript in his hands.

"Your secretary's dream. It's not believable."

"It's a tactic used over and over again in literature." Not to mention the fact that it was based on my own.

"I know but...," he hesitated delicately and sighed. "Have you considered..." He stopped and looked up at me. "No, I see you have."

"What?"

"I just wondered... Have you considered changing the machinations themselves?"

I cocked my head and crossed my arms, stabbing myself with my pen before realizing I'd carried it over with me. "What do you mean?"

"I mean: Have you considered changing the contrivances, the ploys, the very parts that are considered 'standard devices' in literature? Have you considered throwing out the old laws and coming up with your own?"

"Like the female detective you so thoroughly disliked?"

He shook his head and looked at the fire. "No, I mean like having the dream be a lie. Readers will naturally assume it is truth because it is a common belief in this day and age that dreams tell you more than reality."

I considered my own dream, the dream that had neatly vaulted me into this writing foray. "I must admit, even I have difficulty separating dream from reality these days. It's this story..." I waved the pen in my hand. "I have to write this story. There's something compelling me to do it."

"Then don't stop. But do it your way. Do it in a way that will make you proud to see 'Anna Catherine Green' on the front cover."

I returned to my seat at the desk, my hand caressing the newest pages of my manuscript like the babe in arms they were to me. "I do not know that I have the skills. I am a poetess..."

"Come now, Miss Green." The nearness of his voice surprised me. He stood suddenly at my shoulder. A tender look not far from my own watched my hand on the stack of pages. "You're never going to hide your intelligence. You're going to exclaim it to the world, and to hell with their reactions."

"Watch your language, there is a lady present." I smiled.

"See. You've never been one to bite your tongue, or to hold back on sharing your opinion. I know you won't be able to do so with this." He leaned over my shoulder and laid his hand over mine upon the pages. "Especially with this."

I studied his hand on mine. Although the long fingers were crooked, they were warm and soft. I wondered what they would feel like upon my cheek.

"I...well, I..." The warmth of his hand seemed to be spreading up my arm and into my chest, slowing my heart to an unfamiliar beat. I could feel him looking at me. I didn't want him to stop.

"Anna," he breathed against my cheek, which was better than his hand.

"Yes?" I said, still not daring to look at him.

"Your hand is freezing. You should wear gloves more often."

I pulled my hand out from under his and clutched it in my other one, rubbing them together in embarrassment as much as to warm them.

"Here, let me help," he said, wrapping his hands around both of mine, pulling me to standing, close to him, rubbing my hands gently, tenderly, as he continued to draw me closer, closer.

"Anna," he breathed again, but this time it brushed my lips.

And then more than words were brushing.

33

Ink and Paper

"Now it is a principle which every detective recognizes, that if of a hundred leading circumstances connected with a crime, ninety-nine of these are acts pointing to the suspected party with unerring certainty, but the hundredth equally important act one which that person could not have performed, the whole fabric of suspicion is destroyed."

—*The Leavenworth Case*

The gong rang for luncheon. I blushed and said I really must be getting home, but Sokol wouldn't hear of it. My hands wouldn't stop trembling every time I reached for my wine, which I barely drank, so afraid was I that it would inhibit my thinking, something quite muddled on its own this afternoon.

When we did return to the parlor, Sokol sank onto the couch, returning the hot water bottle to his feet, it having been warmed in his absence. I moved to sit at the desk, when Sokol began coughing again.

I returned to his side, helping him with a glass of water nearby. "That doesn't sound good, Sokol. You really ought to let a doctor take a look at you."

He waved me away. "Don't you worry, my dear Anna. I'm not going anywhere without catching that murderer first."

"Sokol—what is your first name?" I asked, a small smile upon my lips as I realized I'd never heard it.

His own lips twitched in response. "Ebenezer."

My eyes widened. "No, it isn't."

"It is. It is only by pure luck that the detective you created—who I must say, is not a well-disguised version of myself—was blessed with the same Jewish name."

"I never knew," I breathed. "And when did you realize Ebenezer Gryce was based on Ebenezer Sokol?"

"From the moment you described him as 'smiling darkly at the doorknob,'" he replied, doing so with his own eyes.

I laughed. "I suppose I really didn't do a good job of hiding the true names of my inspirations, did I?"

"Not really—" His words were cut off again by another cough.

I worriedly poured more water and helped him with it again.

"That cough is in your lungs," I said, once I could hear my own thoughts again. "Water is probably not helping much."

He nodded, a deep weariness drawing his face downward. "Don't mind me. You write, I'll read. At least reading doesn't require exertion, like some other activities..." His eyes sparkled at me, something I'd only ever read about in fiction before, and I was too overwhelmed by the fact that they were sparkling at *me* to be embarrassed by the innuendo in his words.

I hurriedly returned to the desk, eager to write something distracting, but realized I was in the midst of explaining the secret love affair between Mr. Clavering and Mary. At least now I understood the words I was writing.

> *"Mary not only submits to the attentions of Mr. Clavering, but encourages them. Today she sat two hours at the piano singing over to him her favorite songs. Mr. Clavering has expressed his sentiments, and she is filled with that reckless delight which in its first flush makes one insensible to the existence of barriers which have hitherto been deemed impassable."*

I sat back, considering my next words for Amy Belden's explanation of Mary's love affair, and the ensuing anger her uncle would display upon discovering the man was an Englishman. It would give him cause to change his will, leaving everything to Eleanore, where before it had all gone to Mary.

I growled inwardly upon the realization that I'd pondered too long, and my pen had dripped ink spatters all across the lower portion of my paper.

Ink on the paper...

"Sokol, wasn't Mr. Jackson found with a pen in his hand?"

"Yes," he said. Although I hadn't turned around, I could hear his head lift from the pages he'd been reading.

"Wouldn't..." I stopped.

"Go on."

"The paper, beneath his pen," I turned so I could watch Sokol's face, "was there ink on it?"

Sokol frowned at the pen still clutched in my hand. "It was clean."

"Clean," I breathed. "Sokol, why would the paper beneath a pen held by a man who'd just been shot be clean? Shouldn't there have been ink—and blood? Lots of blood?"

Sokol's breath stopped as his eyes locked with mine.

"Where is the paper that he was writing on?"

The rheumatism in Sokol's limbs seemed to evaporate instantly, and before I knew it, we were cloaked and in a carriage, racing back to the Jackson home.

Boyle let us in, surprised to see us without warning, but I didn't stop to explain, following Sokol as he practically leapt up the stairs, his cane seemingly only there for balance.

We entered the study and immediately went to the desk, the dark splotches no longer bothering me because my mind was so intent on finding the missing letter. Sokol took a seat heavily, heedless of the coughing that returned as he did so, and began opening drawers at random. He stopped when he reached the bottom drawer, and pulled out a stack of blank manuscript paper.

"That's the drawer where you found the gun?" I asked.

Sokol nodded, pulling the drawer farther out as though checking to be sure it wasn't still there. But the Bulldog had taken the gun with him as evidence after the inquest, so I prayed it was locked up in a safe place at the jail, waiting for its moment to testify before the court. I smiled at the image of a gun speaking, but Sokol seemed to think I was smiling about something else.

"I noticed you included that little bit of information in your book."

Now I smiled for the same reason. "Yes. I included many things you've said during the course of this case."

"I noticed," he said, with a pleased look at the drawer.

"I did wonder if maybe it wasn't the murderer hiding the gun after the fact, but Mr. Jackson who moved the gun from his bedside table to his desk because he was expecting trouble? Maybe the murderer put it back here because he thought that was where it belonged."

Sokol checked the bottom of the stack of papers first, then moved the pile to the side. "Then why didn't Mr. Jackson use it to defend himself?"

"I'd assume the trouble he was expecting was different than the one that found him."

Sokol stuck his hand farther into the drawer. "No secret compartments hiding a bloody piece of paper," he said with a sigh and a short cough.

I shook my head. "I knew it was a far chance. It's more than likely been burned."

My gaze traveled about the room to the mantelpiece. I considered the items I'd catalogued before, but stopped when I saw the vase full of lighting paper.

I crossed quickly, my bustled skirts flowing behind me as I moved surely, praying my instinct was right.

I lifted down the vase and removed the rolls of paper from within. Sokol joined me by the fireplace, where we began to unroll the pieces, laying them out on the table between the armchairs.

He grunted and reached for my hand, and I looked up. Together, we'd unrolled several pieces of paper with scratched out lines of Mr. Jackson's memoir upon them, but four of the ones Sokol had unrolled had more than writing on them. Something dark red had splattered across them, seeping into the grains of the paper, marring it forever.

I recoiled.

Sokol assembled the pieces, matching the lines and torn edges until before him lay a complete letter. Complete, with blood.

"Ingenious," he murmured, looking up at me as the corners of his mouth almost broke into a smile. "Every fireplace in the world has a vase of lighting paper, which makes it the perfect place to hide a letter in plain sight. Even I would have never thought to look there—" His compliment was interrupted by another hacking cough that forced him to lean back in the chair for a minute.

He pushed the letter toward me, but I couldn't bring myself to touch it. Thankfully, the words were still mostly legible through the red stains, so I focused on them instead.

It began, "Dear, Mr. Green."

I looked up at Sokol.

"As it's addressed to your father, I do not think he'd mind you reading it," Sokol said, having caught his breath.

I agreed, so I read aloud.

"'Dear, Mr. Green,

"'Every rose has its thorn, and my rose is no exception to this rule. Lovely as she is, charming as she is, tender as she is, she is not only capable of trampling on the rights of one who trusted her, but of bruising the heart and breaking the spirit of him to whom she owes all duty, honor, and observance. I have been a fool. Perhaps not an old fool, but a fool nonetheless. It has come to my attention that my niece has kept a secret love affair from my tender gaze, and, therefore, is no longer worthy of that love and trust which I had intended to solely bestow upon her after my death.

"'To that end, I wish you to draft a new will for me and deliver it at your earliest convenience. Hitherto, I had intended to leave all to Lenore, as my sole heir, but I have decided it is necessary to divide my trust equally between her and her sister, my sister's second child, Emily. I shall be inviting Emily to join us here, in my home, as I am much desirous of knowing her better. She may prove to be the more trustworthy of the two sisters. Until such time as I am proven otherwise, I desire to have it written that neither shall inherit upon my death until both girls are eighteen. Perhaps in a few years, my niece will have learned it is better to—'"

Here the letter broke off.

Sokol sat back in the chair and considered his fingertips.

"So Mr. Jackson didn't know Emily was already living in his home," I whispered, getting to what I considered the heart of the matter. "I wonder if Miss Kelthorpe knew she had a sister, even if she didn't know that sister was Emily."

Sokol did not respond, but continued to examine his cuticles.

I watched his face.

Finally, he asked his fingers, "Your father was unaware that Mr. Jackson wished to change his will?"

"Yes."

"He knew the facts of the original will?"

"Yes."

"So as of his death, Mr. Jackson has left everything to Miss Kelthorpe, as this letter did not come to light?"

"Yes," I said slowly.

"Unfortunately the finding of this letter does not bode well for Miss Kelthorpe."

I nodded. "I have a difficult time understanding why Emily would blackmail her. She had no reason to, since things were working out for her better than she might have ever hoped, without her having to lift a finger."

"It does support our little theory of the secret lover being uncovered by Mr. Jackson," Sokol said. "I suppose Emily was blackmailing Miss Kelthorpe with the fact that if Mr. Jackson found out, she'd be written out of the will. In fact, that wasn't the case. Instead, his reaction was to add Emily to the will, so it would have been to her benefit for him to learn the truth."

"Yes, but which lover did Mr. Jackson learn about?"

"I see you found the letter," a voice said from the doorway.

34

Confession

"[Anna Katharine Green's] criminals are creatures of circumstance rather than hard-hearted wretches. They have an air of relief at being tracked down—a sure sign of a redeeming flaw in their devilry."

—**T. Fisher Unwin,** ***Good Reading About Many Books Mostly by Their Authors***

Mr. Farwell closed the door to the study behind him, keeping his eyes and a gun trained on the two of us beside the fireplace.

I grasped the four parts of the letter together and clutched them to my chest, determined that Mr. Farwell would not get ahold of the evidence.

"You know what this letter contains?" Sokol asked.

"I'm the one who put it there. I didn't need to read the letter to know what it said, however." Mr. Farwell moved to stand behind Mr. Jackson's desk, looking at the top and running his empty hand across it as though he could still see it sitting there beneath Mr. Jackson's pen. "I'd already overheard them arguing—Miss Kelthorpe and her uncle. Heard him telling her she would be written out of his will over the folly of her loving me."

I opened my mouth, but didn't speak.

"Instead, the estate would all go to his sister's illegitimate child, the daughter of a whore. I couldn't let that be, not on my account. Transitory emotions with some are terrific passions with me. To be sure, they are quiet and concealed ones, coiled serpents that make no stir till aroused; but then, deadly in their spring and relentless in their action. And so..." Mr. Farwell paused and made a fist against the desktop. "I shot him."

Sokol's eyes narrowed. "When did you shoot him?"

"When? Why does that matter?"

I wondered the same thing.

"*When* did you shoot him?" Sokol repeated.

"I did not check the time. I just walked in and shot him, while he was writing that letter." He pointed with the gun to the torn pieces of paper in my hands.

"When?"

Mr. Farwell threw his empty hand in the air. "I don't know. One o'clock?"

"Are you certain?"

"Yes."

"It wasn't earlier?"

"Earlier?"

"Yes, perhaps before the maid knocked to ask if you'd be joining for lunch."

"I...I don't think so." Mr. Farwell scratched the back of his neck nervously.

"You don't think so?"

"No."

"What are you getting at, Sokol?" I murmured.

"Mr. Jackson was not shot at one o'clock," Sokol said, his voice strong and sure. "He was shot sometime before lunch, most likely while the staff were all downstairs having lunch, so they most certainly wouldn't have heard anything."

"But I heard it out in the street. I may not have had the time exactly correct, but it was certainly after lunch and not before."

"Yes, you heard the shot you were all meant to hear," Sokol told the gun in Mr. Farwell's hand. "Your experiments and discoveries of just how little sound leaves this room told me something quite important. I do not think it was coincidence that the window—the only way someone might have heard the shot from outside this room—just happened to be open when Mr. Jackson was 'killed.'"

I looked to the window, currently closed as before.

"The murderer shot Mr. Jackson earlier, and then shot a second bullet out the window later, to call everyone to the room to discover the body and to hide the real time of death."

"But the coroner..."

"It is difficult to pinpoint the exact time of death. When surgeons are capable of doing that, murders in this state will be solved in half the time."

"The only person in this room was Mr. Farwell." I waved toward the secretary, who stood there listening, still as stone.

"Correct."

"So when Bridget knocked to ask if they'd be having lunch and Mr. Farwell declined, Mr. Jackson was already dead?"

"Correct," said Mr. Farwell. "Are you two finished?"

"Not quite," said Sokol. "Mr. Farwell, you say you shot Mr. Jackson for Miss Kelthorpe's sake, before he could change his will to say otherwise."

Mr. Farwell nodded slowly, as though thrown off by the change in subject.

"But you also said—" Sokol suddenly broke into chest-wracking coughs, unable to continue. He slumped into a chair, clutching his cane for support as his breath left him over and over again, and my fears followed it. Why would this chest cold not leave him?

"May I get him some water?" I asked the secretary.

Surprisingly, he said yes, and I moved to the sherry cabinet, hoping there was still some water stored within alongside the alcohol. I flung the doors open and bit my lip in dismay when only sherry greeted me, and less than what had been there the last I'd looked. I quickly poured Sokol a glass, hoping some liquid in any form would help.

While my torso was hidden by the sherry cabinet doors, I took the opportunity to slip the torn bits of letter into the belt along my shirtwaist, praying Mr. Farwell wouldn't notice.

I returned with the sherry to Sokol and he took small sips. Thankfully, it seemed to help.

I took the opportunity to run through my thoughts. I wasn't certain where Sokol was headed with his questioning, but I did know there had been something else the secretary had said, that I was fairly certain he'd misinterpreted.

Sokol finally gathered his breath and nodded to me.

I stood slowly and faced the man with the gun. "I believe you when you say you didn't read the letter, Mr. Farwell. For there was some information there that might have changed your mind about your actions."

"What are you talking about?"

"If you'd read the letter, you would have seen that Emily was Mr. Jackson's *second* niece. And that Lenore was Emily's sister."

"Emily's—but… How can that…"

"Mr. Jackson adopted his first niece when she was born out of wedlock, but when he learned his sister had fallen into trouble a second time, he refused to help the second daughter, as a lesson to his sister, in hopes that she would change her ways."

"But…"

"In the letter, you would have also read that Mr. Jackson had decided, based on Lenore's actions breaking his trust, that he would be adding Emily to his will, not striking Lenore out."

"So…Emily…she would have inherited…"

"Yes. You and Emily might have been happy together, would you not?"

Mr. Farwell frowned in confusion, the gun slowly lowering in his hand as he tried to work through what I was saying.

"I know you loved Emily, even if you later killed her."

"She's…dead? I didn't—" He stopped himself.

I raised a brow and waited for him to continue.

When he did not, Sokol said in a low voice, "What's more, you said, 'not on my account.'"

Mr. Farwell nodded slowly. "Mr. Jackson was about to write Miss Kelthorpe out of his will because she was in love with me." His chest puffed slightly at this statement.

"I know for a fact that Miss Kelthorpe is soon to be the elated and happy Mrs. Rohlfs," I said.

Mr. Farwell's face became marble—pale, cold stone. "She is not."

"Yes. She is. He's been at our house almost every day since her arrival, and there has been nothing in her manner toward him to suggest otherwise. I can show you his love letters to her, or you could ask her yourself. They had planned to elope the night Mr. Jackson was killed. She's going to marry Mr. Rohlfs as soon as the charges against her are dropped."

"No. She. Is. Not. She loves me." The words were cold as ice, the sting of them flung in my face. My heart pounded as I kept my eyes focused on the gun in the madman's hand, which had raised once more to aim directly at my heart.

"I'm afraid it is true. Although Mr. Jackson was about to change his will on account of forbidden love, it was not yours."

"NO!" Mr. Farwell screamed, the word bouncing off the walls of the room.

I took a step back in surprise. His calm demeanor had finally cracked. We'd just had to find the right crevice in which to slip the dynamite.

Sokol rose shakily from the chair to stand in front of me, leaning heavily on the head of his cane as though he wished he had two.

"Miss Green's words are truth. To deny them is to admit your own folly."

"No! No!" Mr. Farwell continued, bringing both hands to his head as he shook it back and forth, the gun pressed against his temple, forgotten.

"It...it was all for her," the secretary cried, letting his hands hit the desk with a thud, his anger falling like a curtain, the gun dropping from limp fingers. "Emily...oh, Emily, what have I done?" His eyes were wistful, no longer seeing me and Sokol. "She and I were... But then I thought Lenore... We would be so happy, living on her inheritance. We'd have everything we'd ever wanted, with no one in our way. But Emily..."

"She was sent poison under the guise of a dream potion," Sokol finished for him.

We'd deduced as much on our own. I couldn't believe how accurately we'd pieced it all together.

Mr. Farwell sank into Mr. Jackson's chair. "Poisoned for a dream..."

He let his head fall into his hands. A wave of pity passed over me, as though it had begun with Mr. Farwell and then crested, now filling the entire room.

"But...you're wrong...," he whispered.

Sokol and I exchanged a glance.

"She was always having headaches. It started with a pill every once in awhile. But then it grew to every day, and then more than one. She asked me to cover for her, to say the orders for more pills was due to their use by others in the house. She said she loved me..."

He looked up at me, his eyes heavy. "I didn't have the key to the medicine cabinet. I didn't send Emily that poison. But I might as well have..."

Horror skittered across Mr. Farwell's face. "My God! What have I done!" He pounded the desk. "Lies...lies...all because I thought... I thought Lenore loved..."

Her name sounded dreadful upon his lips, half curse and half prayer.

His eyes fell on the gun on top of the desk. He looked back up at the two of us.

I saw it. The switch.

"I was nothing more to her than another cog in her dreadful machine. Show her the letter. If you don't believe me, ask her to her cruel, bewitching face. She'll tell you what I did for her. Then she'll hang for this broken heart that is as much hers to bear as it is my own."

He grabbed the gun.

I had just enough time to swing my head into Sokol's back to hide the sight.

The gun went off.

35

Home

"I will not lose body and soul for nothing."

—*The Leavenworth Case*

When I raised my eyes again, another body lay upon the desktop, this one with the gun still in hand.

Thankfully, no one had heard the shot, leaving us alone with the body while we considered our next steps.

My next step was to throw up in the fireplace.

"Anna, I'm so sorry," Sokol said, wrapping his arms about me after I'd wiped my mouth with his handkerchief. "I'm so, so sorry."

Shock rolled through my body from my head to the tips of my shoes. I focused on the strength of Sokol's arms pulling me into his shoulder, my head tucked beneath his chin in a spot that

I might have enjoyed if the circumstances had been different. Then he began to cough and he pulled away. I kept my eyes on him, the one I cared about, and not on the body at the desk.

Sokol sank into a chair once more, and eventually stopped coughing. Then he tried to distract me with business.

"We must call for one of the staff. They need to call the coroner."

I nodded.

"Then we need to get to your house. We're not finished yet."

I nodded again.

I felt terrible informing Boyle he must call for the coroner once more—another dead body in the study.

While we waited below in the front parlor, Sokol jotted off a letter to my father, and asked Boyle to send it post-haste, so it would arrive before we did.

Thankfully, Mr. Hammond was as prompt as before, and we were able to give him our statements, leaving his declaration that Mr. Farwell had died by his own hand clear as crystal.

We were silent as the carriage took us from Mr. Jackson's to my house one more time. As Sokol and I alighted, I gripped his free hand tightly. We would need to do this together.

I entered the front parlor with Sokol and my father behind me, mentally preparing myself for the coming interview that must happen while we waited for the police.

Over the past few weeks, Mother Grace and Sarah had often kept Lenore company over their embroidery, helping to keep her spirits up with plans for the future, whilst I had been distractedly writing in my room. I was grateful to see that today they'd gone out to call on friends, so they would only learn later of the sad denouement that had occurred in their absence.

Unfortunately, however, Lenore was not alone.

"Mr. Rohlfs," said my father upon entering and finding the two lovers standing before the fireplace, hand-in-hand.

Lenore looked up, her blue eyes studying each person's face.

"What seems to be the trouble?" Mr. Rohlfs asked, taking in our countenances with a glance. "Shouldn't Miss Kelthorpe, who is awaiting trial, be the one with the long face? And yet the three of you come as though there should be a fourth horseman behind you."

Sokol stopped at the window, while my father and I each took a seat facing Lenore, who slowly let go of Mr. Rohlfs's hand.

"I fear something has not gone to plan," Lenore said, dropping her eyes to mine.

She was right. "We have some news," I began. "You might want to sit down."

"Oh?" Lenore lowered herself into a chair.

Mr. Rohlfs rested his hand on her shoulder in a sign of protection. I wondered how far he would go.

"Mr. Farwell is dead."

Lenore's eyes lifted in surprise, but a look of satisfaction crossed her brow slowly enough for me to catch it. She was clearly relieved rather than saddened by this news.

"I am sorry to hear it," she said, clasping her hands in her lap. "Can anything be done?"

"No," Father replied. "The coroner has confirmed suicide."

"Oh, dear!" Lenore said, raising a hand to her mouth.

She was almost as good an actor as Mr. Rohlfs.

"Emily is also dead: poisoned."

Lenore's eyes flashed. "Poison? I thought she, too, was a suicide."

"Where did you hear that?" Father asked.

Lenore sat back in her chair, fingering the arm. "Didn't the paper say something about it this morning?"

All three of us shook our heads. Sokol's request that nothing be reported until at least that evening had, thankfully, been followed to the letter.

Unfortunately for Lenore.

"I thought I… Perhaps I heard it from someone?" She looked up at Mr. Rohlfs, as though he might have the answer, but he shook his head to indicate he had not said anything.

"Who is Emily?" he asked.

"No one," said Lenore dismissively, then seemed to think better of her response. "Only the maid who tried to blackmail me the night before my uncle died. Oh, my head," she said, raising her hand to her forehead dramatically. She reached for a small box on her chatelaine, removing two pills, which she drank down with some water on a table beside her.

"If she was murdered by Mr. Farwell, does that mean…does that mean he also murdered my uncle?" She looked to Sokol, but he was studying the bay window curtains as though the answer was behind them.

"What makes you say Mr. Farwell murdered Emily?" my father asked.

"Oh…I…," she flustered again. "I just assumed from the manner of your telling. You said she was poisoned."

"Yes," I said. "But Mr. Farwell did not kill Emily. He did not kill your uncle."

"How could you know that for certain?" Lenore asked, and I could hear the disdain hiding behind her teeth.

"Before he died, he revealed a few things to Mr. Sokol and myself," I said.

"You were there? How terrible for you!" Mr. Rohlfs said, and I appreciated his concern.

I removed the strips of letter from my belt and laid them out together on the table between us. "He said you could enlighten us about this."

Lenore and Mr. Rohlfs leaned forward. He glanced at the beginning of the letter, looked up at Father, and then continued to read.

When Lenore was finished, she put out a hand upon the letter. "So he did intend to change his will," she said slowly, sadly. "He must have learned of Charles, after all." She reached out to take his hand.

I raised a brow. *That* was the part of the letter she chose to remark upon?

"It does not seem so terrible," said Mr. Rohlfs. "After all, wasn't it odd that he hadn't included your sister in the inheritance originally?"

"Not at all," said Lenore, though she took another look at the letter, as though realizing she'd missed something. "I...I did not know I had a sister."

"So, you were unaware Emily was your sister?" Father asked, his lawyerly voice covering his concern.

"I had no idea." Lenore shook her head, her hand crumpling the bottom portion of the letter.

"Why didn't you mention it then, just now?" I asked. "Upon reading the letter, that was the first thing I noticed."

"She… I did not know she was my sister." Lenore glanced at the letter and then to Father. "I…"

"I think you did," I said.

Lenore's eyes flashed in anger, but I was done dancing around the truth.

"I am sorry, Lenore. I believe you shot your uncle and killed Emily, though you tried to make it look like Mr. Farwell did it for you."

Lenore laughed. Her blonde head tilted back, revealing her perfect white throat.

No one else laughed.

Mr. Rohlfs moved so he could see Lenore's face, though she avoided his eyes.

When she stopped, she looked at Sokol, who of course was still questioning the curtains, and finally to my father, who was the only one brave enough to meet her gaze.

"Tell me what happened, Miss Kelthorpe," he said, as though it were only the two of them in the interview.

"I already told you. At one o'clock I met with the cook to discuss the week's menu, as we always did at the beginning of the week."

Father sighed and shook his head. "Miss Kelthorpe, I am your lawyer. I can only defend you if I know the entire story. The true story." He looked at Sokol and back. "We know Mr.

Jackson was not shot at one o'clock. Where were you earlier? Before luncheon?"

Lenore searched the room again, looking for a friendly face. Mr. Rohlfs was stepping back from her, his brow furrowed as he tried to work out in his head what this all meant. I wished him luck with it, for it had taken me the better part of the carriage ride over to piece it all together in my own head.

Lenore contemplated her fingers before finally looking up resignedly.

"I lied."

When she didn't elaborate, Father asked, "About what?"

Lenore's lips pursed, as though considering which one to admit to, which lie was the one with the lesser consequences.

"The night before my uncle's death, after Emily came to my door, I went and knocked at Mr. Farwell's. I told him what she had just done to me, how she'd tried to blackmail me by telling me she knew about Mr. Rohlfs, and she also knew my uncle was going to write me out of the will if he knew about him. She claimed she would keep silent for one hundred dollars. One hundred dollars! Can you believe it? I figured Mr. Farwell deserved to know what kind of woman he'd fallen in love with. He claimed he knew nothing about it, and was shocked by Emily's behavior, renouncing his affections for her on the spot and swearing he'd do anything, anything to help me." Her hands gripped the flounces of her skirts. "I didn't know he meant killing two people."

Sokol cleared his throat, drawing all eyes to him. "Try again, Miss Kelthorpe," he said in a low tone.

"Excuse me?"

"Try telling the truth again. That wasn't it."

Lenore flushed red, perhaps in embarrassment, but most likely in anger that her lies weren't working this time. She was playing to a crowd not interested in her best recitations.

She turned to Mr. Rohlfs and pleaded. "That is the tru—"

Sokol raised a hand, the other still clutching his cane. "You claim Emily blackmailed you with a threat that would cause Mr. Jackson to change his will, but this does not make sense. If she knew how to make Mr. Jackson write a new will, she wouldn't have blackmailed you at all, as that meant she was to be the new co-heir—to a tune much higher than one hundred dollars."

Lenore's color heightened. "I couldn't let her touch—" She stopped too late.

"Touch what, Miss Kelthorpe?" Sokol interrupted.

She paled.

"Did you dismiss Emily O'Connell for quite different reasons, Miss Kelthorpe?" Sokol asked. "Perhaps on the grounds of her relationship with Mr. Farwell?"

Lenore's grip on her skirts tightened.

"She didn't blackmail you. You'd discovered the truth of her identity. You knew she was your sister. You couldn't have her hanging around, winning over your uncle, getting him to add her to his will so she could inherit all that money—"

"Never!" Lenore spat, the cobra revealing its venom. "I *earned* that money. I gave everything, *everything* for that man. Fifteen years kept inside, never knowing the beauty the world had to offer, and then he dares to disinherit me just because I fell in love?"

She turned fully to Mr. Rohlfs, her eyes searching his. "He wanted to keep me locked up forever, caring for him, doting upon him, like some slave. And then Emily came along, and... She would have... If only she hadn't been... My sister..." Her face softened suddenly, and I wondered at the change in countenance which seemed to fly across the young woman's face with each passing statement.

"Precisely: she was your sister, Lenore," said Mr. Rohlfs softly. "Was it really so bad to have to share?"

"Yes," Lenore snapped. "I shouldn't have to, not after all I'd been through, after all I'd done for him. I didn't complain once. Not once. All those times he kept me in."

"He only did it out of love," I said. "He wanted to protect you—"

Lenore screamed. "There it is again! That word: protecting. I. Don't. Need. Protecting!" She pointed to the letter. "She just waltzes in, out of nowhere, and announces she's my *sister*? Like she thinks that will make me pleased?"

"Well, shouldn't it? You wouldn't have been alone," I said.

Lenore shook her head. "She wasn't worth it. She came to me, said she felt it was time I knew the truth, since we were so close, and would I help her speak with our uncle, persuade him to let her be a part of the family. Little did she know, my uncle and I were not on good terms at the moment. We'd just had an argument after he discovered I was in love."

Mr. Rohlfs smiled but Lenore spit out, "Not with you."

She couldn't have hit him harder if she'd used her own hand.

I looked from Lenore to Mr. Rohlfs and back again. "But I thought—"

"I don't need a man to save me. I'm perfectly capable of doing so myself. I told my uncle so, that I was not in love, but he wouldn't believe me. I had played the part of the young girl falling for her first love too well. But no matter. I had it all planned out. Farwell made a perfect scapegoat, and then Charles turned up to speak with my uncle. Either of them would have taken the leap for me and I couldn't have cared less. Charles and Farwell, they were just...fun." She gave a cruel smile toward Mr. Rohlfs. "So much fun. But with my inheritance, I could have any man I wanted. *Any* man! Who'd settle for a secretary or an actor?"

I watched Mr. Rohlfs's face crumple. I wanted to reach out to him, to comfort him, but now was not the time.

"What happened to Emily?" my father asked softly.

Lenore shrugged. "I told her I had a plan to get her into my uncle's good graces, but that she must leave so that I might enact it. She did what I asked. She disappeared. Then it was a small matter of writing her a letter from her lover, 'Mr. Farwell,' with a 'magic sleep potion' that would help her dream of her 'future husband.'" She patted her chatelaine, from which hung the key to the medicine cabinet. "Those sorts of girls are always so gullible."

"Your own sister...," Mr. Rohlfs whispered, his disgust clear across his face.

"A sister who'd lied to me. Who made me care for her only in the hope of stealing my inheritance." Lenore's voice began to rise again in her passion, as though the word were a provocation, reminding her of what all this had been for. "An inheritance which *I'd* earned. It was mine by right. *Mine.* I had to be rid of her. And him. And then I'd be free. Free! To live on the money I'd *earned*."

Lenore grasped the bits of letter and threw them into the fire as we all rose to our feet and cried, "Stop!"

But it was too late; each scripted letter burned quickly, becoming one with the fire.

"He told me he would do that for me. He promised he'd take care of it," she muttered, watching the flames devour the last words her uncle had ever written.

"Mr. Farwell?" I asked quietly.

Lenore nodded. "He promised he'd do anything for me."

"He lied for you." I was astounded by this young woman. How had she come to this point? Could protecting someone from the world really have such a drastic opposite effect? "He came back from gathering his notes and found you holding a smoking gun, your uncle dead at your hands. But you knew he loved you, even more than Emily, and would do anything for you. That part of your little story was true. He lied to Bridget through the door, said he and Mr. Jackson would be working through lunch. Then he fired a gunshot out the window for you while you were meeting with the cook, giving you an alibi, reloading and cleaning the gun so it would appear that only one shot had been fired, and not two."

"When would he have time to do that?" Mr. Rohlfs asked.

I paused. I walked through the study mentally, and then remembered how there wasn't any water in the sherry cabinet, which meant… "When Lenore fainted—though really she *pretended* to faint. Just like she did at the inquest: at the opportune moment. When she originally told us about finding her uncle," I motioned to my father, "she was able to do so without fainting, but at the inquest, well, it was beneficial to her to get out of having to lie more than was absolutely necessary, and to earn a bit of pity with the jury."

Perhaps I hadn't been so creative in giving my women fake fainting spells in my book after all...

"While Mr. Farwell sent the others for water and smelling salts, he took the opportunity to get rid of the evidence, including the letter Mr. Jackson was in the middle of writing." I waved to the fire. Then, a light went on in my head. "But then he put the gun back in the desk, and not in Mr. Jackson's bedside table, which was where you'd found it." I pointed at Lenore. "You lost your key in your uncle's fireplace when you went to take it. Which was why you seemed surprised at the inquest that the gun had not been found in your uncle's bedroom."

Lenore shook her head. "I should have killed that silly secretary sooner. He was a loose end that I thought I had time to tie off. But I guess I didn't."

"He would have told us the truth eventually, once he learned you had no intention of marrying him." I glanced at Mr. Rohlfs. "Or anyone."

"By then he'd have been dead," said Lenore matter-of-factly. "A little extra something in my uncle's sherry and he'd have painlessly joined Emily in sweet dreamland."

I tried to keep the horrified feeling in my stomach from rising.

"Don't look so shocked. Everyone takes one look at me and thinks I need help. It was worth it, just to know I did it all *myself*."

36

Summation

"And leaving them there, with the light of growing hope and confidence on their faces, we went out again into the night..."

—***The Leavenworth Case***

My father walked with Lenore between two policemen to the door, grabbing his case as he went.

There was nothing more we could do for her now. The rest was up to Lady Justice.

"Mr. Jackson said it himself standing in this very parlor, not one day before he died," I said with a sad shake of my head as the front door closed. "One should never deliberate upon the causes which have led to the destruction of a rich man without taking into account that most common passion of the human race."

Sokol nodded. "In the end, the motive was the usual one of self-interest."

"How could I have been so blind?" Mr. Rohlfs said, sinking onto the edge of the couch like a man in quicksand. He let his head fall into his hands.

Sokol moved to sit across from him, his hands on his cane before him. "She certainly put on quite a performance."

"No one saw the truth," I said comfortingly, sitting beside the actor at a discreet distance.

"You two did," Mr. Rohlfs said from between his hands.

"The blessing of experience," Sokol said modestly.

"She played the role of doting lover to perfection," said Mr. Rohlfs, and I noticed he had yet to use Lenore's name since she'd slapped him with her words. "She made me believe every word."

"I've often been struck by how even my father, in the role of lawyer, seems to be playing a part. He even practices his lines before he delivers them to the court." I looked at Sokol. "The detective must often disguise his intellect to lull the people around him into a false sense of security. I suppose even I must play a role now and then, depending on who I am around."

"Daughter, sister, author?" Sokol suggested.

"You forget detective." I smiled.

"It appears Shakespeare was right." Mr. Rohlfs lifted his head.

"About what in particular?" I asked.

"'All the world's a stage, and all the men and women merely players.'"

* * *

Mr. Rohlfs excused himself shortly after, leaving Sokol and I alone in the front parlor.

We stood together, gazing out the window. The gray sky was a painted mural of our thoughts.

"You were quite marvelous," I said, allowing myself to say aloud what I never would have before.

Sokol moved closer to my side. "And you made me believe a female detective might not be such a bad idea after all."

I blushed. "Detective Gryce has made *The Leavenworth Case* worlds better by his presence. But perhaps in a future book—"

My thoughts were stopped with a kiss.

Father returned alone that evening, long after Sokol had made his own way home.

"Miss Kelthorpe?" I asked.

Father shook his head wearily. "I thought it might do her good to consider her next steps from inside a jail cell."

"Won't that cause the judge to think you believe she's guilty?"

"I won't have her staying in this house," he responded.

I went to my father and hugged him. "I'm so sorry," I said.

He held me out by my shoulders before him so he could look me in the eye. "At least one good thing has come of this whole affair."

I raised a brow.

"If I'm not mistaken, you've completed your first mystery novel."

I smiled.

"And Sokol asked if you'd come by first thing tomorrow morning."

I blushed.

"Now, is there something you'd like to tell me?"

"Nothing yet, Father," I said. "Not yet."

***

"I've written a new poem," I said upon arriving at Sokol's the next morning and finding him again confined to his couch, bandaged and bundled in blankets, though the room was quite warm with a roaring fire.

Sokol's response was to break into coughs that caused me to run to his side, leaning over to help him with the glass of water that stood ready on the table beside him.

"Please," he finally croaked out, and beckoned with his bandaged hand for me to read to him.

I stood and moved to the end of the couch, so he could see me without effort.

"Shadows," I began.

"A zephyr stirs the maple trees,
 And straightway o'er the grass
The shadows of their branches shift;
 Shift, Love, but do not pass.
So, though with time a change may come
 Within my steadfast heart,
The shadow of thy form may stir,
 But can not, Love, depart."

I ended and considered the man on the couch, whose penetrating gaze was studying my lips as though he wished they were not so far away.

Finally, he looked up, and our eyes met. The sadness within his did not prepare me for his next words.

"I love you, Anna Green. I'm sorry it took me too long to say it."

"It's only been a few weeks since we first met," I said, flushing at his words.

Sokol coughed, but then it turned into another hacking fit that drove him forward, bent over his hands. I came to him and offered water once he had paused long enough to breathe.

After I'd set down the glass, I found a chair and moved it closer to him, so that I could hold his hands, even if he could not hold mine.

"You didn't answer," he finally whispered.

"I didn't hear a question," I said, though I knew to what he was referring. "You know I love you, Ebenezer Sokol. I love you enough to create a detective entirely in your image. You shall live on for eternity as Ebenezer Gryce, the world's greatest detective."

"Oh, Anna," he said, and I realized suddenly that his voice was choking not just from irritation by the cough, but from something else.

"Sokol, what is going on?"

He shook his head, and when his eyes connected again with mine, the piercing look was dampened by tears.

"Sokol," I said, grasping his hand tightly. "Tell me what is going on."

He tried to take my hands in his, laying one bandaged hand over mine, and one underneath. "The doctor was here this morning," he said slowly. "He gave me a week at most to live."

My breath left me. I reached for a second glass on the table and poured it for myself, taking large gulps that hurt my throat on their way down.

Only then did I look at Sokol again.

"The rheumatism? The cough?"

"Pneumonia."

I nodded perfunctorily. I should have seen that. No doubt his lungs were weaker already because of the rheumatism.

"Was it from standing in the rain at the funeral?"

"It might have been. It doesn't matter now."

"You didn't have to come to the funeral. You could have stayed away, like every other normal person in New York City."

Sokol shook his head. "And miss even a single moment more with you? Never."

He held his hand out to me and I took it, unwrapping it so I could hold his crooked fingers, feel them pressed against my own one…last…

He drew me to him. I fell to my knees beside the couch so that I could rest my head on his chest, beneath his chin, where it fit so perfectly.

He brushed my hair gently, kissing my head, my forehead, whatever he could reach.

"Have you ever heard of a lodestar?"

I shook my head into his chest, still fighting the wave of despair threatening to push me under.

"It's something my mother told me once. She said, 'Someday, you will meet a girl, and she will be your lodestar. You will be unable to escape her pull, and she will draw you ever closer to her, guiding you home.'"

Sokol lifted my head so that he could look into my eyes.

"You are the lodestar of my life," he said.

It was then the tears began to fall, quietly, softly, like rain.

* * *

"How can I lose him?" I whispered into Mother Grace's shoulder, my arms and fingers wrapped around a pillow like it might be able to draw some of the anguish from my heart.

She ran a comforting hand over my head, though nothing could fix the pain, would ever fix the pain.

"It shouldn't hurt so much when I've only just realized how much he means to me—but it does! How can something so beautiful become so terrible in an instant, to the point you wonder why it had to happen at all? It's like I only just sucked in a mouthful of air and already the waves are thrusting me back under..."

Mother Grace quietly continued the motion across my hair. "I suppose you will have to learn how to breathe underwater."

I squeezed the pillow harder. "What if I can't? I can't eat, I can't sleep, I can't even write. What am I going to do?"

Mother Grace lifted my face to look at her, just as Sokol had done.

"Who are you? Some dime novel heroine who swoons and faints? You're the brave one, the brilliant one. You must find a reason to go on. Your family, your friends, your faith. Life is full of sinkholes. If we let them pull us under every time we meet one, there would be none of us left."

I sat up. "But what if...what if..."

"Let God handle the 'ifs.' He's had more practice." Mother Grace smiled softly. "You just keep moving forward. You're not dying. You've got more to do in this life. I don't know what, but it's out there, waiting for you, so long as you get up and go for it."

"But without Sokol—"

"Yes, but with me. With your dad, your sister, your brothers—there are so many people who love you. We're all here for you." Mother Grace put a hand to my cheek and looked at me directly. "Now snap out of it."

I tried to smile. "You sound like Sokol."

"Maybe that's who you need to hear from right now."

* * *

It took all my strength to leave Sokol's side each evening, and I returned before light the next day, and the next.

On the fourth day, when I entered, he wasn't on the couch, and my throat slammed shut like the gate to a castle.

Fobbs came forward, however, and motioned that I follow him upstairs. I did so slowly, my breath only returning to me when I saw Sokol's open eyes and the twitch of his mouth that was his smile beckoning me from where he lay propped up in bed on pillows. I ran to him.

He wasn't gone yet. He hadn't left me...yet.

I still had more time.

His hand raised to my cheek, not bandaged for once, perhaps in realization that nothing could help him now. I rested my face against the knobby fingers, then took them and kissed them.

"I'm so sorry, Sokol. I'm so sorry."

"Whatever for?" His voice was so weak.

"It was all for nought. She was guilty. I have to change the ending of my book. I was wrong."

"No. Don't change it. It's how it's meant to be. A happy ending."

"But not in real life." I tried to hold back the tears. I wanted to be brave for him. But I was finding my heart couldn't resist much longer.

"Novels aren't meant to be reality. Readers don't want a real ending when they finish a book. They want a happy ending. They want to know that good conquers evil, that the murderer is caught, that the right man ends up with the girl—"

"And then leaves her?"

"True love conquers all. Especially in fiction. If a person wants to read about reality, they can pick up anything that's not a novel."

"I want my happy ending, Sokol. I want it with you."

"I know, my love. I know." He pressed his thin but still warm hand against my cheek and wiped the tear trickling down it. "It seems God has other plans for our story. But your story, this novel, is your creation. Give it the ending you want."

I kissed his hand. "I will, I promise. And they lived happily ever after."

"Well, something less trite than that, of course." He knew me so well.

"You will always be the lodestar of my life, guiding me home."

"That's better," he said, and so went into a dream from which he never woke.

Epilogue

Six Years Later

"Have I read *The Leavenworth Case*? I have read it through at one sitting.... Her powers of invention are so remarkable—she has so much imagination and so much belief (a most important qualification for our art) in what she writes, that I have nothing to report of myself, so far, but most sincere admiration.... Dozens of times in reading the story I have stopped to admire the fertility of invention, the delicate treatment of incidents—and the fine perception of the influence of events on the personages of the story."

—Letter from Wilkie Collins to George Putnam, reprinted in *The Critic*

The line to meet me was out the front door and around the corner; according to my publisher, George Putnam, it stretched all the way to the tavern on the next corner, and still the people preferred to wait rather than settle for a drink instead of my book.

My book.

I couldn't believe it. Every author's dream, and I was living it.

Certainly there were those who doubted. A man in the Pennsylvania Legislature had reportedly protested that I must have used a *nom de plume*, that a man wrote the story—maybe a man already famous—and signed a woman's name to it. "The story was manifestly beyond a woman's powers."

A New York lawyer had happened to be present at the politicians' discussion. "You are mistaken," he'd said. "I have seen the author of *The Leavenworth Case* and conversed with her, and her name is really Miss Green."

"Then she must have got some man to help her," the more obstinate theorists had retorted.

To which my father had stated, upon hearing this story related, that they strongly reminded him of the characters whom I had portrayed so skillfully, the self-willed characters that aimed so well, but did not hit even the target, not to mention the bull's-eye.

Mr. Putnam told me *The Leavenworth Case* was an immediate bestseller. I was "an overnight success"—they'd never sold so many copies so quickly. Even Yale College had been in contact with them because they wanted to use my book in their law classes to illustrate the perils of trusting in circumstantial evidence.

"They want to make certain we have enough copies to supply their students!" Mr. Putnam told me excitedly.

But it was still hard. Six years and it was still difficult not to wince whenever someone asked me where my inspiration had come from for Detective Ebenezer Gryce.

"Why did you choose to give him rheumatism? I have an uncle who suffers from rheumatism. He says maybe he'll take up detecting, too."

They'd laugh at this, like it was a joke, not understanding how deeply the comment pained me.

"I didn't choose to give him rheumatism," I wanted to say. "He came that way. I didn't choose to give him eyes that pierced and at the same time never rested on you unless he wanted to make absolutely certain you were listening. I didn't choose...because he came that way."

I could never admit aloud that my greatest creation was not my own, but someone God had sent to me already packaged too perfectly for me to change.

It had taken me four years just to consider returning to the manuscript. In the meantime, I'd written enough melancholy love poetry to fill a book, and though Father said they were wonderful, no publisher was interested in them.

Then one day, my father opened the paper and gasped before handing it wordlessly to me. There I read that Lenore Kelthorpe had been found dead in her jail cell. Her doctor had continued to prescribe her the migraine pills she required, but instead of taking them, she'd hidden them in a loose stone in the cell wall. Then, once she'd collected enough, she'd taken them all at once, and, being not much more than a condensed form of morphine, she'd overdosed and died.

The murderer who had inspired *The Leavenworth Case* was now dead. I was compelled to tell her story, even if the end result was a piece of fiction.

When I finally sat down to rewrite, I only saw the manuscript's flaws. Because I'd taken years to return to it, it greeted me like a fresh piece of writing that wasn't even mine. Which meant I was less timid in the editing.

Some chapters of *The Leavenworth Case* were rewritten as many as twelve times. I spent two years lost in my own world, and much of the writing had to be done over and over again. On several occasions I felt sorely tempted to burn the manuscript and forget it. It was not until the story was two-thirds written for the fourth time that I dared say anything about it to anyone, admitting that after all these years, once again I was trying my hand at mystery.

After reading the first half of my book, Father agreed I had found my place. And then he became my critic, immediately suggesting many modifications, as I'd always suspected he would. I accepted them without question, as his suggestions were all along the line of practicality, logical development, and conformity to the legal technicalities in the parts which had to do with the courts. I was grateful to him for his kindness in helping me, but I had to confess that the way he tore some of my most cherished constructions all to pieces was almost disheartening. Not least because it reminded me so much of another man who'd done the same to my first draft. However, I'd reconstructed and pieced together the parts which he had condemned, and set about completing my work.

Before taking it to a publisher, Father had insisted that I have a judge he knew read it. Thankfully, the judge was encouraging in his report on my work. It had held his interest from the first to last, he said, and the only criticism that he could offer was on my use in one place of the word "equity." So far as the word's ordinary meaning was concerned I had used it properly, but it had a significance in legal parlance which I had failed to grasp.

One word later, and the book was off to Putnam, who'd told me to cut sixty thousand words from my precious one-hundred-fifty-thousand-word manuscript. Like a dagger to the heart that was, but I'd saved what I'd cut, hoping perhaps I'd be allowed a second chance at writing a mystery.

Mother Grace, the one who'd first encouraged me to try my hand at mystery, had not made it to its publication. Just last year she had passed away, though she'd held my hand as she died and told me how proud she was of me, and that she knew, just knew *The Leavenworth Case* was going to change the mystery genre itself.

And it looked like I just might have the chance to do so. My publisher was asking what I thought of writing a sequel, a recurring detective series with Gryce at the center of more mysteries. It was an intriguing idea, but if it had taken me six years to write and publish my first one, I couldn't imagine getting many more novels on the shelves before I was too crippled by age to hold a fountain pen.

But already new ideas were coming to me. Almost every day something would inspire me and I'd jot it down in my notebook—the notebook Sokol had given me that rainy day six long years ago.

Maybe the next book wouldn't be so hard. So painful. After all, there was no Lenore or Sokol in my life to complicate matters this time. It could be entirely mine. Just mine.

"Miss Green," a soft voice said before me, and I realized I'd drifted off in my thoughts in between customers. The young man before me was tall with handsome, though somewhat comedic features, and for some reason seemed quite familiar. "I see you've chosen to play the role of author to its fullest."

"I'm sorry, do I know you?" I asked, taking his copy of my book in my hand.

He blushed and cleared his throat. "I was worried you wouldn't remember me. I was much younger then. I'm an actor—"

"Mr. Rohlfs!"

His face brightened. He really hadn't changed much in six years, except perhaps by becoming even more handsome. My gaze drifted to his eyes.

His eyes. They were piercing black eyes. Like a falcon's.

"It's been a long time," I said, focusing on dipping my pen in the ink carefully, though my hand shook.

"I left the city for awhile, but I've recently returned. I'm a member of the Criterion Comedy Company now."

"Oh yes?"

"In Manhattan." He shuffled his feet. "I'm, uh...I'm a great admirer of your writing. Your grasp of the law and unparalleled ability to take the reader step by step through a murder case from start to finish—I felt like I was there, investigating right alongside Mr. Raymond." He ran a nervous hand through his hair. "I mean, I know I *was* there, but..."

He seemed quite anxious. It was flattering.

Mr. Rohlfs leaned over the table. "I was sorry to hear of Mr. Sokol's death." He put his hand out like he was about to take mine, but then decided against it. "I know we didn't meet under the best of circumstances. We've both loved and lost, Miss Green," he said tenderly.

I tried to think about something else other than how close he was, and how he smelled like fresh air and sunshine.

"I wondered if...perhaps...you'd join me for a walk in the park when you're finished here? The trees are so lovely this time of year."

I looked up at him. "Thank you, Mr. Rohlfs. It's a pleasure to see you again." I hesitated, then decided. "I think I will take you up on your offer."

He smiled broadly.

I signed my name in the front of my book and held it out.

The tips of our fingers brushed as he reached to take the book, and for a moment, I was lost in eyes that seemed to magnetize me, pulling me further and further in.

"You will laugh at me," he said, "but I must tell you: I felt drawn to meet you here today. Like a lodestar calling me home."

I dropped *The Leavenworth Case.*

"Indeed, Mr. Rohlfs?"

"Please, call me Charles."

THE END

Author's Note

"A.K. Green Dies. Noted Author, 88. 'The Leavenworth Case' in '78 Followed by 36 Other Books. Wife of Charles Rohlfs. Wanted to Write Poetry. Wrote Detective Stories to Draw Attention to Her Verse. Changed Mystery Fiction."

—*New York Times*, **April 12, 1935**

The writing of this book began, as most mysteries do today, with Agatha Christie. In *The Clocks* (1963), Christie has her own renowned detective, Hercule Poirot, refer to *The Leavenworth Case,* saying, "*The Leavenworth Case* is admirable. One savors its atmosphere, its studied and deliberate melodrama. Those rich and lavish descriptions of the golden beauty of Eleanor, the moonlight beauty of Mary!... and there is the maidservant, Hannah, so true to type, and the murderer, an excellent psychological study."

Christie mentions it again in her autobiography, saying it was one of the first mysteries she read that fascinated her: "the seed had been sown...the idea had been planted: some day I would write a detective story." Who was this woman who inspired the Queen of Crime herself, I wondered?

A quick search told me *The Leavenworth Case* was Anna Katharine Green's debut novel, and being a lover of all classic detectives, familiar with the works of Poe, Conan Doyle, Collins, and the like, I picked up a copy and dove in.

When I was introduced to Detective Gryce, it was love at first sight. I was immediately attracted to the way he was described—so different from your average classic detective, more like Columbo than Dupin.

The next section dove right into an inquest. Being an historical mystery author, I immediately did a little research to determine if this was truly accurate: Would they really have called for a coroner so soon after discovering the body? The answer was yes, and not only that, my online search began a rabbit hole dive into the author and her life.

Before Anna, Metta Victor published the first American detective story, *The Dead Letter*, in 1866. However, she published under the non-gender-specific pen name Seeley Regester, so it was only in recent years the author's true identity was revealed. Louisa May Alcott published her novella, *The Mysterious Key and What It Opened*, in 1867, but this story did not include a detective, nor did she publish it under her own name, but instead used initials to evoke the sense that the mystery had been written by a man.

This makes Anna the first woman to publish a full-length American detective novel under her own name—and to make it big. Anna proved with her first book that women could write detective fiction, and not only that, but that people were willing to buy and read it. Because her portrayal of the law was so detailed, she was one of the first overnight sensations in American literature—the Agatha Christie of her day.

In *The Leavenworth Case,* she incorporated and often invented many of the devices recognized by mystery authors today as essential pieces, such as cliffhanger chapter endings, the locked room mystery, a plot carried forward mostly by dialogue rather than description, the importance of ballistics, an inquest, the detailed surgeon's report, a crime scene map, a secret marriage, a missing key, a vanished servant, a forged confession, ciphered messages, overheard arguments, a changed will, a second murder, and a memorable denouement with a classic trap into which the killer falls. And all of this just in her *first* novel!

In addition to defining the foundational conventions of the detective mystery genre, she is also noted for introducing several new concepts. The first was the flawed professional detective: Ebenezer Gryce. Before him, detectives like Poe's Dupin and Gaboriau's Lecoq were perfect examples of intelligence. With Gryce, she showed that even a detective with rheumatism and a tendency to avoid eye contact could solve mysteries, and be an engaging, thought-provoking character.

It is clear Sir Arthur Conan Doyle was greatly inspired by Gryce when creating Sherlock Holmes: from giving his detective an amateur sidekick, to Sherlock's Baker Street Irregulars who would help in collecting information for him, to the bumbling police in need of his expertise. Anna would even publish a sympathetic letter from Gryce to Sherlock when that world-famous detective found out he, too, had rheumatism.

By the time Sherlock's first mystery was published in 1887, Anna had published six more novels and two books of poetry following *The Leavenworth Case.* Gryce was well on his way to becoming the first American literary detective to enjoy such a marked career, with continuations of his exploits in an extensive series of full-length detective mysteries.

Another new concept employed by Anna is the female detective (yes, she finally did get her in there!), who took on the guise of the spinster amateur detective in Miss Amelia Butterworth (1897). Miss Butterworth's escapades would inspire another well-known creation, that of Christie's Miss Marple.

After Butterworth, in 1915 Anna introduced Miss Violet Strange, a girl detective who would inspire the stories of Nancy Drew and many others in years to come.

Those are just the big ticket items. Anna's stories included so many of the ingredients of modern detective mysteries, it's difficult to note them all.

One of the pleasures of writing historical fiction is in finding ways to bring history to life, while staying as true as possible to historical events, people, and locations. In historical fiction, we get to fill in the crevices left by history. Thankfully, Anna left me a pretty broad outline of what brought her to the point of writing *The Leavenworth Case* in her own words, through letters, articles, and more.

Anna did work with her father on cases, laying the foundation for her acclaimed legal knowledge evident in all of her books, which really did cause Yale to add *The Leavenworth Case* to its list of required reading. Her stepmother, Mother Grace, was credited as the first to encourage her in writing a novel rather than poetry, and Anna really did correspond with Emerson about her poems, though he also suggested she pursue other avenues of writing.

Anna wrote several articles about the long steps required to get her first book to publication over the intervening years, though she would write a letter to Mary Hatch about a dream that caused her to dive head first into the writing of it. By the time she shared it, "*The Leavenworth Case* was the strangest looking mass of paper you ever saw. You see, I had written part of it at home in Brooklyn, part of it at the seashore, part of it in the mountains and other parts wherever I had chanced to be as a guest, on journeys and so on. I had procured my paper and ink from the nearest dealer in every case without a thought to uniformity. Chromatically the copy was more like Joseph's coat of many colors than anything else I can compare it to, for some of the paper was white, some blue, some pink and some buff" ("Writing Her First Book," *Kansas City Star*, 1900). Upon publication of *The Leavenworth Case,* she legally changed the spelling of her middle name in homage to her mother, and the world would know her by her full name even after she married.

Even with all of this, the actual birth of *The Leavenworth Case* left some holes to be filled. Several sources suggested Anna had been working on the book a total of six years, starting and stopping, rewriting and reworking, until finally sharing it with her father, who passed it up the line until it was picked up by a publisher and presented to the public in 1878. I decided to move forward with that idea, setting the stage for this story in 1872, and fictionally answering the question of what occurred in those intervening years before her debut novel was finally published.

Patricia Maida in her biography *Mother of Detective Fiction* wrote, "Anna may well have experienced a personal loss. Considering the fact that she did not marry until age thirty-eight, late for a woman of her generation, she herself may have had an unsuccessful relationship." There are many indications of this throughout Anna's writing, both through her fiction and in her interviews and articles. Anna would not marry until after she became famous in her own right through her writing, having published four more novels and a collection of poetry. Why didn't she get married until much later? Was it simply a fact of not meeting "the right man?" Or had she met him, but lost him? I agreed with Maida, and my love for Gryce became such that I knew who my mystery man must be, the man who would inspire her creation long before she met her future husband. And so, although Sokol was created for story purposes, inspired by Gryce, rather than vice versa, it is absolutely possible that someone like him really did exist in Anna's past.

Although Anna did eventually get her poetry published, it was done more as an act of gratefulness by her publisher for her success with her mystery fiction. She would never be famous for her poetry, though in addition to the ones published in collections, she would occasionally include them in her mystery novels. All of the poems included in *A Deed of Dreadful Note* were Anna's, since they were written prior to the publication of *The Leavenworth Case.* I found it fascinating how easily they fit and seemed "meant to be" when writing this fictionalized account.

Regarding *The Leavenworth Case,* I've attempted to weave that story beat-for-beat with Anna's personal history, sometimes using Anna's own descriptions from the book. In fact, wherever

I couldn't find the actual history, I went with what Anna had written instead. For example, when the one year I couldn't find a named coroner for Manhattan was 1872, I went with Anna's Mr. Hammond from *The Leavenworth Case.* So although he may not be a real person from history, he's still a person from Anna's "history."

I chose *Macbeth* as the influence for the title because each chapter in *The Leavenworth Case* opens with a quote, several of which are from *Macbeth,* including the first one: "A deed of dreadful note." It then seemed fitting that the first time Anna met Charles Rohlfs was at a showing of *Macbeth,* though I could not find any record of where or when they first met. Although both went on to become prominent members of history, tracking down specific records of their earlier life has proven quite challenging.

I'd like to especially recommend the one and only biography of Anna Katharine Green that I've discovered as yet, written by Patricia D. Maida, *Mother of Detective Fiction.* Also motherofmystery.com, where I was able to find the perfect jumping off point for almost all of my articles required for first-hand research, including those where I found quotes that I incorporated into the novel. If you'd like to learn more about Anna straight from her mouth, this is a fabulous place to start.

Wherever possible, I have used Anna's own words or words published about her by friends, critics, and other contemporaries. Thanks to public domain, it was quite satisfying to place the words back in her own mouth, although sometimes I would put the words into the mouths of those around her, like Sokol, her father, or Mother Grace, as it seems to me she might have formed the opinion she later shared based on what someone else said to her earlier in her life.

Anna was clearly a great student of people and their personalities, what drove them, and how to manipulate them, as this is at the heart of all her books. Long before Sherlock Holmes read people in a mere glance, Anna quietly studied them and took notes, which in some ways was easier for her, as since she was a woman, she was often overlooked.

Though she certainly changed that.

If you'd like a complete list of which quotes came from Anna's personal writing, interviews, articles, and *The Leavenworth Case*, or to learn more about Anna Katharine Green, my sources, and all the ways she changed mystery fiction, please visit my website at Patricia-Meredith.com and check out my YouTube channel @pmeredithauthor.

Acknowledgements

This book was made possible by the help of many dedicated friends and family. I could not have done it without you, and I look forward to learning more alongside you about this incredible author.

First and foremost, praise to my Lord and merciful Savior, Jesus Christ, with whom nothing is impossible, who led me to this woman who has more of a spiritual connection with me than any other author I've discovered.

Thank you to my husband, Andrew, for his never-ending encouragement and love. Let's be honest: every good and positive relationship represented in my books is inspired by ours. Thank you for being my best friend and writing partner, my lodestar ever guiding me home.

My kids, who have patiently listened to my references to Anna Katharine Green throughout our homeschool time for years now.

My parents, especially my father and his patient, dedicated love for me which is seen in this book in Anna's relationship with her own father. I am so very thankful to be blessed with such incredibly supportive and loving parents.

A special thanks to Patricia Maida, author of *Mother of Detective Fiction*. I am very grateful to her for her kind words regarding the first draft of this novel, and the encouragement to continue in the hunt to bring Anna back to the forefront of readers' minds.

Also a huge thank you to my editor, Corin Faye, who brought this book out of first draft stage and into its present state with much deliberation and effort. I appreciate every word of critique!

My amazing team of Beta Readers: Kathy Buckmaster, Anne Fischer, Diane Gordon, Andrew Mattocks, Andrew Meredith, Maggie Meredith, Renae Meredith, Scotte Meredith, Su Meredith, Lydia Pierce, Dean Rizzo, Sue Rizzo, Layla Sollazzo, Niko Sollazzo, Kini Sunny, Sue Walker, and Rebecca Writz.

And you, dear Reader. Thank you for taking the time to read this book! Please leave me a review so I know how much you loved it.

Thank you for reading!

Photo by Angus Meredith

ABOUT THE AUTHOR

Patricia Meredith is an author of historical mysteries. When she's not writing, she's playing board games with her husband, creating imaginary worlds with her two children, or out in the garden reading a good book with a cup of tea.

For all the latest updates, you can follow her as @pmeredithauthor on YouTube, Goodreads, Instagram, and Facebook, and sign up for her newsletter at Patricia-Meredith.com.

DID YOU ENJOY *A DEED OF DREADFUL NOTE?*

Pick up a copy of *The Leavenworth Case,* Anna Katharine Green's 1878 bestseller! Get a special edition with introduction by Patricia Meredith for free by signing up for her newsletter at her website Patricia-Meredith.com. Find the audiobook read by Andrew D. Meredith everywhere audiobooks are sold!

Printed in the USA
CPSIA information can be obtained
at www.ICGtesting.com
LVHW040007010924
789817LV00004B/878